# SAVE ME

## JENNY ELLIOTT

Swoon Reads   New York

A Swoon Reads Book
An Imprint of Feiwel and Friends

Swoon Reads books may be purchased for business or promotional use. For information on bulk purchases, please contact the Macmillan Corporate and Premium Sales Department at (800) 221-7945 x5442 or by e-mail at specialmarkets@macmillan.com.

Library of Congress Cataloging-in-Publication Data Available

ISBN: 978-1-250-06147-8 (Trade Paperback) / 978-1-250-06179-9 (ebook)

Book design by Ashley Halsey

First Edition: 2015

10  9  8  7  6  5  4  3  2  1

swoonreads.com

*This book is dedicated to Christine Sneddon-Renzie,
my first true fan and the truest friend I've ever known.
Love always.*

# ONE

Cara Markwell pulled into the lot above the dock at Liberty Charters and glimpsed the grille of a red sedan barreling toward her. Panicking, she jerked her steering wheel hard right. The front of her Honda Civic scraped against the bumper of Captain Rick's Chevy Tahoe, and she cringed at the grating sound.

Stomping on the brake pedal, she slammed her car into park and blasted the horn. Her heart pounded harder as her panic turned to anger. She smacked the dashboard and watched the offending vehicle peal out of the lot.

It was a Volkswagen Jetta, just like the one her freshman-year boyfriend, Chris Adams, used to drive. She hadn't seen Chris around town in two years, so it probably wasn't him. Whoever it was had to be a jerk like him, though. Anyone with a sense of common courtesy knew the importance of driving carefully in parking lots.

She inched her car into the nearest spot and stepped out on shaky legs to check the damage. A long, black scrape marred her Civic's right front panel. But she was more concerned about Rick's Tahoe. A thick, white stripe of paint coated its rear bumper.

It might be better to come back a different day for a tour. She could just tell Rick about the accident and head home. But she'd be starting her senior year in another week, and she hadn't seen her whales in over a month.

She grabbed her backpack from her car and popped the locks. Zipping up her windbreaker, she ignored the wobble in her legs as she walked toward the office door. A strong summer breeze blew her long, dark hair across her face. She used the tie around her wrist to gather it out of the way, and took deep breaths of crisp, early morning sea air.

The bell above the door jingled when she swung it open and she instantly relaxed inside the familiar, dimly lit office, with its fake wood plank walls covered by framed photos of the area's whales, including the grays she'd grown to love over the last few years.

Captain Rick's wife and business partner, Sherry, sat behind the front desk. She wore her regular work attire: a gray windbreaker with an embroidered navy Liberty Charters whale tail logo. Cara owned a similar jacket, but hadn't worn it that day, as she wasn't officially volunteering to assist.

Sherry set down a paperback. "I didn't know you planned to go out today, kiddo. But you're in luck. We only have one customer signed up."

Rick's boat held six passengers, and as long as there was a seat available, he always let Cara ride along for free.

Cara stopped in front of Sherry's desk.

"Something wrong?" Sherry's eyebrows rose, pulling the wrinkles around her eyes up with them.

Cara fumbled for her wallet and insurance card as she explained how she'd ended up scraping Rick's truck.

When she set her insurance information down, Sherry patted her hand. "Accidents happen. I'll call down to Rick and have him take a quick look."

While Sherry got a hold of Rick on her cell phone, the bell above the office door jingled again and a tall, dark-haired guy entered.

Sherry said good-bye to Rick and tapped on her laptop keyboard. "David Wilson, I presume," she said to the new arrival and gestured toward Cara. "This is your tour mate."

Cara put up a hand in greeting. "Cara Markwell, resident whale-watching addict."

He turned to her with a crooked smile and raised his hand in response. "David Wilson, whale-watching first timer," he said, his voice deep and soft.

When he met her gaze, she was struck by the color of his eyes, which reminded her of mixed shades of green from area forests. A hint of stubble covered his smooth, pink-cheeked face, and his straight white teeth were no doubt the product of braces. She figured he was in his early twenties. His nose was on the slender side and his smile was lopsided, but those oddities somehow added to his appeal.

Catching herself staring, she tore her gaze away, flustered.

Her first instinct about guys wasn't that they were hot or charming, but that they should be avoided. Chris had broken up with her when she wouldn't sleep with him, then spread rumors that she slept around. And her father had left her mom when he'd gotten her pregnant. Dating wasn't worth the risks.

She shook her head and bent over Sherry's desk to fill out her paperwork.

"Rick said not to worry about the bumper," Sherry whispered. "We'll take care of it."

"At least take a copy of this," Cara said, moving her insurance card on top of her forms.

Then she slipped out the back door that led to the dock and shut it behind her, as Sherry explained the documentation to David.

Cara descended the stairs and crinkled her nose at the fishy stench that wafted across the harbor. Seagulls squawked, clamoring over the remains fishermen tossed aside as they cleaned the early catches. Briny sea air misted over her face. She stopped in front of the *Lookout*, the twenty-six-foot Zodiac-style inflatable boat that floated flush with bumpers against the dock. Its four rows of seats were currently empty, three in front and one behind the center console, where Captain Rick readied the controls.

Rick came over to her with an outstretched arm. Both his jacket and his tanned, leathery wrinkles matched Sherry's. "No worries about the bumper, kiddo."

She started to object, but he shook his head. "I'm just glad you're back."

His booming voice made her smile.

"I'm really sorry about your truck. And I'm glad you're doing a tour. I know you like to have at least two paying customers."

He took her elbow to help her aboard. "Nah, you know me. I'd go out anyway. How was Seattle?"

"The orcas were fun," she said, stepping into the giant raft. "But I miss the grays."

She'd just slipped her arms into a life jacket when he pulled her into a sideways hug. "And I'm sure they've missed you. I have, too. It's not the same without my first mate." He gave her a light squeeze, then let her loose. "So, who's our other crew member today?"

"A young guy." She shot him a warning look. "Behave yourself."

He gave her a sly smile. "I don't know. I don't get many opportunities like this."

One pout and he caved.

"Fine, I'll behave. But you're no fun."

She chose a seat in the first row, keenly aware of David coming down the stairs and boarding the boat. Rick greeted him and suited him up with a life jacket. Cara dug her cell phone out of her backpack and texted her friend Rachel. Instead of saying, *Wish you were here*, she keyed in, *You'll wish you'd been here.* Rachel didn't like to go out on the water, but she never turned down an occasion to appreciate an impressive male specimen.

Rick guided the *Lookout* out of the harbor and began his spiel on spots they'd visit and marine life in the area. Cara dropped her phone in her pack and swapped it for a camera and binoculars.

They hit open water and Rick sped up. The boat's motor buzzed loudly as they bumped across the waves. Cold wind roared in Cara's ears. From her seat up front, she could barely hear Rick's voice, but it was no big deal. She'd heard the rundown so many times, she could deliver it herself.

She snuck a glance behind her. David sat one row back, looking out over the waters of the Pacific. An overcast sky created a dome over the ocean's rippling surface. No other boats were visible as far as she could see.

They reached Seagoer's Cove, and she spotted the heart-shaped spray of a gray whale.

Rick turned the boat toward the cove and killed the engine. "Grays to the right!" he called out. "Orcas to the left!"

Cara spun around toward the orcas. Their dorsal fins were tall, black, and triangular, different than the shorter, curved dorsals of the residents she'd seen in the San Juan Islands. These whales—technically dolphins—also looked smaller and sharklike. She knew orcas sometimes traveled along Oregon's coast, but she'd never seen any in the waters off Liberty.

Rick pulled out his camera. "I'll be darned. I've only seen these transient orcas show up in spring, not late summer."

"I guess I came out on the right day," she heard David say.

She lifted the camera from around her neck. Zooming in on the approaching orcas, an odd chill snaked up her spine. She snapped a couple of pictures.

From the right, a large gray whale slipped underneath the *Lookout* and surfaced next to the boat's side. It spyhopped, its giant head rising up out of the dark blue water.

In a daze, Cara followed David over to kneel before the whale. She watched in awe as David ran a hand over its mottled, slate gray face, next to its baseball-size eye. A low rumble, like a purr, poured from its mouth.

"Unbelievable," Cara said.

She'd gone on dozens of whale-watching tours, but had never before seen a whale spyhop this close. The crisscrossed markings on the back of the large whale's head told her this was Crossback, a gray she and Rick thought was migrating through the area in late spring, along with her baby, Bobbi. Now that the summer was almost over and the other migrating whales were gone, Cara was delighted to see that the mother and baby had chosen to stay in the area.

"I can't believe she's letting you touch her," Cara said to David.

"It's amazing," he said.

She readied her camera and snapped shots of Crossback, and then Bobbi, who poked his smaller head out of the water behind his mother.

"What brings you so close today, Crossback?" she asked.

"You know this whale?" David asked.

In the excitement of the moment, she ignored the impulse to lean away from him. She inched closer, until her arm brushed his, and spoke in his ear. "This is Crossback. And that's her baby, Bobbi."

She reached out to smooth a hand over Crossback's face and savored the cold, slippery sensation. An instant later, even though her fingers didn't touch David's, a warm tingle tickled her fingertips where they met Crossback's skin. The warmth trickled up her arm, spread through her chest, and exploded outward, as if along a tether, seemingly toward David.

With both their hands still touching Crossback, Cara and David turned to look at each other. The intensity of his gaze told her he also sensed the warmth that wrapped around them, the invisible energy radiating between them, connecting them.

Unsure of what was happening, and just as unsure of how she felt about it, she pulled her hand away from Crossback. She stood, and David did the same. Crossback and Bobbi dipped beneath the surface of the water and disappeared.

Cara tried to disappear, too, heading back to her seat to stash the camera and binoculars. No way was she going to crush on a tourist. She pulled a diet soda from her backpack, uncapped it, and took a long swig.

For the rest of the tour, she'd stay by the controls with Rick and try to clear her head. She capped her soda, dropped it in her bag, and turned around.

Just then she heard a loud thump, and the boat rocked. Off balance, she scrambled to find her footing. Over her shoulder, she spotted shiny black whale skin and two rows of gigantic, cone-shaped white teeth as the orca again bumped the boat.

Reaching for something to hold on to, she only grasped air as she fell over the *Lookout*'s side.

*This can't be happening*. The thought played over and over in her mind.

Frigid water hit her face and chest, lapping at her cheeks and biting her skin. She gasped reflexively, thankful her head was above water. Her breaths came hard and fast as she shivered.

"I'll throw you a life ring!" Rick hollered.

The freezing water pierced Cara's fingers, and swell after swell washed over her face. Gasping for breath, she choked on a mouthful of seawater. Her life jacket pulled from her arms and sprang up over her head. Somehow, she'd forgotten to fasten it.

Her arms and legs flailed as she sank beneath the surface. The water was as black as tar, the only visible light shining from a spot above that grew more distant with each second.

Something bumped her leg. Opening her mouth to scream, a stream of salt water rushed down her throat. Her lungs heaved and demanded air. She pressed her lips together and struggled harder to flap and kick with her heavy limbs.

From beneath, she was lifted and thrust upward. Above, the muted glow grew brighter. A pair of strong hands reached down and pulled her up.

As her head cleared the surface, her vision blurred. Her chest convulsed and she coughed, forcing the water she'd inhaled out of her lungs. Salt water burned her throat and nose until she finally drew in long, rasping breaths.

She caught a glimpse of Crossback's markings as the gray surfaced for air, then dove back underwater.

"I got you. We need to get back on the boat," an urgent yet soothing voice told her.

*David.* He'd rested her on top of his life jacket. She looked into his intent green eyes. The water had frozen her to the core, yet a touch of warmth filled her chest. David floated, partially on his back, and held her hands behind his neck.

"Hold on to me. Don't let go," he said.

She hardly felt her numb fingers as she tried to clasp them together. David moved one of his hands to her lower back and held her to him while he used his other to sling the life ring's rope over them.

Rick towed them in. At the same time, a tall, black dorsal fin pierced the water on the other side of the boat. Cara sucked in a painful breath and clasped her hands more tightly around David's neck. The fin skimmed across the water, away from them, toward the open sea.

Letting out a weak sigh, she let her head fall against David's chest. Rick helped them over the side tube. She continued to cling to David as they lay on deck, shaking.

"That water is barely fifty degrees. I'll need to get you two into some dry clothes." Rick grabbed the items he needed from the emergency bins under the *Lookout*'s seats.

Cara's teeth chattered and she was too shocked and frozen to protest when Rick removed her clothing until all that remained were her bra and panties. He bundled her up in thermal underwear, thick socks, a stocking cap, and a waterproof jacket, then did the same for David.

"Don't you worry," Rick said, gripping her shoulder. "I radioed for medical help."

She exhaled and forgot her concerns about David as she huddled closer to him.

"You two lie down on deck until we get back," Rick continued.

"Exposure like that can cause heart troubles." He hurried back to the boat's controls.

Seeking extra insulation, Cara wedged her hand between David's arm and side and slipped a leg between his. He tucked her head under his chin and clutched her to him. No one had ever held her so securely. Her body warmed quickly in his arms.

# TWO

The *Lookout* reached the dock beneath Liberty Charters and a frantic Sherry led paramedics to the boat. The medics climbed aboard and separated Cara and David to examine them. Cold seeped back into Cara's bones.

She and David were given clear bills of health, but still needed assistance getting off the boat and up the stairs to the office. Cara felt an urge to see if the strange connection between her and David remained, but she resisted the desire to catch his eye. Instead, she took her backpack from Rick and stepped into the restroom.

Standing in front of the small mirror above the sink, she dropped the blanket that wrapped around her. The thermal underwear was a faded red color that reminded her of dried blood. She pulled off the stocking cap and set it aside.

Working her fingers through her hair, she fluffed it until it resembled its post-shower condition. She ran water in the sink until it turned tepid, wet her hands, and scrubbed at her face. Color rose in her cheeks.

The no-makeup look was normal for her, so other than her paler skin and red-rimmed brown eyes, she didn't look much different than usual. She swept up the blanket and hat, slung her backpack over her arm, and made her way to the break room.

David sat on the sofa. Sherry sat Cara down next to him, wrapped the blanket around her shoulders, and handed her a steaming mug.

"Spiced apple juice and honey," David told her, raising his own. "It's really good."

"I hope it helps," Sherry said, the lines on her forehead deepening with worry.

The office phone rang and Sherry headed out and shut the door behind her.

Cara blew into her cup and peeked at David. Their eyes met and energy sparked between them, a light buzz now, rather than the stronger surge she experienced when they'd both touched Crossback.

"I probably look like I drowned," she said.

He sure didn't. He looked even more handsome, with pinker cheeks, brighter eyes, and the sweetest smile she'd ever seen.

"You look great," he said, his lopsided grin turning up one corner of his mouth.

He held her gaze, but she looked into her mug. "Only because I snuck to the restroom to try to make myself look less scary."

"You don't look scary to me."

She took in a large gulp of hot juice that blistered her tongue and scorched her throat.

He held up his cell. "Can I get your number?"

She coughed and stared at his phone. "My number?"

His cheeks turned a deeper shade of pink. "Yeah, I'm hoping you'll go out with me this weekend, to celebrate our survival?"

He sure was cute. And he'd helped save her life. She wanted to say yes, but she couldn't be sure he was trustworthy enough to date.

In her head, a small voice said, *You can trust him.*

She'd heard the voice before. It often warned or encouraged her, though it usually sounded like more of a whisper and had never been as clear as just now. She'd never regretted heeding its guidance.

"How long are you going to be in town?" she asked.

"I moved here last month, actually."

"Wow, a new local." And finally a dating prospect she felt good about.

"I figured you were a local, too, when you told me you knew the grays. Do you work here at Liberty Charters?"

"I volunteer as an assistant once a month. But I'm planning to take marine biology courses at the University of Washington."

David set his mug down on the table. "Then you'll be moving?"

"Not till next summer."

"That's good," he said with what sounded like relief, and ran his fingers through his hair. "I mean, the University of Washington's a great school."

He couldn't get much cuter.

"So, if you want to go to dinner Saturday, maybe you could pick the place?"

She set her mug down and gestured for him to give her his phone. As she sent herself a text to swap numbers, she brainstormed for restaurant options. After waffling between fancy and casual, she opted for comfortable.

"There's a great place that overlooks Seagoer's Cove, where we fell overboard."

His lopsided smile returned. "That seems fitting."

"It's called the Cove. It has the best clam chowder in town." She handed back his cell.

He stood. "Can I pick you up at seven on Saturday, then?"

Best not to have him pick her up at home. "How about I meet you there?"

"Okay." He laid his blanket over her lap. "I'm gonna head out, but I'll talk to you soon." His smile turned into a concerned frown. "Are you sure you're feeling okay?"

"I'm fine. Thanks to you."

David held out his hand. Surprised, she placed her hand in his. That same strange energy flowed more strongly between them when they touched.

"I'm glad I got to meet the grays." He raised her hand to his lips and kissed the back of it. "And I'm especially glad I got to meet you."

***

Cara called her mom and left a long-winded message about the overboard incident and how she'd accidentally scraped Rick's truck. After she hung up, she took a few minutes to analyze her encounter with David. For once, she welcomed sappy thoughts about a guy.

Rick and Sherry came in and interrupted her reverie.

"I'm sorry this happened, kiddo," Rick said, pulling off his cap. "It was my fault. It's my duty to make sure everyone on my boat is safe."

"No. I'm the one who forgot to fasten my life jacket. I promise it won't happen again."

Sherry handed over Cara's insurance card, along with the outfit she'd worn when she'd fallen overboard, which was warm from the dryer. "We'll give you a ride home."

Cara shook her head, grabbed her backpack, and stood. "Thanks, but I'm fine. And I don't want to leave my car in the lot."

"You go ahead and change, then, and we'll send some of that spiced apple juice home with you," Sherry said.

Sherry and Rick both turned to leave, but Cara couldn't get one question out of her head. "Do you think the orca's bump was a friendly one?"

Rick faced her with a frown. "Not sure. I've never seen a transient that close and this is awful late in the season for them to be here." He scratched his head. "Don't you worry, though. They never stay in one place. I'm sure they'll be gone soon."

"The orcas in the San Juans were social . . . playful. Hopefully these transients were just curious," she said.

Rick nodded. "I'm just glad you're all right, kiddo."

Cara was all right, physically. But just thinking of the transient killer whales caused a cold, dark feeling to creep into her soul.

# THREE

In the lot, David's green eyes and bright smile lit up on the screen of Cara's mind as she pulled out of her parking spot. She felt a sickening thud against her car's rear bumper. Yelping, she slammed on the brakes. Her head flew forward, then whipped back.

Her fingernails dug into the vinyl on the steering wheel and a heavy weight sank to the bottom of her stomach. Her heart stopped, then took off at a gallop.

In the rearview mirror, she saw the face of a teenage boy, about her age. She had no idea where he'd come from. Twisting around, she got a better view of the guy through the back window. Sky blue eyes stared back at her.

She thanked God he was standing. Her trembling hand fumbled with the gearshift until she managed to put the car in park. She left the motor running, stepped out, and drew in a strained breath of seaweed-scented air.

Inching over to the stranger, she saw that—by some miracle— he stood straight, apparently unaffected by the impact of her car.

"I'm so sorry," she said, shaking inside and out. "Should I call 911? Are you hurt?" Her cheeks flamed.

"No, you just tapped me," he said, his voice deep and melodic. "I'm fine."

A smile turned up his lips, and his bottomless eyes brightened in the morning sun. She sank into the depths of those eyes and a softness enveloped her, like an invisible hug.

That morning, when the red Jetta had nearly crashed into her, she'd been furious. Yet this guy, whom she'd actually *hit*, didn't look or sound mad at all.

"You should be careful and remain alert when you're driving. Over ninety percent of car accidents are due to operator error," he said.

Normal people didn't say things like "remain alert" or "operator error." And he'd just spouted a statistic. Maybe he was going into shock.

"Are you sure you're okay?" she asked.

He nodded, but his face remained expressionless.

"Did you want to report this?" she asked, dreading the trouble she could get in, yet knowing it would be the right thing to do.

"No. I thought I'd look into a whale-watching tour."

She considered warning him about the transients, but she didn't want to relive the events she'd just been through. Rick could fill him in.

"You live here," he said.

She wasn't sure how he'd gathered that just from looking at her, but she nodded.

"I'm new in town. My name's Garren."

Odds were slim that she'd meet one new local, let alone two in the same day. The people she met on whale-watching tours typically came from a steadily streaming pool of tourists who passed through the tiny seaside town.

"I'm Cara. Liberty doesn't get many new residents. What brings you to the Oregon coast?" She realized she'd been too caught up in her connection with David to ask him the same question.

"My family loves the ocean."

She waited for him to elaborate, to tell her his dad decided to become a fisherman or something, but he just said, "I'll be a senior at Seaside High."

That was a surprise. The way he talked, he seemed older. Or maybe just odder.

"So will I."

He continued to stare at her. Maybe he was surprised, too. She did look older than her age.

As she examined him more closely, she saw that he was flawless. Loose, sandy-blond curls brushed his jaw line, his nose and cheekbones were magazine-ad worthy, and he had a perfectly proportioned mouth. His build appeared trim, yet firm, outlined by jeans and a white waffle-knit shirt. He stood a few inches taller than her, at least five feet nine.

Cara suddenly realized she was staring at a guy for the second time that day. Yet, despite his perfection, she knew her rapid heartbeat now was only an after effect of having hit him with her car. She searched his eyes again. All she felt was a calm comfort, as if she could float away on their currents.

A boat's horn blasted in the distance, jolting her back to her senses. She glanced back and forth between the stranger and her idling car. After what she'd done, she was leery of maneuvering a car again.

He walked over and put a hand on her shoulder. She tensed, but then her tight shoulder muscles relaxed and her shakiness subsided. Gently, he guided her back to the open driver's door. He was being awfully nice, considering she could have killed him.

"The best thing for you to do would be to learn your lesson and get back behind the wheel," he said.

Not seeing any hint in his face that his weird words were anything less than sincere, she eased into the driver's seat.

"Take care, Cara." He smiled and stepped away from the car.

She shut the door and secured her seatbelt. Checking both the rearview and side mirrors, then looking over her shoulder, she slowly backed out of the parking space. With a feeble smile in Garren's direction, she drove out of the lot and kept her full attention on the road as she made her way home.

# FOUR

Cara's mom must have left work early after she got the message about the overboard incident, because her Outback sat in the driveway. Cara parked on the street, closed her eyes, and leaned against the driver's seat. If circumstances that day had been different, she could have wrecked, drowned, or killed someone. She had a lot to be thankful for.

Grabbing her backpack and the jug of apple juice concoction Sherry had given her, she sighed and climbed out of the car. As she walked up the path to the front door, she drew comfort from the details of the modified Cape Cod perched on a hill a few blocks from the water, the home she often took for granted. From the inside, many of the house's large windows showcased ocean views. Sometimes she didn't need to venture farther than her bedroom to score sneak peeks of her whales.

In the family room, her mom sat in her usual spot on the blue gingham-covered love seat. Spotting Cara in the doorway, she set down the stack of college students' psychology assignments she'd been grading and hurried over to pull Cara in for a hug.

"I'm so sorry this happened to you, honey. Are you sure you're all right?" Her mom held her by the shoulders, examining her.

"I'm fine. It probably wouldn't have been as big of a deal if I'd remembered to fasten my life jacket. I won't make that mistake again."

"Did something else happen?" her mom asked, releasing her and watching as she absentmindedly sloshed around the contents of the jug.

"Sherry sent this home with me." Cara gripped the jug's handle with both hands and made a conscious effort to hold it still. "The guy who helped me in the water is a new local. We're going to dinner at the Cove this Saturday."

Her mom looked at her with her characteristic sideways gaze. "You don't have much dating experience. What do you know about this guy?"

"Not much," Cara had to admit. She and David had shared an intense experience, but they were still strangers. It might be wise to talk to him on the phone first, or by text or email—to get to know him better before she went out with him—especially since she hadn't dated in over two years.

"Even if I decide to wait to go out with him, though, it can't hurt to have something to wear. I'm hoping you'll take me clothes shopping, to help me pick out an outfit?"

Cara knew her mom would say yes to this. Clothes shopping ranked at the top of Mary Markwell's list of Most Favorite Activities. Cara liked shopping, too, for books and music and whatnot. But since sophomore year, she usually only picked up the basics for her wardrobe. She just hadn't cared what anyone thought of how she looked. Until now.

"You actually want to go clothes shopping? Today?" her mom asked.

"If you're up for it."

Her mom only hesitated for a second. "You sure *you're* up for it?"

"I'm good. Really."

Her mom sprang up off the love seat. "Then it's a date."

---

"What style are you going for?" her mom asked, as they left the station wagon behind in the outlet mall's parking lot.

"Mature and responsible?" was the best Cara could come up with.

"How old is this guy you met?" her mom asked, with a suspicious sideways gaze.

"I'd guess he's in his early twenties."

"I'm not sure I like the idea of you dating someone older."

"Trust me, younger guys aren't necessarily safer. Besides, David can't be that much older than me. And I'm sure I'll meet guys his age in college next year."

Her mom's steps fell short. Then she continued walking. "Let's try feminine, but conservative."

They walked along a concrete path lining a row of storefronts. Her mom ushered her through a glass door and sifted through items on the store's racks. She mixed pieces to create outfits with the expertise of a professional shopper.

Cara's phone buzzed in her purse. She pulled it out to read a text from David:

Watching the water and thinking of you. Hope you're doing well?

She drew in a heady breath and masked her sigh with a cough. He was thinking of her. Any thoughts of canceling their date that weekend dissipated as she reread his sweet message.

Her mom looked over and her brows furrowed, likely because she couldn't make sense of Cara's giddy grin.

Cara slipped the phone back in her purse.

"I knew you just needed to go clothes shopping to fall in love with outfits like these." Her mom loaded her up with clothing hanging from a tangle of hangers and shut her inside a changing room that felt like an upright coffin.

Cara hung up the clothes and pulled out her phone.

*Keep it casual*, she thought, as she shot David a response:

I'm out and about. Doing good. Hope you are too?

Facing the full-length mirror, she undressed and stood in her bra and panties. She wondered if David had seen her body this exposed on the boat. God willing, he'd been too busy trying to get warm.

Her skin still looked blotchy from her morning dip in icy ocean water. And the harsh overhead lights spotlighted every freckle and dimple. Still, she had curves in all the right places.

Her phone buzzed again. She grabbed it and read:

Looking forward to seeing you Saturday.

"Do you have one of the outfits on yet?" her mom asked from the other side of the door. "I'm dying to see you."

"Hang on." Cara tapped out a quick reply to David:

Me too.

She pressed "send," satisfied her answer didn't sound too enthusiastic. And it was the absolute truth. If someone had told her the day before she'd be this excited about a guy, she would've laughed.

But as things were, it would be a long three days until she saw David again.

———

Early Saturday evening, Rachel burst into Cara's bedroom, armed with a surplus of makeup and hair supplies to prep Cara for her date. Cara groaned when Rachel dragged her away from the Scrabble game she was winning on her laptop. Scrabble was Cara's main method of meditation and was currently her only means of keeping her jitters at bay.

Rachel arranged her arsenal on Cara's desk. "I still can't believe you didn't get photo evidence of those beautiful boys you told me about."

Cara pushed her hair back with a headband. "Don't worry, you'll meet David soon enough. And I have no doubt you'll be impressed with Garren."

*You and every other girl at Seaside.*

"It's been a while since you've noticed any guys," Rachel said, and dotted concealer under Cara's eyes. "I'm worried your judgment might be off. *Two* hot new guys in Liberty? That's hard to believe."

"Believe it."

"Guess I'll have to take your word for it for now," Rachel said with a smirk. She puffed a light coat of powder over Cara's face and brushed on blush.

"Thanks for helping make me look pretty," Cara said.

Rachel snorted. "You're already pretty." She smiled down at Cara and placed her hands on her shoulders. "I'm so happy for you." Her smile drooped. "To be honest, though, I'm also super jealous."

Cara took Rachel's hands and held them. "Don't be."

Rachel hadn't been part of the popular clan that had adopted Cara as a freshman. Back then, Cara learned from the "It" girls that, rather than the buxom beauty Cara saw, a lot of guys saw Rachel as a big-boned girl with a big mouth.

But Cara had faith that the right guy would come to appreciate Rachel's unique appeal. Someone who would take the time to get to know and love her exuberant spirit.

Cara gave Rachel her most encouraging smile. "Your time will come."

Rachel grabbed a hand mirror and showed Cara how her makeup job was coming along. The blush looked a tad heavy.

"Let's make a little go a long way," Cara said. "Only, I don't want to look too young."

Rachel swiped at Cara's cheeks with a tissue. "Doesn't David know how old you are?"

Cara continued to stare into the mirror. "It didn't really come up."

"Cara. Marie. Markwell." Rachel drew out her full name in mock chastisement, grabbed the mirror, and set it down on the desk. "What if you guessed his age wrong and he's in his thirties or something?"

Cara envisioned David's emerald eyes, dark hair, bright smile, and pink cheeks. "No, I'm sure he's not much older than us. I just don't know how he'd react to my still being in high school."

"Well . . . I assume you don't plan to sleep with him anytime soon?"

"Definitely not."

"Then your age difference shouldn't be that big of a deal, right?"

"Right."

Way for Rachel to say just what she needed to hear.

# FIVE

At precisely seven o'clock, Cara pulled up to the Cove and drew in a deep breath. She walked inside on unsteady legs. Her gaze immediately fell on David, and her heart stuttered.

David stood beside a familiar brunette girl with blunt-cut, shoulder-length hair and starkly drawn-on eyebrows. Lori Johnson. She'd been a senior at Seaside a couple of years back. And at the moment she sure looked a lot like David's date.

Cara's first instinct was to turn around and walk out. Then she noticed Lori's nametag and how she posed next to the hostess stand. She must be a new hire.

Cara relaxed and approached David.

He held his hand out. "It's great to see you again."

His crooked smile and rosy cheeks caused a tickle in her chest, as if her heart had sprouted wings that fluttered against her rib cage. She smiled and placed her hand in his. Warmth flowed between them, but she didn't look him in the eyes yet, for fear of swooning in front of Lori. Instead, she admired the contours of his chest underneath the white button-down he wore with khakis and casual brown dress shoes.

Lori eyed Cara. "Kathy has a table set up for you by the back window." Her words were polite, but Cara sensed an underlying gruffness in them.

Lori had been one of the popular girls that befriended Cara when she'd dated Chris and then axed her when he'd broken up with her. Apparently, Lori didn't leave those types of petty things behind with high school.

"Thank you," David said, his tone neutral as he led Cara by the hand and followed Lori through the large dining area.

Lori left them at their table without another word.

Not wanting the warmth between her and David to end, Cara fought the urge to cling to him. He gave her hand a light squeeze and let it go to pull her chair out for her.

Breathing in the scents of baked bread and fish, she sat and peered out the window beside them that framed a breathtaking view of Seagoer's Cove. David did the same. It was Labor Day weekend, the last weekend before school started. The restaurant was full of hushed chatter and clinking silverware.

David must have made a reservation. She hoped he felt as comfortable as she did here. It was as though they were cradled in the belly of a boat, its wooden sides adorned with peepholes and life preservers.

"So, what will you be doing . . . ?" Cara meant to add "while you're here?," but just then Kathy, a middle-aged waitress with copper curls and a maternal smile, stopped at their table with pen and pad in hand.

"I worried you'd grown tired of our chowder, Cara," Kathy teased.

"Never," Cara said, then introduced Kathy to David.

Kathy took their orders for diet soda, water, and chowder. Then she unsuccessfully attempted to give Cara a clandestine thumbs-up.

Glancing at David, Cara saw him struggling to suppress a smile, and she couldn't control her own as it spread across her face. She rolled her eyes at Kathy's back as the waitress walked away.

Then she pointed down at the cove. "Recognize that rock wall?"

"We were in the water just outside of it."

Cara shuddered at the memory.

At the cove's outer edge, tall white spray spouted high in the air. Another shorter spray shot up beside it.

Her jaw dropped. "No way."

"That's not Crossback and Bobbi?" David asked.

She turned from the view to look into his eyes. "You remember their names."

"I remember everything about that day."

Warmth brimmed in her chest and spiraled toward him through the invisible tether. He held her gaze and she felt sure he sensed the connection between them. If she mentioned it, though, he might think she was overly emotional, or crazy.

Steadying her breaths, she said, "That has to be Crossback and Bobbi. They're the only mother and calf I've seen out there in a long time."

They kept a lookout for more whale spouts, all the while sneaking glances at each other, until Kathy tottered over balancing a tray. Kathy set their drinks, chowder, rolls, and a bowl of butter on the table. This time, she gave Cara a not-so-clandestine wink.

David hid a laugh by coughing into his fist. Cara just shook her head. They cut and buttered slices of bread, then scooped spoonfuls of chowder into their mouths.

"You weren't kidding," David said, after he swallowed another mouthful. "This is the best clam chowder I've ever had." He pointed at his pot-size bowl, then held up his roll, which was the size of a small loaf of bread. "And also the largest portions I've ever had."

Cara chuckled. "You'll leave here full, that's for sure."

"I'm already full," David said, and blew out a breath. Then he gave her his lopsided smile and took another bite of chowder.

They looked down at the cove, but there was no further sign of the whales.

"I still can't believe we fell overboard into that frigid water," she said.

"You didn't fall. You were knocked in, remember?" David said, his voice soft.

"Yeah, for a second it felt like the orca was attacking us, but I'm thinking it was probably just curious."

"Maybe. Doesn't make it less scary. . . . I was startled myself, and I wasn't the one falling overboard."

"Wait . . ." Cara's lips parted and she stared at him as his words sank in. "You jumped in? To save me?"

He nodded and his cheeks turned a deeper shade of pink at the same time that she felt the heat rise in her own.

"You could've just thrown me a life ring."

"I saw you go under. I didn't realize until I was in the water that I needed to take my life jacket off to dive down after you, though. I was trying to get out of it when you suddenly came to the surface."

How amazing of him to risk his life for a stranger. "I got a boost."

"From a whale?"

"Yep, probably Crossback."

"Those whales really are highly intelligent, aren't they?"

"They are."

"They're also humongous." His lopsided smile returned.

She laughed. "True. And those transient orca teeth are like five inches long. Weren't you scared to jump in the water with them?"

His expression turned serious. "Not as scared as I was that you'd drown."

She looked into his eyes again and worried she might melt into a puddle in her seat.

Kathy brought David their check. He insisted on paying and held Cara's hand again on their way out of the restaurant. Lori eyed them curiously, almost with hostility, as they left. Cara brushed it off. Tonight was too perfect for pettiness.

Outside, the sun had descended toward the horizon. A muted, pinkish-blue hue filled the sky. Twinkle lights sparkled along the edges of the restaurant's awning, imbuing the lot with a fanciful luminescence.

David walked Cara over to her car. She faced him, leaning against the driver's-side door, and drew in a deep breath of courage. "Did you notice something unusual when we both touched Crossback?"

A light smile touched his lips and he nodded, but said nothing. Most likely, he didn't want her to think he was nuts, either.

She gazed into his eyes and basked in the warmth that radiated between them. It felt as though a tropical spring bubbled up within her.

"Can I take you out again next weekend?" he asked.

Her heart rate sped up, silently answering his question. "I'd like that."

"I'll call you."

The ocean breeze blew wisps of her hair in her face and David ran his fingers through a few tendrils. She glanced at his mouth and he leaned down and brushed his lips against hers. The kiss was light, but the flood of warmth between them was the greatest yet, like a fire that turned her bones to ash and set her skin aflame.

His lips sought hers again, first her bottom lip, then the upper. Kissing him back, she pressed her body more fully against his. Her fingers touched his cheek as he buried his deeper in her hair. She was molten lava in his arms.

He pulled back and looked at her with a soft glint in his green eyes. "This might sound crazy, but I'm glad we ended up overboard together."

Cara's mom called out from the family room when Cara shut the front door behind her a little after ten o'clock. Cara practically floated down the hallway and rested her weight against the family room doorframe.

"Looks like you had a good time," her mom said from the love seat.

"David's a great guy. He loved the chowder at the Cove as much as we do."

"Who wouldn't?"

"You'll like him. We're going out again next weekend. I'll introduce you."

"I look forward to it."

Cara could tell by the way her mom inclined in her seat that she hoped to get more details. Not sure whether she wanted to share, Cara paused. Even though this was all new and wonderful, the idea of talking to her mom about this kind of personal experience with a guy seemed awkward.

"Clam chowder always makes me tired," she said, and yawned for effect. "I'm going to head up to sleep. 'Night, Mom."

"Good night."

Cara winced at the disappointment in her mom's tone.

# SIX

Texting Rachel as she navigated her way through a throng of students on the first day of school proved difficult for Cara. By the time she'd crossed the blacktop and reached the school's metal double doors, she'd only managed to tap out a brief text:

Are you here yet?

Inside, sounds of anxious first-day banter and sneakers squeaking on linoleum echoed all around. Cara's phone vibrated in her hand. She flipped it around to read Rachel's reply:

I'm at your locker.

Cara rounded the corner to find Rachel leaning against the bank of lockers beside hers.

"I'm dying to meet the guy you almost killed at Liberty Charters," Rachel teased.

Cara playfully shoved Rachel aside and spun the combination on her locker. "I told you, I just tapped him."

But Cara had trouble truly believing that. The way she remembered it, she'd definitely hit Garren hard enough to hurt him.

She opened her locker door and set two soda bottles on the top shelf. When she turned around, Rachel was gawking at Garren, who stood there looking godlike in a casual white henley and jeans.

"Garren. Hi," Cara said. She had an irrational inclination to reach out and hug him, probably because she was still relieved he was alive. He looked out of this world, as perfect as the first time she'd met him. Yet, oddly, her pulse maintained a steady pace in his presence, not even a blip to hint at physical attraction.

Rachel, however, was undressing him with her eyes.

"This is my friend Rachel," Cara said, smacking her arm. "Rachel, this is Garren."

Garren flashed his brilliant smile. "Nice to meet you."

Rachel breathed out a hello.

"I hope you ladies will join me for lunch."

It was odd that he phrased his request as a statement rather than a question, but the invitation was nice.

"Of course," Cara said.

"I'll meet you on the stone wall," he said, and left them with one last dose of his mesmerizing smile.

As he slowly walked away, Rachel pulled out her phone and held it up to aim the camera lens at Garren's backside. She snapped a picture.

"What are you doing?" Cara said, snatching Rachel's phone away.

"Getting that photo I wanted."

"You can't even see his face." Cara shoved the phone back in Rachel's bag.

"His face isn't his only asset," Rachel said, continuing to appreciate the view. "You must really be into David to not be hot for this guy."

"I told you, David and I really connected."

"And I really am happy for you. But I'm also happy you're not interested in Garren. You won't mind if I go for him, will you?"

Garren would likely have plenty of options for girlfriends, but Cara would happily take this opportunity to give Rachel an early shot at him. He seemed like an exceptionally nice guy. "Have at him."

Rachel groaned. "You're not going to believe this, but Garren wasn't the first guy to ask me to eat lunch with him today."

Cara masked what must have been a look of surprise on her face with a smile. Rachel receiving two lunch invitations before the first day of school started seemed as unlikely as Cara meeting two new, good-looking local guys on the same day.

"Who's the other guy?" Cara asked.

"Ethan Thomas. He's in our class. You know, the cute, quiet, mysterious musician."

"Cute" might be a stretch, "quiet" was common, and "mysterious" struck Cara as code for "drug user." "Musician" called to mind a guy who always carried around a guitar case. "I've never talked to him, but I know who he is."

"I've never talked to him, either, until this morning."

"Did you tell him no?"

Rachel gritted her teeth. "I said yes. But I'd hate to miss out on a chance with Garren."

"You could always reschedule with Ethan and give Garren a chance first," Cara suggested.

Rachel was quick to bite on that option. "Good plan. Game on."

At lunch, Cara and Rachel hunkered down on the low stone wall bordering the upper-level lawn. Most of the students around campus either clustered at the few picnic tables on the school's lower level or sprawled on the grass. Sun hid behind wisps of clouds and cool air blew across campus. Animated voices and laughter carried over to where they sat.

Garren approached and shared his dazzling smile as he sat on the rough area of stone beside Cara.

Rachel sighed. Loudly.

Setting a messenger bag on the wall beside him, Garren said, "It's not a great feeling to be the new kid in town at a small school."

Cara had felt the same way when she'd been the new girl as a freshman. After Chris and the popular clan rejected her, Rachel had come to her rescue sophomore year. Their "group" had consisted of just the two of them since.

Grinning, Cara nudged Garren with her elbow. "It's probably not such a great feeling to almost get run over by the first classmate you meet, either."

His laugh was resonant and harmonious, just like his voice. He pulled two shiny, red apples from his bag and held them out in offering. They looked like pieces of waxed fruit. Their heart shape and deep ruby skin reminded Cara of the Red Delicious variety.

"No thanks," Rachel said. She didn't like to eat things that mussed up her lipstick, especially in front of boys.

Garren's face fell. He held up an apple for Cara.

"Thanks." She accepted the apple and bit into it. It was the crispest, sweetest, and juiciest piece of fruit she'd ever tasted.

From her backpack, she pulled out chips and a diet soda. She uncapped the bottle and took a drink, then tore open her chip bag and tilted it toward Garren.

He thanked her and selected a single chip. Twisting it back and forth in his fingers, he observed it. Then he held it up to his nose and sniffed at it.

Rachel giggled into her water bottle.

"It's jalapeño cheddar," Cara said. "Spicy, but tasty."

Garren bit into the chip and took his time chewing and swallowing. "Nice."

Cara held the bag out for him again. He took several this time.

Rachel had spotted Ethan, who stood a short way down the wall. He was brawny and his eyes remained narrowed, as if he was perpetually suspicious. He wore his chin-length brown hair parted down the middle.

Cara pictured him in her mind as she'd seen him in past years. He'd always worn hoodies, jeans, and sneakers, and he often carried an acoustic guitar case. Now he wore black clothes that matched his combat boots, and he'd ditched the guitar. His jaw was taut, his lips pinched together.

"Ethan looks creepily upset. Didn't you tell him you were eating with us?" Cara asked Rachel.

"He wasn't happy that I decided to eat with you instead of him. But it's not like he's my boyfriend," Rachel said, glancing at Garren to check his reaction.

His expression was unreadable.

"How are you liking Seaside?" Rachel asked him, twirling a silky strand of hair into a curl around her finger. It stubbornly bounced back into its favored straight state.

Cara registered Rachel's flirtatious grin, but wasn't sure if Garren did.

"There's good and there's bad," he said. "You just have to make sure to choose the good."

Garren prompted them to fill him in on their plans for the next year. After listening politely to Rachel, his attention turned back to Cara, who did her best to answer his questions between mouthfuls of apple. Cara tried to steer the conversation toward Rachel, but Garren always ended up switching the focus back to her.

It flattered her to think he might be attracted to her. Since she'd met David, she'd taken more care with her appearance, happy she'd finally found a guy she didn't want to hide from. Each day, she applied light makeup, tousled her hair with mousse, and wore clothes that revealed her curves.

She finished off the luscious apple. Garren took the core and deposited it in his bag.

Rachel's attention had shifted back to Ethan. He wore a sad frown now as he returned Rachel's gaze. Hunching his shoulders, he shuffled away toward the school building. Rachel looked at Cara and cocked her head toward him, said a quick good-bye to Garren, then hurried off.

Garren rose from the wall. "If you want, I'll join you for lunch again tomorrow."

Hopefully, like her, he only wanted to be friends. "Don't feel obligated." She held out her half-full bag of chips. "Here, take the rest."

"Thanks." He accepted the chips and smiled before he turned his face up to the sky and walked away.

She wondered how he saw where he was going, looking up while he walked.

# SEVEN

Two periods later, Garren passed Cara and Rachel in the hallway and entered the journalism classroom. Cara prodded Rachel from behind to get her moving in that direction. Inside, Cara chose the middle desk in the back row. Rachel sat in the seat to her left.

Garren stood in front of the teacher's desk, blocking her view of Ms. Burg. For some reason, Mr. Cutter, a young teacher who taught English and creative writing, stood at the head of the class.

More students filed into the room. Garren came over and took the seat to Cara's right.

Cara glanced toward the front desk. And her heart sank deeper than she'd sunk beneath the ocean's surface. Her head swam and she thought she might pass out. Which would be okay. At least then she wouldn't be conscious of what was happening.

David looked up and his green eyes froze on her. His face paled, his chest expanded, and he let out a deep breath.

Cara was too taken aback to stop staring at him. Her heart lay in a cold puddle in the pit of her stomach. David was her teacher.

Her gaze dropped to her desk. There was no way she could hide. And she'd have to see him every day at school.

Mr. Cutter interrupted her horror by addressing the class. "I recognize many faces here. Welcome to the new school year. For those who don't know me, my name is Mr. Cutter. Ms. Burg accepted a last-minute job offer in Portland." He waved David over, spoke in his ear, and handed him a stack of papers.

David distributed small piles of the papers to the first person in each row to pass back.

Mr. Cutter continued, "Fortunately, Mr. Wilson is an intern from Washington who'd already signed up for student teaching this semester. He'll be your new lead. My job here is to observe."

"Hello, everyone," David said, claiming Mr. Cutter's former space.

Mr. Cutter continued, "You should all receive a ballot listing newspaper staff members' names. Please check the box next to the candidate you think deserves the position. You can leave your votes on the teacher's desk at the end of the period. Mr. Wilson will announce the winning candidate tomorrow."

Mr. Cutter sat at the teacher's desk. "Mr. Wilson, I'll turn things over to you."

David stood tall in front of the class. "I want to give you all some time to think about your votes before we begin with today's lesson." His words weren't smooth, as they had been when she'd spoken with him before, but were cut off neatly at the corners.

His eyes never met hers.

Grateful to have something to focus on, Cara bent over her ballot. She concentrated on four names in the column of staff members, each next to a corresponding check box: John Albright, Rachel Clark, Cara Markwell, and Jeff Peters. John was a star athlete and strictly a sportswriter. Jeff loved to argue and covered editorials. Rachel was the least qualified staff member, but she wrote an advice column students loved. Cara wrote the most diverse articles and had assisted previous years' editors.

She was certain she wanted the editor position more than the other candidates. In past years, she'd worked the hardest, and she expected to win the vote. But if she did get the position, David would be her lead. At the moment, working closely with him seemed like it would amount to utter humiliation.

Rachel doodled in a notebook, unaware that Cara's recent hopes for love had just been doused, in the worst way.

Students finished with their ballots and many of the girls' eyes turned to Garren. Several girls also turned their attention to David, and not just because he was a new student teacher, if their flushed cheeks and silly smiles were any indication.

Jealousy ignited in Cara's chest and fanned into flames. She wanted to tell the girls to stop being ridiculous. "Mr. Wilson" was a teacher. But she'd have to tell herself to stop, too. For the rest of the period, she tried, with little success, to concentrate on the lesson as much as she did David.

After class, Garren stood with his back to the teacher's desk and looked down at her. She could swear she saw sympathy in his tempered smile.

"Sorry about the student-teacher situation," he said, his voice quiet.

He couldn't know about her feelings for David. "What do you mean?"

"It must be awkward."

This wasn't the first time Garren had made odd comments. Maybe he assumed she'd miss Ms. Burg or something, since they'd worked together on the paper for the past three years.

"It'll be fine, thanks," she said.

"Good luck on the editor vote," he said with a wink, and walked off.

She turned to talk to Rachel, but she'd already snuck to the front of the line to drop off her ballot. Ethan stood in the doorway, waiting for her. Rachel disappeared with him down the hallway.

Mr. Cutter shook David's hand and left the room.

Cara waited for the other students to drop off their ballots before she approached David at the teacher's desk. The connection she felt with him was a mystery she didn't understand. But as her eyes held his, warmth coursed through the invisible tether. Energy spread within her, then rushed back toward him.

Her ballot shook in her hands. She quickly set the paper facedown on top of the others.

David's smile appeared strained, a counterfeit version of his natural, lopsided grin.

"I'm sorry . . ." she began.

"Don't be sorry." His forearm caught the stack of ballots and the papers fluttered to the floor.

She leaned down, picked them up, and set them back on his desk.

"I don't know what to say, other than I wish you luck on the editor vote," he said, his voice as shaky as she felt.

"Thanks," she said, knowing he also knew the true reason for the tremor in her voice.

# EIGHT

At home, Cara absently walked into the kitchen and dropped onto the kitchen nook bench. Her mom stood at the stove with a spatula, pushing meat around in a sizzling skillet. Cara and her mom usually prepared dinner together after school, so her mom had set out a cutting board and fixings for an avocado salad for Cara to work on.

Seeing Cara's face, her mom turned down the heat on the stove. "Not up for fixing dinner today?"

Cara shook her head. "Sorry."

"Looks like this calls for ice cream," her mom said, and dished up two bowls of Cara's favorite peppermint candy flavor.

She set the bowls on the table, sat, and gave Cara a concerned sideways gaze. "The first day of senior year didn't go so well, I take it?"

Cara picked up her spoon and poked at her ice cream. "David was there." Her words sounded flat.

"What?" Her mom dropped her spoon and it clanked against her bowl. "Why?"

"He's the student teacher for my journalism class."

"Oh, no." Her mom took her hand. "How could he not know you were in high school?"

Cara sighed. "I didn't tell him. I was going to tell him next month, after my birthday. I didn't know if he'd want to date me if he knew I was seventeen."

"Did he say anything to you today?"

"He wished me luck on the editor vote."

Her mom let go of her hand and clasped her own together on the table. "You know you need to give up on this, right?"

"I wouldn't do anything to cause problems for him."

"Well, I'm a little unnerved that he didn't make sure you weren't too young. I hope he regrets his mistake."

A *mistake*. That's what she was to him now.

No longer able to hold back her emotions, she grabbed her things and ran for the front door.

Cara sniffed and blinked the tears from her eyes, doing her best to focus on the road as she headed for her favorite overlook at Maritime Bay. A few minutes later, she arrived at the lot above the lookout point. The only other car was a silver Toyota truck with Washington plates, and any tourist who saw her tear-stained face probably wouldn't bother her. She parked far from the truck, stepped out of her Civic, and sucked in a salty, cleansing breath.

The rhythmic sound of the waves crashing against the rocks below calmed her. She shuffled down the grassy hill that led to a fence lining the cliff top. The owner of the truck leaned against the railing. His head was bent, as though he were watching the waves below him.

Veering left, toward the farthest length of fence, she glanced over at the guy. His eyes met hers and she stopped breathing.

David froze in place, staring at her. She did the same, paralyzed with disbelief that he was there. Her cheeks lit on fire, and not because of the connection between them. They were too far away for that.

He might think she'd followed him after school. She turned to leave.

"Cara, wait."

Taking in another deep breath of sea air, she hesitated, then turned to face him. He didn't smile, but waved her over.

She walked over to where he stood and gripped the cool fence railing. The waves smacking the rocks below echoed her desire to smack herself in the head. She wasn't sure if she could speak without her voice breaking.

"I'm sorry, too," he said. "I shouldn't have assumed you were older. I should've asked."

She cleared her throat and repeated his earlier words. "Don't be sorry." Her voice cracked.

He took a step closer and studied her face, zoning in on her eyes and cheeks. "Are you okay?" He cringed, as though he were in pain.

She most definitely didn't feel okay. More than anything, she wanted to wrap her arms around him and have him do the same, for him to hold her like he had on the *Lookout*. Amazingly, she felt colder now than she had then, only on the inside this time.

But he was her teacher. And she didn't want him to feel guilty about anything. She needed to pull herself together.

This was too much, though. Tears rolled down her cheeks. She cursed them, unable to control the flood of emotions that assaulted her.

Standing up straight, she scanned the water to distract herself.

Two tall, black dorsal fins and three shorter ones clustered in the water not far from the cliff face. She shivered and wrapped her arms around herself.

"They're still here," she whispered.

"That's weird," David said. "Rick said they should be gone."

"I need to get back out on the water," she said, eyes still on the transients. "I just don't know if I can. Especially if they don't leave."

"You can." His words were firm.

She met his gaze, not bothering to wipe away her tears. Her shivering ceased when their warm connection took hold.

"I know the orca who knocked us overboard was probably just curious, or playful," she said, more to try to convince herself than David. "But I'm used to baleen whales. These transients. Those teeth. They're like sharks."

"They're whales."

"Actually, they're dolphins."

The corner of his lip turned up. "So they're dolphins. As far as I know, not one has ever harmed a human in the wild."

*Maybe because humans rarely swim with transient orcas in the wild,* Cara thought.

"Don't let fear rob you of something that means so much to you," he said before he took a few steps back.

Cara relished the last shower of warmth between them, then nodded and broke their gaze.

"I should go," he said.

She wasn't sure if she'd imagined a hint of regret in his tone.

She nodded again, but didn't look at him.

Not long after, she heard the hum of his truck motor as he drove off.

She dropped down on the wet grass and hugged her knees to her chest. The transients had disappeared the moment David left.

In the overlook parking lot, Cara sat in her car and texted Rachel about David. Rachel texted back that she was home, so Cara drove over and parked in front of the Clarks' brown bungalow. Ms. Clark welcomed her in and Cara let herself into Rachel's room.

Rachel, who'd been lying on her belly on her bed reading a paperback, hopped up into a cross-legged position and patted her mattress for Cara to sit. Cara dropped down next to Rachel and pulled a diet soda from her backpack. She cracked the bottle open and swigged from it.

"Smile for me?" Rachel asked.

Cara gave her a bogus smile and worked on screwing and unscrewing her soda's cap. Her vision blurred as she tried to make out details in the pictures of her and Rachel taped to Rachel's vanity mirror.

Rachel walked over to her vanity, grabbed a tissue, and brought it over to Cara, who stashed her soda in her bag. Cara swept at her eyes, then stared at her hands as she folded and unfolded the tissue.

"Busy hands are a sign of a busy mind, as your mom would say," Rachel teased.

Cara balled the tissue up and tossed it at Rachel.

"I'm really sorry about David," Rachel said, lobbing the tissue at her trash can and missing. "But I'm glad you got to talk to him at the overlook. How weird that you ran into him. It's a small town, but still."

"I know. I hope he didn't think I was following him."

"You didn't follow him, did you?"

Cara glared.

Rachel broke out in a grin. "Kidding. So what's the deal with these orcas?"

"They're transients that should have left the area a while ago. I keep having nightmares about them coming after me in the water, mistaking me for their next meal."

"Oh, please. You don't have enough meat on your bones to satisfy some orca that has its pick of a gazillion seals and sea lions. No wonder they don't want to leave. David's right. You need to get back out there."

"I don't suppose you'd go with me?"

"Yeah, no. But just because I'm afraid of monstrously large mammals and man-eating fish doesn't mean you should be."

"That's very comforting, thanks."

"You need to think positive. What are the odds that you'd have a second incident like the overboard deal? Slim to none, I'd say."

God love Rachel.

"You're right. I need to get out there." She smiled. As always lately, her mind circled back to David. Her smile faded.

"Part of the thinking-positive thing is to not let yourself obsess about what you can't have," Rachel said.

"How am I supposed to force myself to act like nothing's going on between us after how we connected? I have to see him at school every day."

"At least you'll get to see him. And you'll want to protect his reputation. So you won't do anything stupid. Maybe you'll become desensitized."

*More like hypersensitized.*

"Or . . ." Rachel tucked Cara's chin up with her fingers. "Maybe you two will get together later." She offered a hopeful smile.

"Mr. Cutter said David's only interning for a semester. He'll probably leave after that."

"So? Yours wouldn't be the first long-distance relationship."

Rachel was sweet to make something so far-fetched sound plausible.

"What about you? Are you still planning to go for Garren?" Cara asked.

"Don't be naïve, Cara, he's obviously into you," Rachel said.

Cara wasn't so sure. He hadn't given off any amorous vibes toward her. Or to Rachel, either.

"Then what about Ethan?" Cara didn't let on that she'd seen Ethan waiting for Rachel after school and didn't share her worry that Ethan might be bad boyfriend material.

"It took some kissing up to get him to forgive me for ditching him for Garren."

*Hopefully not too much kissing up.*

"No worries, though. We're on for lunch tomorrow."

Cara put on a false smile as her chest tightened with anxiety. "You'll have to tell me all about it."

# NINE

Thin fog curled through Seaside's campus and crawled along the stone wall where Cara sat for lunch the next day. She kept an eye on Rachel and Ethan, who had settled onto another area of the wall. Ethan stood, while Rachel sat with one leg crossed over the other.

Rachel flipped her hair back, then fanned it over the front of her white, long-sleeved tee. Ethan fished in a brown paper sack, then offered Rachel something she stuck her tongue out at after tasting. Next Ethan offered Rachel a drink, but after she tried it, her face bunched up and she grabbed a water bottle from her bag and chugged from it.

Ethan noticed Cara watching and hooked his finger toward himself and Rachel, gesturing for her to join them. Cara looked away. The idea of being a tag-along to a twosome wasn't appealing. And she didn't want to seem like she supported Ethan, in case he did end up being bad news. But Rachel might be upset if she didn't accept his invitation.

As she considered how to respond, Garren sat beside her and held out an apple.

She thanked him and took it, doubting it could be as tasty as the one he'd given her the day before. Yet when she bit into it, it tasted at least as delicious as the first one.

She pulled out a bag of the jalapeño cheddar chips he'd liked so much and gave it to him in exchange.

"I voted for you for the editor position," Garren told her, opening the chips. He popped one in his mouth and took his time chewing.

"That was nice of you," Cara told him. "But you don't even know if I deserve the position."

"I can tell that you do."

Instead of arguing that it wasn't possible for him to simply *tell*, she bit into her apple again. Suddenly, she realized she forgot to respond to Ethan's invitation, and she leaned forward to look down the wall. Rachel pulled out a set of earbuds and handed them to Ethan with a shake of her head. He laughed and rested his hand on Rachel's knee.

Cara tensed and turned her attention back to Garren. Just because Ethan had opted for a look she wasn't impressed with and was touching her best friend didn't mean she had a right to judge him. She should be happy for Rachel.

As if in tune with Cara's intuitive suspicions, Garren pointed to Ethan and said, "That one hangs out with a sketchy crowd. You should watch out for Rachel."

"How do you know about Ethan's crowd?"

"I've been around long enough to notice."

Cara wasn't surprised to hear a warning about Ethan, especially since he'd changed so much over the summer. But she was sorry, for Rachel's sake, that her instincts had likely been correct.

She finished her apple as she and Garren sat in a comfortable cocoon of silence. Like the day before, Garren took her apple core and tucked it in his bag. They rose from the wall as Rachel rushed over, wearing a huge grin.

"See you two in journalism class," Garren said, and headed toward the building.

Oddly, Rachel didn't give Garren a second glance as they followed along behind him.

"You and Ethan looked pretty happy together."

They entered the building and headed down the hall and around the corner to Rachel's locker. "He's cute, but he's changed. Last year, I heard him one day after school playing this sweet, romantic music on his guitar. I figured he was the quiet, sensitive type. But just now he had me listen to some heavy stuff. It's probably death rock."

Rachel pulled a textbook from her locker and slammed the door. "Plus, I thought he was after you at first. He kept mentioning you and wanted you to sit with us."

Cara frowned, but kept her mouth shut. Now didn't seem like a good time to bring up Garren's warning.

Rachel shook her head and linked arms with Cara as they walked down the hall. "But I was wrong. He wants to get together after school."

"I was going to say, for someone who was after me, he sure touched you a lot."

"You saw that?" Rachel covered her mouth with her hand, pretending to be embarrassed.

Cara knew better. "I was worried he was trying to poison you. What was he feeding you?"

Rachel wrinkled her nose. "Some weird organic crap that tastes like hell. He's really big on it."

"Gross. You should just say no."

"I don't want to put down his passions."

"So are you interested in him or not?"

Rachel smiled softly. "Yes. He's cute. And potentially sweet. He wants to introduce me to some of his friends tonight."

"He's already introducing you to his friends?"

"I think it's romantic that he's acting so serious about me so soon."

"Just don't swoon too hard over that death rock," Cara teased.

Rachel elbowed her in the ribs.

Cara played hurt and winced.

Garren's warning that she should watch out for Rachel chimed in her mind. "Be sure to watch out for yourself."

Rachel rolled her eyes. "Yes, Mom."

---

Cara sat between Rachel and Garren in the journalism classroom and took a few final deep breaths to slow her racing heart.

David turned from the whiteboard. "Congratulations to Cara Markwell for getting the most votes for this year's editor spot." His words were softer than the ones he'd spoken during class the day before.

Mr. Cutter clapped from the teacher's desk. The rest of the class followed his lead.

David shared his lopsided smile with her. Their eyes met and her heart buoyed in the warm bath of energy that built up within her and flowed out toward him.

"Cara, please see me after class about getting started on the first newspaper issue."

The class period dragged on. Cara hoped she pulled off the right balance between observing David and looking elsewhere. It was hard to turn her eyes away when she had such brief opportunities to admire him.

Finally, class ended. Mr. Cutter stood to write on the whiteboard. David took the teacher's seat. Cara remained at her desk, and several students stopped to congratulate her. Garren was one of them. Surprisingly, Rachel was not. She was the first one out of the classroom. Ethan was probably waiting for her again.

A ball of jealousy flared up within Cara, but it died down when her eyes fell on David's. She waited in her seat until the other students had left the classroom, then walked over to the teacher's desk on rubbery legs.

David swiveled in his chair to face her, but avoided her eyes. "I've been reading the past newspaper issues, and there's plenty of evidence that you've worked hard to earn the position. You're the one I would've chosen for the editor spot no matter how the vote turned out, just so you know."

"Thanks for saying so."

Mr. Cutter paused to look over at them before he continued writing on the board.

David met her gaze, but abruptly looked away, then swung his chair back under the teacher's desk and collected some papers. "I trust that you're familiar with the editor's duties, so I'll leave things in your hands, unless you have questions. Garren has experience with layout and agreed to help with that. I'll want to look everything over. But that should be the extent of my involvement."

"Thanks for your support," she said and walked off.

*So much for working closely with him.*

"Congratulations, Cara," he called after her, sounding more like he was apologizing to her than praising her.

At home, the welcome aroma of sautéing vegetables wafted through the air and lured Cara into the kitchen.

Her apron-clad mom mixed chopped onion, celery, and carrots in a frying pan. She motioned with a wooden spoon for Cara to get started on the two palm-size heads of elephant garlic waiting on the cutting board.

"I thought we'd use one head for lentil soup and bread and save the other for our favorite snack later this week, if you don't mind getting those ready to bake?"

"Sure." Cara felt her mom's eyes on her as she dumped her backpack by the nook and pulled an apron from a hook. "I got the editor position," she said, tying on the apron. She pulled a knife from the block on the counter.

"I knew you would. Congratulations." Her mom continued poking at the vegetables while peeking sideways at her. "You don't look too happy about it. Is it because you'll have to work with the student teacher?"

"Yeah, that's gonna be weird. But David said he's going to leave most of the work up to me and the new guy, Garren." She cut the top off the first giant garlic head, then set it aside and grabbed the other.

"David?" Her mom put a hand on her hip. "You're not calling a teacher by his first name at school, are you?"

Cara sawed the top off the second bunch of garlic. "No. I meant, Mr. Wilson."

Her mom dumped the vegetables from the frying pan into a large pot of beans and broth on another burner. "I'm not trying to upset you. I just know that you wouldn't want to jeopardize his job."

"I wouldn't do anything to hurt him." Cara reached into the cupboard beneath her for the aluminum foil and ripped off a sheet.

"Who's this new guy you mentioned?"

"His name's Garren." Cara set the garlic on the foil, grabbed a bottle of olive oil from the counter, and filled the heads.

"I actually met him at Liberty Charters the same day I met David." She thought better of revealing that she almost ran him over with her car. Her mom was unhappy enough about the scrape on her Civic. "I guess Garren has experience with layout. And he's been eating lunch with me."

Her mom stepped aside so she could fetch a cookie sheet from the small cupboard beside the oven.

"What do you think of Garren?" her mom asked, her eyes never moving from the mass she swirled around in the pot.

Cara didn't want to give her mom the impression she was attracted to Garren, so she decided not to mention how good looking he was. "He acts sort of weird, old-fashioned or something."

"That doesn't sound so bad."

"He's really nice." That seemed like an understatement. "And I'll be glad to have help with the newspaper layout."

"You'll be spending a lot of time with him, then?"

"Maybe."

"Sounds promising." Her mom smiled at the soup.

Cara crushed ends of foil together to encase the garlic heads and placed the bundle on the cookie sheet. "It's not promising."

Her mom stopped stirring. "You're not just saying that because you're hung up on the student teacher?"

Cara opened the oven and shoved the cookie sheet onto the top rack. "No. I'm just not into Garren." She shut the oven door and faced her mom. "But to be honest, yes, I am hung up on the student teacher."

Her mom eyed her warily, then pulled her into a hug. "I know it must be hard, honey. But I'm glad you understand that you need to forget about him."

*Easier said than done.*

# TEN

Cara didn't hear from Rachel Thursday night, although she'd expected an update on the Ethan situation. And Friday morning she didn't find her at either of their lockers, where they usually met. Cara pulled out her phone and sent a text:

> Didn't see you this morning. Are you home? You still
> have to fill me in on how things went with Ethan's
> friends.

Rachel never sent a return text. Cara wondered if she'd gotten sick. Until lunch hour came and Cara sat on the stone wall.

Another pervading fog wove through the campus. Rachel and Ethan had taken up their same spots from the day before. Ethan once again fed Rachel odd food, though Rachel ate and drank the offensive offerings with less of a grimace. She must be getting used to the stuff.

Cara figured Ethan was a health food addict or something. Although he sure didn't look like one. She couldn't remember him ever looking so pale, and his hair hung past his chin in limp, scraggly strands. His appearance had definitely taken a nosedive over the summer.

The only explanation Cara could think of for Rachel's lack of communication was that her phone was broken, or missing. She was about to head over to ask Rachel about it, when Garren sat down beside her.

He took a red apple from his bag and offered it to her. It looked every bit as delicious as the apples he'd given her the past two days. She pulled a ham sandwich from her lunch sack and held it out for him. He shook his head.

"I've got more chips for you, too, if you'd rather have those," she said, setting down a bag. She took half the sandwich from its plastic wrapping. "Take it. If I eat the apple, I'll only be able to eat half of this anyway."

"Deal."

She accepted the apple, bit off a hunk, and let the juices flow across her tongue before she chewed and swallowed. "Where do you get these? They're unbelievable."

"A secret source."

This kind of obscure answer was becoming typical for Garren.

"I'll bring you an apple every day if you love them so much," he said, and bit into the sandwich.

"I definitely won't turn them down," she said, and took another succulent bite.

"I see you're keeping an eye on Rachel."

Cara nodded. "Something's not right with her. I'm not sure what it is, but she didn't meet me this morning and she hasn't been answering my text messages."

"You should talk to her."

"I will. But I don't want to interrupt her time with her new boyfriend. If that's what Ethan is."

"You didn't warn her about him." Cara was glad that Garren didn't sound accusatory. He did sound disappointed, however.

"I had hopes you two would be into each other." She watched closely for his reaction.

"I'm not . . ." He looked up at the sky for a moment, then met her gaze. ". . . *attracted* to her."

So he wasn't attracted to Rachel—or to her, so it seemed. And she hadn't seen him interact with any other girls, though he didn't seem shy. Maybe he was gay and hadn't felt comfortable pursuing relationships with any guys yet.

"Forcing things never works," he said with a hint of frustration.

"I guess I'll just have to keep trying to look out for her," Cara said.

"She's fortunate to have a friend like you."

"I'm pretty fortunate to have her, too."

Cara finished her apple. As was Garren's peculiar habit, he took the core and deposited it in his bag, along with the bag of chips she handed him. As they sat together, swaddled in silence, Garren often glanced in Rachel and Ethan's direction.

When lunch ended, Garren stood to wait while Cara stuffed her lunch sack and diet soda bottle in her backpack. She rose from the wall, and he walked with her as she headed toward Rachel and Ethan. As they drew near, Rachel's and Ethan's eyes narrowed.

"What's going on, Rachel?" Cara stopped several steps farther back from her friend than usual.

Garren remained by Cara's side. Rachel and Ethan backed up and scowled at him. Ethan slung an arm around Rachel's shoulder and the two of them turned and stalked off.

"What's your problem, Rachel?" Cara called out.

Rachel didn't acknowledge her.

Cara pressed her lips together and held back the harsher words she wanted to let loose. In their two years of friendship, she'd seldom known Rachel to be quiet and she'd never known her to be rude. Also, it had only been a couple of days since Rachel had been interested in dating Garren.

Cara slapped on a smile and faced him.

He frowned at her. "You're upset."

She lost her fake grin and sighed.

He offered her his arm. The genteel gesture threw her off. She felt confident this was simply gentlemanly treatment, but from the stares of their fellow students, others didn't find the interaction so casual. She didn't mind if people thought she and Garren were involved, especially if it helped hide her attraction to David. Still, she wondered why Garren wouldn't care.

She slipped her arm through his. "I'll be fine."

They walked toward the building and Garren kept her arm tucked in his. A breeze carried his scent over to her. She inhaled, absorbing the fragrance of what had to be a cologne—a fabulous one, reminding her of freshly dried laundry, lemon candy, and recently fallen rain. The pleasant smell put her at ease. She couldn't imagine how Garren would put anyone off.

"Does Ethan have a problem with you?" she asked as Garren steered her into the building, then down a side hall.

"Most likely." He didn't sound aggravated about it. "Let's hope he gets over it. Please don't let it bother you."

He said good-bye and left her at the door to her chemistry class.

Strange, he hadn't walked with her after lunch before, and she couldn't remember telling him where her class was.

Before journalism class, Cara hurried down the hall toward Rachel, who was heading to meet Ethan at his locker. Cara touched her shoulder, but Rachel didn't stop. When Cara grabbed her forearm, Rachel spun around and faced her with a pinched, annoyed look.

"I'm busy." Rachel's words came out sounding like a hiss. She didn't look Cara in the eyes.

"You and Ethan could have been more friendly to Garren at lunch."

"Ethan has a bad feeling about him."

"What does that mean?"

"Garren creeps Ethan out. He makes me feel weird, too. Ethan wanted you to hang out with us, but not now."

Knots of anger tightened in Cara's chest. "Us? You and Ethan are an official couple now? Forget the fact that, as of yesterday, 'us' would have referred to you and me."

"I hope Ethan and I are a couple." Rachel's words floated from her mouth, dreamlike. She headed off, leaving Cara standing alone in the middle of the hall.

Rachel stopped at Ethan's locker. He slid an arm around her waist, and they walked in the opposite direction of the journalism classroom. Cara watched as they made their way down the hallway and out the exit.

Garren was clearly right about Ethan being a bad influence. Unfortunately, at this point, Cara doubted there was anything she could do to change Rachel's mind about him. She'd just have to try to keep an eye on things.

Cara had hoped to get to journalism class early to talk to David. But after her run-in with Rachel, her nerves were worn ragged. She barely made it to class before the bell rang.

The other students were already seated. Mr. Cutter sat at the teacher's desk with his laptop, and David stood at the whiteboard completing his lesson plan. Garren gave her a sympathetic smile as she slunk over to her seat.

After class, she remained at her desk as the other students streamed out of the room, happy to be free for the weekend. Mr. Cutter remained at the teacher's desk, eyeing her every few seconds. David slowly walked over and sat sideways in Garren's seat. She shifted around in her chair to face him, and their knees nearly touched.

He stared down at their legs. His chair scraped against the floor as he angled away. "Did you need something from me?"

Her heart pounded so hard she worried he could see it through her blouse. She quit fussing with her sleeves and crossed her arms over her chest. "I'm planning to write a 'new teacher feature' for the first newspaper issue."

She knew her mom was right that she needed to put David behind her. But she couldn't resist a school-approved way to get to know him better and to spend time with him. "I'm hoping you'll be available for an interview, maybe Monday after school?"

He hesitated.

She forced a thin smile.

"I'd be happy to do the interview," he finally said, and shared his lopsided smile with her.

She tried to catch his eye, but his gaze dropped to the floor. "We can do it during class. We'll make it a free-for-all day."

She fell back against her chair and felt her face fall, as well. *Free-for-all* didn't sound like quite what she had in mind.

●

Garren waited by her car in the student lot. His rigid posture and steady gaze hinted at an underlying concern.

Reaching out and putting a hand on his arm, she asked, "Is everything all right?"

He moved aside to let her open the driver's door. She tossed her backpack on the passenger seat.

"Rachel skipped class," he said, as though she'd broken the law.

Cara gritted her teeth. "You were right about Ethan. I tried to talk to her, but she said Ethan doesn't want to hang out with us." She gestured between herself and Garren. "Now he's got her skipping school. I don't know what to do."

"You should go see her."

She thought about it for a second. If she could talk to Rachel alone, outside of school, away from both Ethan and Garren, maybe Rachel would act like her normal self again.

She nodded. "It's worth a shot."

●

At home, Cara talked her mom into baking early batches of the oatmeal gumdrop cookies they froze each year, then doled out at Christmas. Rachel loved them. An hour later, the kitchen swelled with warmth and a sweet, buttery scent.

The mixer wound down from a frantic spin to a slow churn. When the machine's groaning stopped, her mom leaned against the counter and stared at her.

"You still seem down, honey. Are you and Rachel fighting? Is that why you want to bring her cookies?"

Cara went to the sink to wash her sticky hands. "Rachel basically ditched me for the first guy who showed interest in her at school. She's all about her new boyfriend."

"The school year just started and Rachel already has a boyfriend?"

Cara dried her hands and popped the lid off a cookie tin to make sure it was full, then clamped it back on. "She's been hanging out with him at lunch and after school since the first day. And she's been distant with me since I started eating lunch with Garren."

"Maybe Rachel's jealous of your new relationship."

Cara shook her head. "Rachel knows I'm not interested in Garren. But she said she and Ethan don't like him."

"Garren's new in town. I can't imagine they'd know him well enough to dislike him."

"I agree. But the only thing I can think to do is to try to talk to Rachel when Ethan and Garren aren't around."

Her mom put an arm around her and squeezed her shoulder. "Sounds like a good plan. And don't worry. Good friends almost always outlast boyfriends."

# ELEVEN

Rachel's Corolla sat parked in front of the Clarks' house. She still hadn't answered any of Cara's texts. Hopefully Ethan hadn't picked her up and taken her away somewhere. Maybe Ms. Clark had found out about Rachel skipping class. Then Rachel might be grounded for life.

Ms. Clark gave Cara an odd look when she found her on the doorstep holding a Christmas tin before Halloween. Cara popped the lid off and held the tin out.

Ms. Clark patted her ample belly. "I shouldn't, but I can't help myself." She selected a cookie. "Thanks, sweetie."

"They're Rachel's favorite. I thought I'd bring her an early batch."

Ms. Clark ushered her inside. "That's nice. Rachel came home sick, though."

Rachel probably told her mom she didn't feel well so she wouldn't get in trouble when the school called and reported her absence. "She can always save them for later, I guess." Cara gestured with the tin toward Rachel's room down the hall. "I'll bring them to her, if that's okay?"

"Sure. I hope she's not contagious."

*Not likely.*

Though Cara had walked in on her best friend in her room count-less times in the past, Rachel shot her a tight-lipped look when she entered without knocking. Sitting on her bed with her knees bent, Rachel held a thick, hardcover book against her thighs. Before Cara could catch the title, Rachel slammed the book shut and shoved it under her pillow.

Rachel eyed the Christmas-themed tin the same way Ms. Clark had. "'Tisn't the season."

Rachel's sense of humor would've been a good sign, if her tone weren't mocking.

"I thought I'd bring you an early dose." Cara walked over to Rachel's bedside and held out a cookie. Rachel didn't take it.

Cara grabbed Rachel's hand, placed the cookie on her palm, and folded Rachel's fingers around it. For a second, Rachel's eyes flashed clear. When Cara let go and took a step back, they clouded over.

With a blank face, Rachel tilted the cookie back and forth in her fingers. Then she crumbled it in her hand and dumped the pieces on her comforter.

"Not cool." Cara snapped the lid back on the tin and hugged it to her chest.

No reaction from Rachel, who stared, expressionless, toward her vanity. Maybe she really wasn't feeling well.

"Your mom said you came home sick."

"I've had some stomachaches and headaches. It happens."

"I wanted to talk to you about today. It's too bad that you and Ethan don't like Garren. But you and I have been friends for years. I don't want anything to come between us."

"I have a boyfriend now. I'm going to spend time with him. You need to understand that."

"I do understand. But you can't spend *all* your time with him."

Again, Rachel offered no response. The reporter in Cara kicked in. She visually inspected Rachel's room, searching for clues as to what could have so radically altered her friend.

Photos of the two of them still covered the sides of Rachel's mirror. But her makeup had been shoved off to one side of her vanity top, her magazines and books to the other. In the center sat two large, cylindrical candles with darkened wicks. One candle was orange, the other black, like Halloween colors. Next to the candles were two alabaster shells. The last item appeared to be a black glass circle.

Strange new decorations, but nothing that bizarre. As always, a heap of clothes lay on the floor by the closet. The only truly unusual thing was that Rachel seemed to hide the book she'd been reading.

Cara wanted to dart over and snatch the book. Instead, she left the cookie tin on Rachel's vanity. "I wish you'd talk to me about whatever's going on with you."

"You want to help me?" Rachel's tone sounded scornful.

Cara took a step back, then stood tall. "Of course."

"Then shut the door behind you."

Cara scowled. But Rachel just sat there, staring off into space.

"And stay out," Rachel added.

Cara reluctantly turned away and closed the door on her friend.

# TWELVE

Cara woke early Saturday morning with visions of gigantic white teeth flooding her mind—a perfect start to the morning she was scheduled to assist on a whale-watching tour. She shrugged into her Liberty Charters jacket and headed to the kitchen. Over a bowl of cereal, her mom wished her luck on her first trip out since the overboard incident. Cara put on a stoic smile.

Outside, she climbed into her Civic and drove off toward the highway. She hung a left into the lot at Liberty Charters and braked as hard as she had the day the red Jetta almost crashed into her. Her stomach flip-flopped with nervous excitement. She was sure that the truck parked next to Rick's was David's. The only unfamiliar vehicle in the lot was a Dodge Caravan.

She parked next to the van. Her mind raced, trying to make sense of why David was here. This was the same tour time as the first one they'd gone on together. But it was a different day of the week. Maybe he'd looked at the schedule on the office wall to see when she was going out.

Shaking her head, she grabbed her backpack, got out, and locked her car. She strode with all the confidence she could muster to the office door.

Whatever reason David was here, this was a good thing. She'd be able to spend another day on the water with him after all. And his presence was bound to calm her, if he'd only look her in the eyes and let their warm connection take hold.

She stepped inside and found the office empty of anyone but Sherry, who sat at her desk.

Sherry closed the book she was reading and smiled when Cara approached. "I'm so glad you're going out with us again, kiddo."

"Of course I'm going out again. I'm scheduled to assist today," Cara said, infusing as much casualness in her voice as she could, considering her fists were clenching as she considered the possibility of seeing the transient orcas, and her heart was beating like a wild creature trying to break free from her chest at the thought of being close to David.

Sherry's eyes twinkled. "You might be happy to know that the good-looking fellow who fished you out of the water is going out on this tour."

News obviously hadn't yet traveled around town that David was the cute new student teacher at Seaside High. Cara would save that news for a time when David was nowhere near. "I saw his truck in the parking lot. What a coincidence."

"Uh-huh." Sherry looked like she was about to laugh.

Cara ignored Sherry's goading and leaned over the desk to sign her paperwork.

"Don't worry, kiddo. Everything will be fine."

Cara practiced her stoic smile again. It came easier this time. She could do this.

David stood aboard the *Lookout*, adorably casual in a navy windbreaker, jeans, and boat shoes. He was talking with what looked like a married couple and their grade school–age daughter. Cara descended the stairs on shaky legs. Thick exhaust fumes from larger fishing boats drowned out the scents of the sea and stung her eyes.

Glancing her way, David smiled and waved before turning back to the man speaking to him. Rick helped her onto the boat and handed her a life jacket, then watched as she fastened it. He appraised her carefully, so she gave her stoic smile another go. She must have perfected it by now because Rick's face lit up.

He hung his arm over her shoulder and called out to the others. "This here is my first mate, Cara. If I miss anything about the grays, she'll be able to answer any questions you have about them."

David aimed his full, lopsided smile at her. She smiled back, then directed her attention toward the other customers, whom Rick continued to address.

"Like David and I told you," Rick said, "we had an incident with some transient orcas the other week. They didn't leave the area as early as they usually do, so we'll steer clear of any if we run into them." He gave Cara a final squeeze and patted her head.

David waved her toward him. Her nerves were even more charged after Rick's mention of the transients. She teetered over.

"Cara, this is Tom and Jean Jameson and their daughter, Katy," David said.

Cara closely inspected their life jackets. "Hi there. I've been coming out with Rick just about every month for the last three years. We have a local pod of over two hundred gray whales here. We've identified and named over fifty of them. Odds are always great we'll see some."

She patted the back of one of the seats. "Please sit while we head out. Rick will give you some information about where we're going and what we're likely to see. When we stop, feel free to ask me any questions."

The Jamesons sat in the row behind the controls. Cara sat in the second row back from the front. David sat close beside her, as though he'd been doing so for years. She angled toward him and looked into his eyes, ready to look away.

His face was free of any of the recent tightness she'd seen at school. And he didn't avert his gaze. Warmth filled her, but her heart continued to beat erratically.

"Rick called and thought it would be good for both us to get back out on the water," David said.

Conflict raged in his eyes. Even though he must have worried that he shouldn't have, he'd come out anyway. For her.

She fought the urge to close the distance between them, to run her fingers through his hair and press her lips to his. Realizing her gaze had lingered on his mouth longer than she intended, she blinked and looked down at her lap. But she couldn't stop herself from looking back up into his eyes. She was sure the longing that burned there was mirrored in her own.

"I'm glad you came out," he said.

Her stoic smile came naturally now. She cleared her throat. "I'm glad you came out, too."

An extra splash of pink washed across his cheeks. He looked away when Rick began his spiel and pulled out of the harbor. When the boat had remained docked, Cara had been able to control her nerves. But now, heading out to sea, she gripped the bottom of her seat. Her body tensed and she took in deep, shaky breaths.

David inclined his head toward hers, close enough that his words sounded soft in her ear. "Try to relax and remember what it felt like in the past when you came out, how much you enjoyed the boat ride, the wind, the grays."

She closed her eyes and recalled tours from the beginning of the summer when she'd first met Crossback and Bobbi. Crossback's markings were distinct and couldn't be missed. And baby Bobbi never went down for a dive without waving good-bye with his tail flukes.

Cara's breathing evened out as she concentrated on pleasant memories of the grays. She opened her eyes and glanced sideways at David, who was watching her.

"Thanks," she told him.

A sweet smile touched his lips.

Instead of heading toward Seagoer's Cove, as Rick usually did, he steered the boat northwest toward Cape Cornell. At least two dozen gray humps dotted the water near the inlet. A few disappeared beneath the surface.

Pulling her binoculars from her backpack, Cara stood and tried to make out any familiar markings. David pulled out his own binoculars and the Jamesons moved to Cara's other side. Cara pointed out the whales she recognized, gesturing toward Barney at the back of the group, whose back was covered with barnacles, and Dotty, a darker gray with circular white spots, who dove underwater.

Rick called out from the controls. "I can't remember a time I saw a group of grays this big feeding together."

Cara leaned down, handed her binoculars to young Katy, and helped her home in on the whales. The little girl giggled and held tight to the binoculars.

When Cara rose to a standing position, David gently nudged her arm.

He passed her his binoculars. "That might be Bobbi in the front. He's the smallest of the bunch."

Cara raised the binoculars and focused on the front of the group. Sure enough, a small whale tail lifted.

She pointed. "Did you see the little whale tail wave?" she asked the others. "That's the signature move of one of our newcomers, a calf named Bobbi. That large whale in front must be his mother, Crossback."

The tension eased out of Cara's muscles. Crossback's head lifted enough for Cara to make out her unique markings before she turned and dove underwater. The other grays all followed suit, many flipping their tails up as they dove and seemed to turn in the opposite direction.

"Everyone take a seat, please," Rick commanded.

To their left, five transient orcas swam at a fast clip toward the boat.

The Jamesons retreated to the third row.

Cara gripped David's arm and dragged him down to sit with her.

"Let's head after those grays," Rick said, sounding jovial as ever, but Cara knew better by the way he sped away from the transients in the direction of the harbor.

David brushed Cara's hair away from her ear and leaned closer to speak over the roar of the boat's motor. "It's not common for transient orcas to overturn boats. Right?"

More muscles than Cara knew she had tensed up. She couldn't answer him, so she shook her head.

He pushed his sleeves up to his elbows and leaned in again. "So we've already learned that at least one of these transients is aggressive. Now we're avoiding them. We're going to be fine."

She sucked in a lungful of air and nodded. Exhaling, she squeezed his bare forearm and her body warmed. She breathed deeply and scowled at the transients as they receded from view.

Rick sped toward safety. David sat close to Cara and let her continue to hold on to him. She couldn't crawl into his lap right now like she wanted to, even if they were a couple. But it would be so easy to lay her head on his shoulder, to forget that he would be her teacher come Monday.

They entered the harbor and pulled up to the dock. She reluctantly let go of David. Standing, they faced each other. She avoided his eyes.

"Thanks for helping me calm down out there," she said. "I'm more angry than scared at this point. I hope the transients will leave soon. But even if they don't, I think I'll be good from now on."

"Don't be ashamed of being scared." He shoved his hands in his pockets.

Rick's booming voice carried over as he spoke to the Jamesons.

"That was more whales than we usually see on a week's worth of tours, even in peak season," Rick was telling them as he helped them onto the dock.

The Jamesons waved their good-byes and Rick came over and clapped David on the shoulder. "Thanks for watching out for my first mate."

Cara and David unfastened their life jackets and handed them over.

"Those transient orcas are a fierce brood," Rick said, stowing their life jackets. "But I promised to steer clear. And I did. So don't you worry about those blackfish anymore, you hear?"

Cara nodded and allowed Rick to ruffle her already windblown hair. Wanting to leave things on a good note, she said good-bye to Rick and David and hopped off the boat before awkwardness could set in.

The guys remained onboard talking. Cara glanced down as she climbed the stairs. David was watching her. Maybe there was hope for their future yet.

# THIRTEEN

The shift and tights Cara wore to school Monday made sitting on a stone wall or the floor in front of lockers impractical for lunch, so Garren joined her in the cafeteria. With any luck, the cloying odor of onions and grilled meat from the cheeseburger line wouldn't cling to her clothes. She plucked a tiny piece of lint from her cardigan and smoothed her skirt.

"You look nice," Garren said. He held out an apple and she offered him half her turkey and cheese sandwich in exchange, along with a bag of his favorite chips.

She bit into the apple's crisp, sweet, juicy goodness. Just like the others Garren had given her, this one tasted unreal, like none she'd eaten before.

"You really can't tell me where you get these apples?" she asked, then took another bite of the delectable flesh.

"Sorry. I'm sworn to secrecy." He smiled and shrugged.

She smiled and shrugged back. He really could be quite odd.

"You're having a birthday next month," he said.

She paused as her teeth sunk into her apple. Pulling off a chunk and chewing, she stared at him. She was getting used to his stated questions, but was starting to wonder if he was psychic. Or a stalker.

"First you know where my class is, and now you know my birthday. How is that?"

He finished a bite of sandwich, chewing slowly, apparently appreciating it more than most would. "Your name's on a list."

No way did the office start posting class schedules and birth dates for all to see. "You sure know a lot more about me than I know about you. What's your story, Garren?"

He let his head fall back before he looked at her. "I need to keep my story to myself."

*More secrecy. Surprise, surprise.* Maybe his father had left, like hers had. Or his family might be dysfunctional. She didn't want to embarrass him or stir up hurt feelings, so she left it alone.

"Tell me how you'll celebrate."

"My mom and I usually have our birthday parties at home. It's been just the two of us since my grandparents died a few years ago and we moved here from Spokane."

"I'll come over and celebrate with you."

She found herself saying, "Sure," without giving the matter another thought.

He brushed bread crumbs from his hands, placed his elbows on the table, and steepled his fingers. "Rachel's sick." The way he said it, he might have been predicting that Rachel had an incurable disease.

"She definitely isn't herself. Whether she's really sick or is just playing it up so she won't get in trouble for skipping school, I don't know. She was horrible to me when I visited her. All she seems to care about is Ethan."

Garren ran his fingers through his blond waves. "I told you Ethan hangs out with a bad crowd."

"Do you think Ethan did something to her?"

"I know Ethan's involved in occult practices."

Fairy tales and horror movies came to mind. "What . . . like witchcraft and voodoo?"

"Sorcery, yes."

"That's just a bunch of myths made up by misfits."

"No." He didn't continue until she looked him in the eyes. "It's not."

She should've known there was a catch when it came to Garren. He was too quirky and too kind. Of course he wasn't sane. She chuckled, but he gave no hint of a smile, so she swallowed her laughter.

"You think Ethan got Rachel mixed up with that stuff? Maybe that's why she's sick?"

"Yes." He took her apple core and deposited it in his bag.

Ethan might be into hokey things, like death rock, and she could see Rachel doing anything he wanted now that she was so gaga over him. Still, that kind of hoodoo stuff couldn't seriously be causing Rachel's problems. She didn't argue with Garren, though she felt silly going along with his foolishness. Even if he truly was crazy, though, her gut told her he was a safe kind of crazy.

During journalism class, the room buzzed with light banter and laughter. Cara made her way around the classroom, jiggling the plastic container of cookies she held. First, she stopped at a group of desks where students were generating leads for the inaugural newspaper issue, due to come out at the end of October. Then she moved on to three game tables set up in the back of the room, one for checkers, one for chess, and one for Scrabble, where other students chose to take a break from newspaper work.

At one of the computers lined up against the wall, Garren sat with the sophomore-in-training who would end up overseeing the layout program. Cara stood beside Garren and pretended to pay attention to his instructions. Really, her focus remained on David, who stood at the front of the room, speaking with a student. Mr. Cutter sat at the teacher's desk with his laptop.

When the girl David had been speaking with left, Cara walked over to him. His eyes turned to her. She didn't meet his gaze, but looked down to admire his muscular forearms beneath his rolled-up sleeves.

She handed him the container of oatmeal-gumdrop cookies. "Thanks for agreeing to the interview."

"My pleasure." He pried the lid off the container and held it out for her.

She took a cookie and bit into it. It tasted buttery and sweet and felt chewy and gooey in her mouth.

He finished off his cookie in two bites, then grabbed two more. "These are great. Thanks." He brought the cookies over to Mr. Cutter, who also took a couple. Then he closed the container and set it on the desk.

Cara walked over to the far corner of the room, where she and David would have more privacy. Mr. Cutter chewed his cookie as he watched David walk over to her.

"I had dinner at the Cove last night," David said.

She was surprised he'd mention anything related to their first date. If anything, she thought maybe he'd say something about their whale-watching trip that weekend. She wondered if he'd eaten alone—or, more to the point, if he hadn't.

"Did you have the chowder again?" she asked, hoping to encourage his openness.

"Of course. Even though the rest of the menu sounded pretty great, too."

It didn't sound like she was going to find out if he'd dined alone. "Nothing's as great as that chowder."

"So how would you like to do this? Do you want me to sit next to your desk? Or we could bring a couple of chairs over here?"

"Let's get some chairs."

"Let me get them." He walked over and picked up the free chair next to Garren. He seemed to concentrate more on Garren than the layout on the computer screen. Then he picked up another free chair closer to their corner.

When he brought the chairs over and set them down, Cara caught a whiff of his minty, musky scent. She wanted to reach out and touch him, to run her hands along his forearms, bury her face in his neck, and breathe him in. He took a seat across from her and she sat and crossed her legs.

Clearing her throat, she pulled her camera from her backpack. Focusing on David's image through the lens, she said, "First, the photo."

He sighed, then smiled.

The photographs she snapped would get more than their fair share of attention from her before the newspaper issue came out. There was no harm in admiring him from afar.

She put the camera away and David relaxed and leaned back in his chair. His khakis pulled tighter over the muscles in his thighs. Averting her gaze, she pulled her cell phone from her bag to record the interview, as well as a notepad and a pencil. She flipped to her page of questions and stared at it. If she wanted to get through the list, it would be best to wait until further into the interview to look him in the eyes.

She rested her phone on her backpack and pressed record. "I didn't ask for a copy of your résumé, so let's start with some basic questions."

"You were going to ask for a copy of my résumé? Yikes."

She shrugged. "What's your date of birth?"

Unless she imagined it, when David revealed his age, he looked closely at her face, as if checking her reaction. He was twenty-one. Considering she'd turn eighteen the following month, he was only about three years older than her. Not that big of an age difference, really.

"Where are you attending college and what degrees are you working toward?"

"I'm studying at Inland Washington University. This student teaching job is part of a reciprocal program Washington has with Oregon. I'm working toward a B.S. in secondary education with an endorsement in English."

"Why do you want to teach high school?"

"I thought it would give me a chance to help students get a handle on the basics before college. This internship came up and felt like the right fit at the time. It almost seemed providential."

Now she couldn't stop from looking into his eyes. There was a knowing look there, emphasized by the flow of warmth between them. She struggled to convey with her own eyes that she agreed that his being here, and their having met at Liberty Charters—their bond—seemed meant-to-be.

Blinking and swallowing, she checked her list of questions. "What are some of your favorite outdoor and indoor activities?"

"Well, whale watching is growing on me." He graced her with a giant lopsided grin.

She laughed. "That's good to hear, especially after all the drama you've been through on the water."

"It hasn't been all bad." He paused before he continued. "I also love running and fishing. My favorite indoor activities are reading, writing, and playing Scrabble."

She perked up at his mention of her favorite game. "Do you play Scrabble with people or against the computer?"

"Against the computer, mostly. I play a lot."

"I play the computer, too, just about every night." She glanced over at the game table, where other staff members gathered, chattering as they played. "I'd love to play you. Maybe after the interview?"

He nodded his assent. "I'm curious to see how we'd compete. We can rotate with the group."

*Great. More group time.*

But she wouldn't complain. She'd take what she could get.

"Where does your family live?"

"My dad lives in the Tri-Cities. It's just the two of us."

"You don't have any brothers or sisters?"

"Nope, I'm an only child."

"Me, too." She tapped her pad with her pencil. "My father left before I was born, so I'm thankful to have my mom."

He frowned. "I'm sorry."

Before she could ask him another question, he looked past her and sat up straighter in his chair. Turning her head, she recognized Principal Roberts by his graying hair and his tie and dress slacks. He strolled across the classroom, accompanied by a familiar, slender blonde female.

Amber Miller. She'd been a senior when Cara was a freshman and had been the girl Chris dated before he'd asked Cara out. Amber looked as eccentric as ever, wearing a pink swing dress with a black trench and heels. Her lips and fingernails were painted pink, like her dress. Her features reminded Cara of a porcelain doll's, with her large, round, cobalt-colored eyes and full lips. Amber had never looked like she belonged in high school, nor in Liberty.

Mr. Roberts and Amber stopped at the teacher's desk to talk to Mr. Cutter, who directed them over to David and Cara.

David glanced at Amber, then turned his gaze toward the principal.

"Good to see you, Mr. Wilson," Principal Roberts said as he strode over with Amber at his side. "You, too, Cara. I hear you're this year's newspaper editor. Congratulations."

Cara pasted on a smile. "Thanks. I'm interviewing Mr. Wilson for a new teacher feature."

Principal Roberts nodded in an a-ha way. He waved a hand in Amber's direction. "You might remember Amber Miller, Cara?"

Amber turned an unsmiling face toward Cara.

"Of course," Cara said, only managing a slight smile in response to Amber's disparaging look. "Nice to see you, Amber."

Amber's "hello" sounded sing-songish and taunting. She cocked her head to the side.

Cara blinked. For a second it looked like Amber's eyes darkened until they turned black, then shifted back to blue.

"Amber graduated from Seaside a few years back," Principal Roberts explained to David. "Amber, this is David Wilson. He's new to Liberty. He's student teaching in English and journalism."

"Good to meet you, David," she said, and held her hand out to him.

He took it and shook it. She cupped his hand in both of hers, only letting go when he pulled his hand free.

Cara hadn't missed the seductive lilt in Amber's tone any more than the handholding.

"Ms. Miller's interviewing for the administrative assistant position," Principal Roberts said. "I thought I'd show her around."

"Good to see you," David said, effectively dismissing the pair.

Principal Roberts guided Amber back toward the door. David didn't give Amber another look that Cara noticed. Amber, however, turned back to eye David.

Amber winked at Cara as Principal Roberts steered her out of the classroom. Cara wasn't sure what to make of that.

After their unexpected visitors left, she turned back to David. "I think I have enough to work with for the feature. Wanna play Scrabble?"

He stood and avoided her eyes. "Would you mind taking a rain check? I should work with a few other students before the period ends."

"Sure." She barely stopped the frown she felt coming.

*Thanks a lot, Amber.*

At home, Cara sat back on her bed with her laptop and downloaded the photos of the whales she'd taken on the day of the overboard incident. The shots of the grays turned out clear and colorful. But for some reason, the transient orca photos appeared dark and grainy.

The difference in photo quality didn't make sense. She'd only used one camera and both pictures were taken in the same setting under the same lighting. The only thing she could figure was that the opposite direction of the orca shots and the greater distance had caused the disparity.

She printed the photos of the grays and tacked them up with the other whale photos on her wall. Back on her bed with her laptop, she scrolled ahead through her pictures and took her time evaluating each of David's new teacher feature photos. She printed the one she finally chose.

In the photo, David looked cute with his dark hair, white smile, and green eyes. Only the smile was straight rather than lopsided, and the depth and warmth she witnessed in his eyes in person wasn't visible. Still, it was better than nothing.

With David's printed photo in hand, she went to her dresser and pulled the backing off two of her frames. She slid a photo of her and Rachel out of one and slipped it behind the picture of the two of them in the other. David's photo fit in the empty frame. She tucked it away in her nightstand drawer, where she'd stash it whenever she was gone, so her mom wouldn't see.

# FOURTEEN

Even after unloading the books she didn't need before journalism class, Cara groaned from the weight of her backpack. Garren met her at her locker, slipped her bag from her shoulder, and slung it over his own.

"Thanks," she said, and rubbed the dent in her shoulder.

Like the day she'd hit him with her car, he offered up some advice. "It's not good for your back, hefting this heavy bag around. You should carry less and stop by your locker more often."

He was right, of course. "I'll work on that."

They walked together to the journalism classroom. Mr. Cutter tapped away on his laptop at the teacher's desk. Cara scanned the room for David, but he wasn't there.

When she took her seat, Garren placed her backpack on the floor.

Rachel sat motionless beside her, wearing a black hooded sweatshirt, black leggings, and new combat boots. Black eyeliner outlined her narrowed eyes. Black was an unusual color choice for Rachel. She must be trying to look more *mysterious* like Ethan.

"So Rachel, who died?" Cara meant the comment as a joke.

Rachel ignored her, staring straight ahead with a blank expression.

David hustled in before the bell rang and dropped his bag behind the teacher's desk. As always, Cara's stomach turned bubbly as he addressed the class. He stood tall and spoke with confidence, using both his voice and his hands to communicate.

Halfway through the period, an abrupt movement from Rachel caught Cara's attention. Rachel wrapped her arms around her midsection and winced, then fell to the floor. Cara's mouth dropped open. Forgetting about their silly fight, she climbed over their seats and knelt beside her friend. Rachel's body went rigid.

"Rachel? What's wrong?" Cara's words choked her as concern crept up from her belly to her throat.

Rachel lay stiff and still. Her wide eyes looked murky like mud, not bright like their usual melted caramel shade.

Garren bent down beside Cara, frown lines puckering his perfect forehead. Other students gathered around them. David knelt on Cara's other side and took Rachel's wrist to check her pulse. Rachel's body remained ramrod straight.

David gently placed Rachel's arm back at her side.

"Do you want me to go tell the office?" Cara asked him.

She was ready to spring to her feet, but David put a hand on her arm to stop her. "Mr. Cutter already called. The nurse is on her way," he said, in the same soothing tone he'd used when they'd last been aboard the *Lookout* together. He gave her arm a reassuring squeeze. When he let go, she missed the comfort of his touch.

Not a minute later, the school nurse bustled into the classroom to evaluate Rachel before calling to instruct the front office to notify both Rachel's mom and emergency assistance. The paramedics arrived and whisked Rachel away.

Mr. Cutter dismissed class early. After a short yet agonizingly slow drive to Liberty County Hospital, Cara passed through the automatic doors. She rounded the corner next to the lobby and made her way down the hall to the waiting area, where she spotted a familiar plump form sitting in a faded armchair.

Cara bent down and gave Ms. Clark a quick hug. "How is she?"

Ms. Clark picked pieces of Styrofoam off the rim of the coffee cup she held in her lap. "Her stomach and head are still hurting her. They're giving her some tests and pain medication."

Cara sat across from her.

Ms. Clark offered her a small smile. "I'm glad you came."

"I hope Rachel will be glad, too. She hasn't wanted to talk to me much lately."

Ms. Clark sighed. "Me, either. It's that Ethan she's so obsessed with. Ever since she started seeing him, she hasn't been herself."

"I know. I just don't know what to do about it."

"The nurse said I could visit soon. Please try to talk to her."

Cara nodded and sorted through the magazines on the small table beside her: *Better Homes and Gardens*, *Parenting*, and *Coastal Astrologer*. The last publication seemed an odd choice for a hospital waiting room. She opened the magazine to the table of contents and found titles like "Harvesting Holiday Herbs," "Moon Cycles," and "Potent Potions."

Glancing up, she found Ms. Clark eyeing her, her mouth open as though a question hung on her tongue. Cara raised her eyebrows, inviting her to ask whatever was on her mind. Ms. Clark hung her head again and resumed picking at her coffee cup.

After Cara had flipped through half the pictures and diagrams in the *Coastal Astrologer* magazine, a nurse called for Elizabeth Clark. Ms. Clark lumbered out of her chair and followed. Cara trailed behind.

The nurse and Ms. Clark disappeared behind a curtain. Cara waited on the other side while they fussed over Rachel. A couple of minutes passed before the nurse walked out and Ms. Clark waved Cara in.

Cara slipped into the small area surrounding the hospital bed Rachel rested on. Rachel lay partially reclined, wearing a standard white gown flecked with tacky pastel splashes meant to mimic waves. A small monitor was clipped to her finger and an IV fed into her arm.

Cara shared her best smile with her best friend. Rachel gave her a blank stare.

Ms. Clark stood on the opposite side of Rachel's bed. "The least you could do is greet Cara, Rachel."

"Hi," Rachel said, her voice as devoid of emotion as her face.

"What do you think's wrong?" Cara asked Rachel, confusion twining with the concern festering in her gut.

"Nothing," Rachel said. But her teeth clenched, and she pressed her forearm against her midsection.

"Then why are you still in pain?" Ms. Clark tilted her head toward the IV fluid bag hanging from the pole next to the hospital bed.

Every now and then, a machine attached to the bag issued a methodical *click*.

"They're giving you morphine, but you're still hurting," Ms. Clark continued. "That's not normal."

Cara took Rachel's hand in hers. A hazy film receded from Rachel's eyes and they widened. Her fingers tightened around Cara's. When Cara's knuckles cracked, she wrestled her hand free. Rachel's eyes clouded over again.

A nurse pushed through the opening in the curtain. Ethan entered behind her. Ms. Clark scowled at him.

"You said you were expecting him?" The nurse looked to Rachel, then to Ms. Clark.

"Yes." Rachel pushed a button that raised the back of the bed until she reached a full sitting position. "I want him here."

Ms. Clark gave the nurse a terse nod, but blocked Ethan's access to Rachel. The nurse backed out of the opening in the curtain.

Shoving his hands in the pockets of his black jeans, Ethan faced Ms. Clark. "I'm here to make sure Rachel's okay," he said, his voice husky.

"Rachel's been given some tests to see what's causing her pain," Ms. Clark said, her tone clipped. "You wouldn't happen to know of anything that might show up, would you?"

"I'm fine," Rachel said.

"Rachel's not taking drugs, if that's what you mean," Ethan said. He and Rachel shared gushy-looking smiles.

Cara shook her head. Maybe Ethan hadn't given Rachel drugs. And witchcraft seemed too wacky an explanation for her behavior. But no doubt something abnormal was going on.

"I'm leaving." Cara edged over to the curtain. "Please let me know what the doctors say," she said to Ms. Clark, who frowned and nodded.

Ethan tossed his jacket on a plastic chair, as though he meant to stay for a while. Hanging from a black leather rope around his neck was a large, white, cone-shaped tooth. It looked an awful lot like an orca tooth.

Cara wasted a glare on him. He and Rachel never took their eyes off of each other.

# FIFTEEN

Playing Scrabble on her laptop as she sat on her bed that night wasn't working to ease Cara's worries. She called the hospital and asked the receptionist to ring Rachel's room. Mindlessly tapping her fingers against the side of her computer, she waited through three rings until Ms. Clark answered.

"Hi, it's Cara. Have the doctors figured out what's wrong?"

A heavy, defeated sigh sounded from the other end of the line. "No. They're going to refer her to a specialist for more testing."

"Is she feeling any better?"

"Not really. They're giving her a higher dose of morphine, but it doesn't seem to be having an effect."

"The medicine isn't helping her headaches?"

"It doesn't seem like it, no."

Cara chased Ms. Clark's words around in circles in her mind. When Cara had her wisdom teeth pulled, even a moderate pain reliever like Vicodin had knocked her out. Morphine was a much stronger drug. She couldn't understand how something that potent wouldn't help ease Rachel's pain.

"When will she be able to go back to school?"

"In a few days, probably."

"That's good. I hope she'll be back to her old self soon."

More than ever, Cara needed Rachel's support. And whether Rachel knew it or not, she needed Cara, too. There had to be a way to help her.

------

The next day at lunch, Garren sat next to Cara on the stone wall, where she'd set down half a peanut butter and pickle sandwich on a napkin for him beside a bag of jalapeño cheddar chips. He handed her an apple.

His face was sober. "Rachel's home from the hospital." He didn't make it sound like that was a good thing.

"I'm not sure if she's home yet, actually." She explained that the doctors didn't know what was wrong and that Rachel was being referred to a specialist. "The weirdest thing is that painkillers don't seem to be helping with her headaches, and no one knows why." She started in on her apple.

Garren looked up to the sky, then leveled his gaze at her. "Painkillers having no effect is a bad sign."

"Sign of what?"

He steepled his fingers in front of him, but didn't answer.

"She's not in excruciating pain," she said. "It's just frustrating not to know what's causing any of it, or how to stop it. Got any theories you want to share?" Somehow, she knew he would.

He held her gaze again. "I'm concerned that Rachel's under demonic influence."

Cara's jaw fell open, exposing a mouthful of apple. She snapped it shut, quickly finished chewing, and swallowed hard. "You think Rachel is *possessed by a demon?*"

"Probably. You can do a test if you want, to see if I'm right."

"What kind of test?" she asked, not bothering to hide her incredulity.

"You can sprinkle holy water over all of Rachel's clothes. If she doesn't wear them, you'll know I'm right."

This was the most weirdness she'd heard from Garren yet. She waited, hoping for a punch line. He didn't deliver one.

"Why wouldn't Rachel wear her clothes if I sprinkle them with holy water?" she asked, playing along.

"Clothes that are blessed with holy water would itch or burn her skin. She would also resist going to church, so you could look into that, too."

Cara was speechless.

"It's your choice whether or not to give the blessing of Rachel's clothes a try."

Cara turned this kooky idea around in her head a few times. Crazy though Garren might be, this plan sounded harmless. "Sure, I'll do it. I'll try to find a way to sneak into Rachel's closet. If you can get the holy water."

"I will."

Cara watched him closely, once again hoping he'd break down laughing and tell her he was joking. No such luck. "You're really not kidding that you think Rachel's possessed?"

"Demonic possession is nothing to joke about."

"But I don't understand. Why would God allow that to happen to Rachel?" Strangely, she felt confident Garren would have an answer to that question, though surely an outlandish one.

"Humans are free to make their own choices. And those choices have consequences."

"That doesn't make sense. Rachel didn't *choose* to be possessed by a demon."

"Unfortunately, Rachel has made innocent choices that nevertheless have consequences. But mostly she's suffering from the consequences of other people's choices. Still, she'll also benefit from having a good friend like you who chooses to help her."

———

"I hope Rachel's feeling better," David said, catching Cara's eye as she was leaving the journalism classroom.

They exchanged concerned frowns.

"I hope so, too."

Mr. Cutter looked over from the teacher's desk. She met his gaze. He tugged on his chin, then turned back to his laptop.

David walked with her to the classroom door.

She stopped to face him. "Rachel probably won't be back to school until next week."

"Unless I'm imagining things, she's been acting pretty strange lately."

"You're not imagining anything. Hopefully the doctors can figure out what's wrong with her."

*Or not, if Garren's right and she's under attack by a demon.*

"How about you? How are you feeling?" he asked.

Her lips parted, but she didn't answer right away, not entirely sure what he meant by his question. He had to know she was devastated that he was her teacher and they couldn't be together. Maybe he worried she was at risk for using drugs or something.

"I'm doing all right. I'm going whale watching again this Saturday." Hopefully he'd take that as an invitation.

"That's good." He shoved his hands in his pockets. "I'm going home to visit my dad," he said with a slight shrug of his shoulders.

*Shoot.* She enjoyed one last moment of nearness before she said, "Have a nice trip," and walked off.

———

That night, Cara leaned against her headboard with her laptop and typed the words *signs of demonic influence* in a search engine bar. She could hardly believe she was doing it.

The first site listed under the search results was titled "Signs of Satan." It included an article outlining clues that people had opened themselves to demonic influence. Cara shook her head as she read:

They disobey their parents.
They want to stay up all night and sleep all day.
They walk around in bathing suits.
They see UFOs or aliens.

*Ridiculous.* She hit the back button. The next site she clicked on was "Demonic Attacks." She skimmed a list of causes and symptoms of demonic influence, pausing when something seemed reasonable:

Irrational fears, phobias, and anxieties
Deep depression
Low self-image
Conflicts with authority figures

Reasonable or not, all of those signs could apply to any number of teenagers. And none of them reminded Cara of Rachel.

Again, Cara clicked the back button. The next site that caught her eye sounded the most promising: "Signs of Demonic Possession." The signs listed resonated more than those listed on the other sites. And the list was provided by a Roman Catholic exorcist.

Changes in personality. (CHECK)
An aversion to religious objects and church. (NOT SURE)
Changes in the way a person dresses. (CHECK)
Occult materials in the person's living environment. (POSSIBLY)
Long periods without blinking and not looking people in the eye. (POSSIBLY)
Appearing catatonic. (CHECK)

She lingered on the next sign.

A person's eyes may turn almost black, like a shark's eyes. (LIKE AMBER'S EYES)

What most surprised Cara about all the sites she visited was how the authors took it for granted demonic influence was real, and noted that it happened more often than people realize. The author of the last site pointed out that the listed signs could signal the beginning of drug use or could be due to psychiatric or psychological changes, or cries for help.

Cara printed out the list of signs and zipped it in a compartment of her backpack. She was just as uncertain now about what was wrong with Rachel as she had been before she began her search.

Sipping on a soda and staring out at peaks of waves resembling fluffy egg whites against the dark sea, she thought of casual, confident David, with his lopsided grin and his enchanting green eyes, of how, when she looked into those eyes, a warm, magical energy connected them.

No, *magical* reminded her of Rachel and Ethan. The best word for Cara's and David's connection was *providential*. David had used that word to describe his idea of why he ended up in Liberty. It was hard to fathom how something so *providential* could be wrong.

---

Garren sat down by Cara next to her locker the following Monday at lunch and offered up his most far-fetched advice yet. "You should try to cut down on your diet soda consumption. Moderation is key."

She laughed before he'd even finished his statement. "Don't hold your breath waiting for that to happen. Diet soda is my sole source of caffeine." She held up her soda bottle before taking a drink.

He shook his head. "I guess we can't win all our battles."

Whatever he meant by that, he was probably right about the soda. Come to think of it, he'd been right about a lot of things. Little things, anyway. Big, bizarre things like her best friend being possessed by a devil—the jury was still out on that one. But she wasn't in a rush to cut back on diet soda.

She handed him a bag of jalapeño cheddar chips.

"I hope I'll have better luck with this." He handed her a full, transparent bottle of water.

No way was she going to give up soda for water. And she hoped this wasn't a new offering to replace those delicious apples. Still, it was sweet of him to worry about her.

"Thanks." She took the bottle and uncapped it.

He set down the bag of chips and eased the bottle out of her grasp. "It's not to drink." He held out his hand for the cap.

She gave it to him and he recapped the bottle before he handed it back.

"This is the holy water to sprinkle on Rachel's clothes," he said, his tone serious. He pulled an apple from his bag and handed it to her, along with the bottle.

Tilting the plastic bottle back and forth, she watched the water slosh around inside while she took a bite of the apple. She'd hoped he would have come to his senses. Since he obviously hadn't, he'd probably overreact if she shared the results of her Internet search with him.

"You still think I need to do that?"

"I do. But it's your choice."

"I want to do it if it could help."

"It could help."

She couldn't say no, regardless of how crazy Garren's plan was. For some reason, he'd chosen her as his one-and-only school companion. She never got the feeling he wanted more than friendship, though she also couldn't consider him a close friend. He was caring, but shared next to nothing with her. Still, she sensed that he only meant to help her with the bits of advice he offered.

She stuffed the bottle in her backpack and tried not to think about it.

When Cara and Garren entered the journalism classroom that day, Cara was surprised to see Rachel was back. When Cara drew near, Rachel jolted upright in her chair, her eyes wide and dark. Cara couldn't find the right angle to see if they looked black. Then Rachel went limp and stared straight ahead again. There was that catatonic thing going on.

"Rachel, are you feeling any better?" Cara reached over and touched the sleeve of her black, long-sleeved shirt.

Rachel snatched her arm away and didn't look Cara's way for the rest of the period.

# SIXTEEN

Rachel continued with her zombified stare during journalism over the next week and a half. Cara was awkwardly aware of the whispers of other students who noticed the huge change in her normally outgoing friend. Rachel, however, didn't seem to notice—or at least to care—about anything that went on around her. More often than not, Rachel skipped class anyway. When Cara saw her in the halls or at lunch, she clung to Ethan, who held on to her possessively and skittered off with her anytime he saw Cara or Garren.

Cara knew she had to do something to try to help Rachel. So she came up with a plan—one that would debunk Garren's ridiculous demonic-influence theory and would also be good for Rachel's soul. She phoned Ms. Clark and suggested the two of them drag Rachel to church that Sunday. It seemed simple enough.

"I like your idea, but I've already tried to get Rachel to go to church." Ms. Clark's tone was light, but Cara sensed her uneasiness. "When I even mentioned things related to it, she spewed all kinds of sacrilegious garbage. Then she locked herself in the bathroom and wouldn't come out until she was sure services were over."

Garren had mentioned Rachel's not wanting to go to church as one of the signs that she was under demonic influence. Cara had also come across *aversion to church* in her online search. But Rachel had always seemed to enjoy going.

Ms. Clark ended their phone call by saying she wouldn't stop Cara from trying.

Sunday morning, dark clouds opened up and pounded Cara with pelts of rain as she stepped onto the Clarks' porch. Ms. Clark let her in, whispering that Rachel didn't know about the plan. Shaking the wetness from her hair, Cara walked down the hall to Rachel's room where her friend lay asleep in bed.

The rain knocked against Rachel's window, as though seeking entrance. Cara went to the closet and flung the doors open so they banged against the wall. Rachel sprang up into a sitting position. Around her neck, hanging on a rope of black leather, was a large, white, cone-shaped tooth. Ethan must have given it to her. Cara gritted her teeth at the sight of it.

From the closet floor, Cara selected a pair of leather Mary Janes and pulled out an outfit to match. "Come on, Rachel. Get ready or we'll be late."

Rachel's head snapped around toward the doorway.

Ms. Clark stood inside the door. With shaking hands, she held a thick book to her chest. "Cara wants to go to church with us, Rachel."

Rachel's mouth twisted into a snarl and her eyes riveted on the book her mom now held out, which displayed a large, embossed cross on the front. A low growl that sounded like it originated deep within erupted from Rachel's throat. Cara dropped the outfit and stumbled around the bed toward the door.

Rachel hissed and clenched her fists around bunches of bedspread. The room grew colder and Cara shivered.

"I thought it might be different if you were the one who mentioned church to her," Ms. Clark said, trembling.

"Rachel needs serious help," Cara said, her voice a weak whisper.

In a daze, she walked out of the Clarks' house, climbed into her car, and drove off. Beastly images of her friend continued on cinematic display in her mind. Those visions alternated with flashbacks of Rachel from the previous year, when she'd sat on her bed, chatting and giggling as she propped one knee up and bent down to paint her toenails red, white, and blue.

The idea that Rachel wouldn't be able to go to church had struck Cara as ridiculous. Yet Garren's impossible theory had just been reinforced, in a way she never would have expected. Now that she'd seen the most bizarre behavior from Rachel yet, she couldn't help but start to believe in negative supernatural possibilities, just as she believed in the positive ones, like her connection with David.

Still, she yearned for a more sensible explanation. So she headed for the best place she knew to seek the psychologically sound and stable.

Cara's mom took one look at her face as she entered the kitchen, rushed over to put an arm around her, and guided her to the kitchen nook. "You look sick, honey. I thought you were going to church with Rachel. What happened?"

Her mom sat her down with a plate of cookies, then went to pour them two glasses of milk. She sat across from Cara and waited for her to speak.

Cara picked up a cookie that shook in her hands, along with her words. "Something's wrong with Rachel."

"Is she still sick?"

"I don't know. I could swear she growled at the Bible her mom was holding. And when Ms. Clark mentioned church, Rachel started hissing. It was like she's possessed."

Her mom set her cookie down and clasped her hands together on the table. "Did Rachel tell you she thinks she's possessed?"

"No." Cara took a drink of milk, hoping it would wet her throat enough so she could get words out properly. She decided not to blame the off-the-wall demonic-possession theory on its rightful origina-tor, for fear of turning her mom against Garren. "But don't you think it's weird that she reacted like that?"

"Her behavior does sound like something out of a horror movie," her mom said. "It's also not untypical of mental illness. But my guess is Rachel's probably acting out, wanting attention, or help."

"What kind of help do you think she needs?"

Her mom gave her a reassuring smile. "Let me call Liz and have a talk with her, okay?"

Cara choked out a "thanks" and took a bite of her cookie. It tasted like gravel. The small, clear voice in her head insisted that whatever was going on with Rachel was something bigger than even her mom could handle.

Cara didn't mention her failed attempt to drag Rachel to church when she sat on the floor by her locker with Garren for lunch on Monday. She needed time to sort all this weirdness out on her own.

Surprisingly, Rachel made it to class every day the following week. Not surprisingly, she still resembled the walking dead whenever Cara saw her. She gave no sign if she was upset about Sunday's events and ignored everyone but Ethan, including the continued stares from other students and teachers, and all attempts Cara made to speak to her.

Ethan continued his habit of picking Rachel up at the journalism classroom door when school let out. He would glare in Cara and Garren's direction as Rachel walked over to meet him. Like he worried they might kidnap her or something.

———

"You're scheduled to assist Captain Rick on the *Lookout* tomorrow," Garren said when they settled onto the stone wall for lunch one day.

He offered up her daily apple. She swapped it for a bag of his favorite chips.

"How did you know?" she asked, and savored the apple as she bit through its skin.

"The office has the schedule posted with 'assistant' on the days you go out."

It would have been a while since he'd seen the schedule, unless he'd visited Liberty Charters since they first met. "Have you gone out on a tour?"

"I'm planning to go tomorrow, if you don't mind the company."

"Of course not."

David was the one she really wanted with her when she went out on the water again. But she was glad Garren was up for the experience. Hopefully the transients had moved on. She still couldn't shake the fear that crept into her soul every time she scanned the ocean's surface.

Pitch-black water and giant white teeth closed in on her so frequently in Cara's dreams that night that, come the next morning, she rolled out of bed with her eyes still shut. She tripped over to her curtains. Dark clouds blanketed a dirty gray sky above whitecapped water. Not good conditions for going out on the ocean.

She grabbed her cell phone from her backpack and called Liberty Charters. Sherry answered after the first ring.

"Hi, it's Cara. Just wanted to confirm that this morning's tour is going to be canceled because of the weather."

"Hey, kiddo. Actually, the dark clouds are moving off pretty fast. We've told the customers we'll go out if the weather calms down in the next hour."

As Sherry predicted, the gray clouds had moved off by the time Cara reached Liberty Charters. Garren waited for her, in the same spot she'd parked in when they'd met so awkwardly that summer. He leaned against the driver's door of his white Chevy Silverado, hands in the pockets of his jacket, looking like a fashion model or a movie star.

She took in his magnificent face and statuesque physique. He was undeniably striking. Yet her body still didn't react at the sight of him in any way other than to give her heart a soft squeeze that made her want to reach out and hug him.

They walked to the office together. Light blue sky poked holes in several spots of the overcast canopy above them.

Sherry winked at Cara when she saw her with Garren. "It's nice to see you've made some friends lately, kiddo."

Cara shook her head at Sherry to quit with the teasing. "This is Garren. He's another newcomer."

"We've met." Sherry sighed and ogled him like a hormonal teenager.

Garren shared his charming smile with her.

Sherry sighed once more, then set two piles of paperwork before them. "Your tour mates will be the Jeffersons, a father and his three sons." She tapped Cara's papers with a pen. "There's been no sign of those transient orcas, and there've been plenty of gray sightings, so it should be a good tour."

Cara waited for Garren, and they walked side by side down the stairs to the dock. Rick helped Cara on board and handed over life jackets as Garren stepped over the side tube.

After making sure they'd both fastened their vests properly, Rick turned to Garren. "Nice to have you aboard—Garrett, is it?" Rick asked.

"Garren. Nice to be here. I'm looking forward to meeting these grays Cara loves so much."

Cara didn't recall ever mentioning the whales to Garren. Her focus at school was most often on Rachel and David, and on Garren's peculiarities. Maybe he just assumed she loved the grays since she volunteered to assist so often. Or Rick and Sherry might have clued him in.

Rick introduced them to the other passengers, who occupied the second and third rows. Cara gave them her usual rundown. Garren stopped at the front seats.

Cara had avoided the front row on the last tour with David. But she couldn't avoid it forever. She walked over and sat in the same spot she had on the day she ended up in the water. Garren sat beside her.

Like the last time, Rick passed on visiting Seagoer's Cove. He sped toward Armory Bay, where another harbor housed boats that traveled in and out from fishing and whale-watching ventures. The street above the seawall fronting the bay was lined by a long walkway for observers. On the other side of the road, numerous gift and candy shops, water sports stores, and restaurants enticed tourists.

At street level, weekend visitors looked down at a giant spouting horn that blew seawater high into the air. The onlookers jumped back too late. They'd already been soaked by the unexpected rush of water.

Near the ocean floor, waves ran beneath lava beds and built up pressure to create the spouts. They were usually only visible when seas were turbulent. This spout must have been a residual effect of the storm that had passed.

After a few minutes of trolling the area in search of any grays, Rick gave up and headed to Seagoer's Cove. Cara figured he thought she'd be ready to face it again by now. Hopefully she would be.

"This is where you fell overboard," Garren said. She knew he wasn't being insensitive by saying so. He was just being matter-of-fact.

"How did you know this was the spot?" she asked. Actually, she wasn't certain how he even knew she'd fallen overboard in the first place.

"You're tensing up."

*True.* She took a deep breath and pulled out her binoculars. Rick slowed the boat and surveyed the water. Garren pointed to a spot to the right, near the cove's wall, almost exactly where Crossback and Bobbi had approached the boat on her tour with David. Two heart-shaped spouts, one higher than the other, blew into the air.

The other passengers hooted and snapped pictures. Cara hopped up and focused her binoculars on the grays. Bobbi's tail flukes rose out of the water and Crossback's markings showed before her hump raised and she and her baby dove underwater. Cara handed the binoculars to Garren.

"That was Crossback and Bobbi," she told him.

She couldn't help wishing David was the one beside her, and that she could be free to cuddle close to his side, and then to go somewhere private later, where she could feel the warm softness of his lips. Thoughts of David caused a tickle in her chest that spread throughout her body.

Just then, Garren gave her a teasing smile that made her think he knew her thoughts had strayed from the whales to something that excited her in an entirely different way. She cleared her throat and looked back toward where the whales had descended.

"Crossback and Bobbi are a mother and calf that came to the area this spring," she said, in what she hoped sounded like her normal voice. "They'll probably be back up within five minutes. You can get a better look with the binoculars."

Seconds later, the grays rose out of the water next to the *Outlook* and spyhopped like they had on the tour when Cara and David had touched Crossback. Cara instinctively glanced around, looking for any sign of the transients. From the surface, there was no sign of any other whales.

She turned back to the grays and found Garren kneeling before Bobbi, stroking his face. The family of four guys crowded in on Garren's sides and took turns touching both whales.

"Your turn," Garren said to Cara, and made room for her to kneel beside him.

Cara sank to her knees and ran her hand over Bobbi's face, while

Garren petted his head. The calf blinked like a dog that had been rubbed in just the right spot. It was the first time Cara had ever touched such a young whale. This was every bit as amazing as when she and David had touched Crossback. Except there was no providential connection between her and Garren.

After petting Bobbi one last time, Garren moved away. The grays dove underwater, Bobbi waving good-bye with his tail. Rick turned the boat around to head back to the harbor. Cara looked once more at the area where they'd seen the grays. She could swear she caught the tip of a gleaming black dorsal fin. When she blinked, it disappeared.

# SEVENTEEN

Cara was counting on Rachel not being anywhere near her house when there was a chance her mom might drag her to church. Sure enough, Rachel's car was gone when Cara pulled up that Sunday. Ms. Clark stepped out in her Sunday best to greet Cara as she reached the front porch.

"I'm sorry, Cara, but Rachel's not here. Do you want me to . . . have her get in touch with you?"

Ms. Clark obviously meant to be polite, but Cara knew there was little chance Rachel would suddenly become open to communication. "It'd be better if I left her a note. Do you mind if I leave one in her room?"

"Of course not, sweetie." Ms. Clark opened the door wide for her to enter and turned to face her in the hallway.

"Rachel doesn't seem like she's feeling much better?" Cara asked, shutting the front door behind her.

Ms. Clark wrung her hands. "She says she is. But she's still not herself. I'm sure you've noticed?"

Cara nodded.

"What do you think of Ethan?"

Cara opened her mouth to say something negative, but

didn't know what to say exactly. Finally she said, "I don't know him."

"I can't keep Rachel away from him. I'm worried he's gotten her involved with drugs."

"Rachel was tested for drugs, wasn't she?"

"She passed all the tests she's been given. But I can't help but wonder if some drug isn't being detected."

Drugs might be the best explanation for Rachel's recent behavior. Or maybe, like Cara's mom had said, Rachel was just acting out, trying to get attention. But that small, clear voice in Cara's head told her something completely different was going on.

Cara shrugged. Ms. Clark bowed her head and continued down the hall. Cara let herself into Rachel's room and noted that the décor had once again changed since her last visit. Photos no longer covered the vanity mirror. Patches of tape were the only evidence the pictures had ever been there. Rachel had stripped away years of memories between the two of them. Cara's heart slipped down a notch.

On the vanity top, Rachel's makeup and perfume were still pushed off to the side. There were a few new candles—two white, and one blue. The shells and black mirror sat near the center, along with one new item. A silver chalice, similar to ones she'd seen on TV that were used as Communion cups in churches, held a central position on the vanity.

The items looked regal and ritualistic, hauntingly beautiful. But Cara couldn't help but see them in a sinister light. A chill tickled her scalp as she mentally checked off one more sign of demonic influence: *occult items in living area.*

She dipped her fingers in the white substance that filled one of the shells and touched her fingertip to her tongue. Salt. She plucked a tissue from its box and spat in it. The bitter taste remained in her mouth, so she grabbed another tissue and scrubbed her tongue clean. Then she pulled a soda bottle from her backpack and washed the nasty bits of cotton down her throat with the soothing fizz of carbonation.

Her gaze fell on the stack of books and magazines on the corner of Rachel's vanity. The selection was innocent enough, mostly textbooks and assigned English literature. The latest issues of *Allure* and *Seventeen* rested on top. But the magazines appeared untouched. The Rachel Cara knew pored over her magazines the moment they arrived.

Cara set her backpack down and ran her hands along Rachel's unmade bed. She shook out the comforter and peeked under the pillow. She checked under the mattress, too. Nothing.

Rachel's closet, which was normally a jumbled rainbow of colors, was now organized by shade. Rachel's white and brighter-colored clothes hung on hangers on the left. Various shades of newer, primarily black and gray tops, hung on the right. Another heap of dark clothing lay on the floor. The items in that pile were pieces of outfits Cara remembered seeing Rachel wear in the past week.

Garren didn't say if laundering the clothes after they were sprinkled would eliminate the holy water's effect. Not that she believed the holy water would have an effect anyway. Digging the bottle from the bottom of her backpack, she kept still for a moment, listening for any sound of Ms. Clark approaching. Too bad there wasn't a lock on Rachel's door.

After a few seconds of silence, Cara opened the bottle and used her thumb to cover the top, as she would to squirt water through a hose. She quickly gave the pile of clothes on the floor a liberal dousing. When she touched them, they felt damp.

It could take a while for the clothes to dry. Rachel wouldn't wear them if they were wet or smelled mildewy. But Cara had told Garren she'd do this and she planned to finish what she started. She lightly covered the clothing on the floor, then sprinkled the dark clothes on the right side of the closet, as well as the white and colored tops, though she couldn't remember seeing Rachel wear anything light or bright since that first lunch with Ethan.

Working quickly, she sprinkled Rachel's pants and the sweaters and sweatshirts lining the closet shelf. Thinking it would be overkill and wanting to get this over with before she got caught, she spared Rachel's underwear and shoes.

She snuck out of Rachel's room and down the hall toward the bathroom, which doubled as a laundry room. After she splashed the last of the holy water in the washing machine, she soft-footed back to Rachel's room and sat on the small stool in front of the vanity.

Looking in the mirror, Cara watched a mixture of emotions cross her face: first a smirk, then a scowl, a frown, and finally a blank slate, which made the most sense, because she didn't know if she wanted to laugh, yell, or cry. Here she was in her best friend's bedroom, performing some loony test to determine whether Rachel was demonically influenced. Meanwhile, that same friend gallivanted around with her oddball boyfriend, not giving Cara a second thought.

From the vanity drawer where Rachel kept writing supplies,

Cara selected a pen and a piece of paper. Skipping the *Dear*, she wrote:

Rachel,
I came to visit you, but you're no doubt out with Ethan.
Interesting redecorating job on your vanity. It would be
nice if you'd be open to talking to me sometime.
   Sorry if I sound angry. I'd just really like to talk
to you.

   Cara

She dropped the pen back in the drawer. It landed on top of a stack of white paper that slid off to the side. Underneath the paper was a black hardcover book. It looked like the same one Rachel had hidden under her pillow.

When Cara picked up the book, something heavy scraped across the bottom of the drawer. At first she thought it was a large letter opener with a black handle. On closer inspection, she saw it was a double-bladed knife etched with elaborate symbols she didn't recognize. The blade was clean, but she shuddered to think what the weapon might be used for. She dropped it back in the drawer and examined the book.

Its title was *Witchcraft: Vade Mecum*, and in the center of the cover was a silver star surrounded by a circle. Flipping through, she found a diagram of another circle, which indicated proper placement of an altar and an "entrance point," whatever that was. There were also pictures of horned men and naked women with flowers in their hair, as well as items similar to the knife in Rachel's drawer and those on the vanity.

All the items were listed as components used in spells. Cara wondered what kinds of spells Rachel might be trying to cast. Spells to make Ethan crazy about her, maybe. If so, they seemed to be working.

Closing the book, Cara set it down on the vanity, then placed her note on top of it. She wasn't so sure about magic spells or demonic attacks, but she fully believed Rachel was under Ethan's influence.

Rachel's recent behavior when Cara had tried to drag her to church wasn't so easily explainable. Still, Cara couldn't accept that Rachel would truly react to the holy water.

Garren met Cara at the parking lot above Rockford Beach that night. It was about two hours after sunset when she parked next to his truck. They walked to the rock wall fronting the parking area. Below, white tips of waves crashed into the ocean's blue-black night waters and swept onto the shore.

They descended the steep set of wooden stairs to the deserted beach. Wind lightly ruffled their hair and clothes as they trekked along the sand. Eventually, they settled on a large piece of driftwood and admired the waves swirling toward them, as well as the few visible stars and the nearly full moon.

With her coat on, Cara wasn't cold. But Garren put an arm around her and pulled her close to his side. She might not feel a spark of attraction with him, like she did with David, but she'd never felt so comfortable with a guy. She let her head fall against his shoulder.

"I sprinkled Rachel's clothes with the holy water today. I left her shoes and underwear alone, though. Will that be okay?"

His chin rubbed against the top of her head as he nodded. "If I'm right, Rachel won't wear anything the holy water touched."

"I'm pretty sure I got every piece of her clothing. I even poured holy water in the washing machine. What will she wear?"

"If she can't find anything you missed, she'll have to borrow something or buy something new."

Cara turned to look him in the eye as best she could in the moonlight and made no effort to conceal her skepticism. "You truly believe Rachel is being affected by a demon and will shy away from holy water like a vampire?"

"Of course not. Vampires are make-believe monsters. Demons are real. And holy reminders make them uncomfortable."

# EIGHTEEN

Cara hadn't seen Rachel all day on Monday and figured she'd skipped school. But in the journalism classroom, Rachel sat at her desk. She wore clothes too big for her frame. A long beige cardigan covered a baggy navy turtleneck and gray sweatpants hung over her combat boots. Maybe the clothes belonged to Ms. Clark. For sure, these pieces weren't victims of the holy water sprinkling.

As usual, Mr. Cutter sat at the teacher's desk, tapping away on his laptop. David was writing on the whiteboard, his back to the class. Cara slowly walked over to her seat. Rachel turned toward her for a change, but didn't make eye contact.

"What did you do to my clothes?" Rachel asked, her voice a rasp that escaped through her teeth.

Cara glanced at Garren, who simply nodded.

Rachel was nearly hyperventilating now.

"Look at me, Rachel," Cara whispered.

Rachel's chest rose and fell heavily with each breath she took. She still didn't look Cara in the eyes and Cara reluctantly checked another item off the list of signs of demonic influence: *avoids eye contact.*

"What's wrong with your clothes?" Cara casually asked.

Rachel stared at the floor. When her eyes widened, they looked like black glass. Then they disappeared behind the slits of Rachel's narrowed eyelids. Cara leaned away, fearing her friend even more as she checked off yet another sign: *black, sharklike eyes.*

Rachel's voice grew louder. "All my clothes are itchy and burn my skin. Tell me what you did."

"Let's keep our voices down, please." David's words were firm.

He and Mr. Cutter both shot Rachel stern looks.

When Mr. Cutter's head bowed toward his laptop again and David faced the board, Cara whispered, "I sprinkled holy water on your clothes."

Rachel stiffened. Her eyes widened and looked like two black marbles. Then they faded back to murky brown. Her face went blank and she resumed her comatose state.

Before the bell rang at the end of the period, Ethan was at the door to collect Rachel. Even from a distance, Cara was sure his eyes also looked black and sharklike, though they narrowed as he glared at her and Garren.

Mr. Cutter kept busy with his laptop at the teacher's desk.

David spoke from the front of the room. "Have a nice evening, everyone. Cara and Garren, I'd like to talk to you for a minute before you leave."

Remaining in her seat, Cara watched Rachel shuffle off with Ethan. She took her time stowing her notebook and pen in her backpack and mentally prepared to face David after having little close contact with him lately.

Garren remained close beside Cara when they stood before David, whose voice and shoulders sagged.

"The computer lab is reserved for the first two hours after school,"

David said. "But I'd like to get together a couple of nights this week to work on the layout for the first newspaper issue."

Cara was glad he'd dropped the formal teacher treatment he usually used with her at school. Still, she kept the joy that lit within her off her face. His current subdued behavior confused her.

"It should only take a couple of hours each night. I know it's short notice, but could you make it tomorrow night and the following night at six?"

"I can make it if Cara can," Garren said.

David stared at Garren for a moment, then looked to Cara. She nodded. Inside, she was dancing.

David offered a small smile. "Good. Mr. Cutter will also be there."

Cara glanced at Mr. Cutter, who was tugging on his chin as he watched her, before she headed for the door with Garren.

"Cara, wait," David said.

With her back to him, she stopped and took a deep breath as she waved good-bye to Garren and mouthed, "Wait for me."

Garren nodded at her and left. She turned and headed back toward David, thankfully on steady legs. He grabbed something that rested against the wall behind the teacher's desk, where Mr. Cutter sat with his laptop. Her heart tripped around in her chest to think he was going to give her something.

Mr. Cutter watched David closely, still tugging on his chin, as David held a grocery bag out to her. "I'm sorry, I forgot to return the container from the cookies you gave me."

"Oh." She heard the frown in her voice as well as she'd heard one in his.

David turned his back to Mr. Cutter. "The cookies were terrific." His voice was softer than normal and his smile was small.

She looked into his eyes. Warmth surged between them. He didn't look away and she thought her heart would combust from the heat. But then his smile disappeared and the resulting frown reflected in his eyes.

Cara wanted to reach out. She wanted to tell him she'd keep him company. They could play Scrabble. Or go whale watching. She'd hold him like he'd held her on the *Lookout*.

But all she could do was say, "Thanks," and walk away.

In the parking lot, Garren waited next to her car.

"I cannot believe you were right about Rachel's clothes," she called out, before she reached him.

Garren maintained his common calm demeanor. "I told you. Rachel's under demonic influence."

"I know what you told me. And I looked up the signs. I've been ticking them off every time I notice one in Rachel. But I still think there could be another explanation."

"There is no other explanation."

"How do you know about these things?"

"Rachel is going to need prayer to get rid of the influence. Right now, she's not open to it. Hopefully, she will be soon. You got her thinking. Good for you."

Cara ducked inside her car and shut the door before she started the engine and rolled her window down. Garren bent over with his elbows on the window frame and his hands clasped together in front of him.

"You didn't answer my question," she said. "How do you know about this stuff?"

He tipped his head back and stared at the sky. For a second, she thought he was bothered by her questioning. Then he looked at her with a soothing smile.

"I've seen demonic activity. It's dangerous. The good news is the influence can be eliminated."

She gripped the steering wheel, perturbed as much by his vague answers as she was by her interactions with Rachel and David.

He squeezed her shoulder. "You're making good choices," he said as he pushed away from the car. "Try not to get frustrated."

# NINETEEN

Cara's mom had left to teach a night class by the time Cara headed out for the layout get-together. Wanting to make things easier on Garren, she arrived at the school a little after five o'clock, almost an hour earlier than David, Garren, and Mr. Cutter were expected. That would give her time to work on finishing up her editing before they started on the layout.

She drove by the nearly empty students' lot. Past that, only a handful of vehicles were parked in the teachers' area. David's truck wasn't one of them, though she'd hoped it would be. She parked close to the door that led to the journalism classroom.

At the entrance, she punched in the access code, let herself into the building, and walked down the brightly lit hall. The classroom door was unlocked and the fluorescents glowed. She set her coat and bag down on a desk and dragged a chair in front of a monitor.

Once the computer booted up, she called up the layout program and opened the files containing the pieces she'd already edited, as well as those that still needed work. She completed an edit of her "Whale Tales" update, an editorial, and a brief, before she found Rachel's advice column saved in the journalism classroom's folder.

Rachel hadn't turned in a hard copy. Cara had figured she'd have to either ask someone else to complete the Q & A at the last minute, or would have to fill the slot with another article. Looking at the topic, she saw Rachel had titled it "Make Believe or Magick?" Included was a copy of the email Rachel sent to students, requesting they send in questions. Cara frowned. She'd never received the email.

The first inquiry Rachel answered came from a student who asked why Rachel's spelling of *magick* included a "K." Rachel answered that *magic* with a "C" usually involved a guy in a silly suit and hat who did parlor tricks and sleights of hand. *Magick* with a "K," on the other hand, created true change by harnessing and using energy from the world around us.

As far as Cara knew, neither *magic* with a "C" nor *magick* with a "K" had ever been part of Rachel's interests, before Ethan.

Another student asked whether a spirit in her boyfriend's house might be causing him to get angry all the time. Rachel answered that, no, he was getting angry because he had grown comfortable in their relationship and was showing his true self. He was a jerk.

Cara laughed at that one.

The last question was whether magick could help someone accomplish whatever he or she wanted, whether good or bad. Rachel answered that, yes, magick could work to reward you with anything you wanted. Cara worried Rachel must believe what she wrote.

Leaving the Q & A alone and planning to deal with it later, Cara moved on to the photos for her "Whale Tales" update and her new teacher feature. She found her camera in her backpack, plugged it into the computer, and downloaded the pictures she'd taken of Crossback and Bobbi, and David. The gray whale photos fit well on either side of her update at the bottom of the first layout page. She added a small copy of David's photo alongside her feature at the top.

Her focus remained on the picture of David, and it took a second before she noticed the sound of high heels clacking into the classroom. An emphatic huff near the teacher's desk made her turn, and Cara's teeth ground together at the blonde hair, sexy figure, and doll-like face.

Amber's hands were on her hips. "What are you doing here?" she asked in a high-pitched, irritated tone.

Cara gripped the edge of her chair and struggled to keep her voice level. "I'm the newspaper editor. What are you doing here?"

Amber cocked her head to the side and looked Cara up and down. "Where's David?"

Cara's heart deflated and her hands loosened on her seat. "I haven't seen him."

Just then, she did see him, through the doorway at the far side of the classroom. He looked at her and graced her with his lopsided grin as he walked through the open door. When he saw Amber, his grin faded.

He stomped over and faced Amber, so Cara could only see his back.

In an exasperated voice, he echoed both Amber's and Cara's words. "What are you doing here?"

"I should ask you the same question," Amber said, glaring at Cara over his shoulder.

David turned to Cara and shook his head. "I'm sorry. I'm not going to be able to stay. I'll talk to you and Garren tomorrow."

He took Amber by the elbow and hauled her toward the door. Amber twisted her head around to smile at Cara, as if she'd won some childish game. Cara half expected her to stick her tongue out.

Cara continued to gape at the door when Garren walked through it.

He stood before her chair. "Tell me what's wrong."

She finally tore her gaze from the doorway and shared the facts of what had happened.

"Sounds like an angry girlfriend," he said.

She frowned.

"From what you said, though, Mr. Wilson didn't seem happy to see her. Maybe she's harassing him."

That idea sounded better. Amber was attractive, though, and David had paid her attention, even if it was negative. They seemed to have dated, and whether or not it should, that broke Cara's heart. If they weren't already a couple, Cara worried they could become one.

"You're really bothered about it," Garren said.

She pressed her lips together.

"It's obvious you have feelings for him."

She thought she'd made a good effort to conceal her feelings for David from others. People at school had paid more attention to her lately than they had in years. But that was because of the changes in her appearance and how they thought she had a thing going with Garren, the hot new student, not David, the cute new teacher.

She would never forgive herself if people truly thought anything was going on between her and David. Better that they think she was involved with Garren. "Why would you say that?"

"You talk about him more than you realize, and you stare at him like he's the only man on Earth."

She hung her head. "I can't help it. We dated before school started. And we really connected. Now I can't stop thinking about him."

"Well, it doesn't seem like this girl has captured his attention the way you have."

Her head snapped up. "What do you mean?"

"I've seen the way he looks at you, how he's always dropping papers when you're around."

Had Cara known she'd get a promising response from Garren, she would have shared her feelings with him sooner. She wanted to trust not only in the connection between her and David, but also in the signs of continued attraction she hoped she recognized from him, like the special grin he seemed to reserve for her, and the way he quickly looked away when she caught him watching her, even the overly formal voice she'd only noticed him use with her.

She wanted to believe he felt the same way she did, despite the fact that he ignored her most of the time. Hearing someone else confirm his attraction to her made it more believable.

"I hope other people haven't noticed," she said. She worried for a second that Rachel might start rumors. Then she remembered how uncommunicative Rachel was these days. Ethan, too. "Please don't tell anyone."

"I won't say anything. And he seems to be trying to find someone closer to his age. Only it doesn't sound like he's been successful."

She groaned.

Garren placed his hands on her shoulders. Countless girls would be overcome with envy if they saw how tenderly he gazed at her. He was like a combination of an ideal friend, brother, and father.

"If you don't already have a date in mind, I'd love to bring you to the Halloween dance," he said.

She eased his hands off her shoulders and held them. On the few dates she'd gone on after her breakup with Chris, the guys had quickly come to understand that she wouldn't participate in the extracurricular activities they had in mind. Then she'd given up on dating altogether.

In the past couple of years, she'd done just fine with her mom and Rachel, her whales, her newspaper work, and Scrabble. Then David had come along. And Rachel had deserted her.

But David was off limits, at least for now. Maybe forever. And standing in front of her was the most perfect boyfriend material she was likely to ever come across.

Only a fool would fail to give this relationship a shot at romance. Maybe the reason she'd never felt a spark between her and Garren was because neither of them had attempted to ignite one.

A smile played at the corners of Garren's lips as he looked at her. "You're going to kiss me."

*Awkward.*

She blinked. "It's probably a bad idea."

"Actually, I think it's a good idea."

She looked into his eyes and was calmed by their kaleidoscope effect, though, as usual, she didn't feel aroused. A kiss could change that, though.

She placed her hands on his shoulders and leaned in. His eyes remained open, but when their lips met, she shut hers. His mouth felt soft and warm and nice. But still, there was no real heat. She pressed her lips more firmly against his and felt them mold with hers. Still nothing.

As a last resort, she stretched her tongue out to meet his. She pulled away as though she'd been burned. But not by passion. If she'd had a brother, she imagined kissing him would feel the same as it had to French-kiss Garren.

Her lips felt cold and wet as she stepped back. She stared at Garren's sneakers. When she dared to look into his eyes again, he didn't flinch away from her gaze. His face was perfectly composed.

"You're not attracted to me. That way," she said.

"You're not attracted to *me*. That way."

*True.* She shook her head.

He nodded, which she took to mean he wasn't upset about it.

"Not because there's any reason I shouldn't be attracted to you. I just can't force myself to feel something I don't. Trust me, I know I'm crazy."

Now he shook his head. "You're not crazy. You're human. And not every relationship between a male and a female is meant to be romantic."

"Well, then, the answer is yes. I'd love to go to the dance with you, my friend."

# TWENTY

Rachel was absent on Wednesday and Cara was grateful to be able to focus solely on David in journalism class. She expected him to offer an explanation for his abrupt departure the previous night. After class, he again asked her and Garren to stay.

In the far corner of the room, Mr. Cutter talked on his cell phone. He looked at David, pointed to his phone, and walked out.

Cara stood next to David, where he sat at the teacher's desk. She was hopeful, but kept her expression blank. Garren stepped close to her side.

"I apologize for not being able to work with you last night," David said in his formal teacher's tone. "Thank you both for the work you did. I saw you got most of the layout done, but I'm hoping you won't mind meeting again tonight."

Disappointed that David seemed ready to dismiss them, Cara offered a curt, "Sure," and turned to follow Garren out of the classroom.

Like the day before, David called out, "Cara, wait."

Garren waved good-bye and left.

Cara's breath hitched. She and David were alone. And he didn't have any containers to return this time.

She was dying to know what he had to say, but first, she needed some answers. She swallowed and focused on his desk.

"Amber was pretty rude last night." She spoke lightly in hopes of sounding more sympathetic than annoyed.

"I know she was. I'm sorry. I made it clear she'd better not bother me at work, so we shouldn't have to worry about her intruding again."

"Are you dating her?" She looked him in the eye now.

He met her gaze and warmth flooded through her.

"No, I only took her out once."

"I'm sorry she's bothering you."

"Me, too."

Satisfied by the irritation in his tone, she let the subject go and asked, "What do you need from me?"

He drew in a big breath. "I wanted to ask if you'd like to cash in on that Scrabble rain check I promised you?"

"Tonight?" Her question popped out before she thought to tone down her surprise and delight.

"Why not? We're ahead of schedule. We'll have plenty of time to finish things up."

"What about Mr. Cutter and Garren?"

"Mr. Cutter can't make it. And Garren can either play with us, work on the layout, or both."

"You're on," she said as she walked away.

*Score one for Cara. Take that, Amber.*

---

Around four thirty, Cara's mom came home from shopping, ready to cook dinner. She found Cara in the kitchen nook eating a micro-waved macaroni and cheese.

"Hi, Mom. I forgot to tell you that I'm going to the school to work on the newspaper layout tonight." Really, Cara hadn't told her so her mom wouldn't have a chance to consider saying "no."

As expected, her mom asked, "Who'll be there?"

"Garren and Mr. Wilson."

Her mom's eyes narrowed. "What time will you be home?"

Figuring discretion was the better part of valor, Cara got up, tossed the macaroni and cheese in the garbage, and placed her fork in the sink. "In a couple of hours. See ya."

Her mom didn't protest as Cara picked up her backpack and hurried off.

At the school, David's truck sat in the teachers' lot. She grinned at it and parked a few spots away. Garren must not have arrived yet.

She slung her backpack over her arm and made her way to the building's entrance, where she keyed in the door code. In the journalism classroom, David sat at a table in the back, where a Scrabble game was laid out. Garren showed up as she set her jacket and backpack on a desk.

"Thanks for coming, you two," David said, standing to greet them.

"Of course," she said.

"You got a lot more done last night than I expected. There should be plenty of time to get the rest of the editing and layout done tonight if you want to play Scrabble with us afterward, Garren?" David asked.

"No thanks. I'll just finish up with the layout," Garren said. He walked over to an already glowing monitor.

David joined him and pointed out a few things on the page displayed on the computer screen. "Let me know if you need help."

Cara sat at the computer next to Garren and started in on the rest of her editing. That amounted to committing to add Rachel's "Make Believe or Magick?" Q & A to the newspaper issue, sans the question and answer about magick being able to reward a person with whatever he or she wanted. When Cara finished, she stood behind Garren and watched as, like the night before, he scrolled up and down the computer screen, calling up articles and placing and sizing them with speed and skill she thought would take many years to achieve.

"You're really good," she said and squeezed his shoulder. "I was going to offer to help, but it doesn't look like you need me."

Garren turned his head toward her and smiled. "I couldn't do this job if you hadn't done yours. I can handle the rest if you want to play Scrabble."

Did she ever. "Thanks."

She headed over to David, who flipped through a Scrabble dictionary.

He gestured to the seat across from him. "Ready to play?"

She rubbed her hands together. "Let's do it."

As they began their first game, David held her gaze and she immediately sensed the familiar warmth between them. She relaxed and gave him a sly smile that bunched up at one corner as she placed a Bingo on the board, using all her tiles to score fifty extra points, in addition to the double points for her first word. The word she'd arranged on her rack was C-O-M-P-L-E-X, of all things.

David nodded, not surprised by her play. Or her luck. She let out a quiet sigh. Playing with him was something she'd looked forward to, but she didn't want to look stupid if he creamed her. Luck or not, the Bingo would help her save face if she lost.

"So did you end up going out to see the grays?" he asked before he made a strong play using an "H" two ways.

"Yeah, Garren and I went out a couple of weeks ago," she said, then bit the inside of her cheek when she realized she'd made it sound like it had been a date.

David focused on the tiles on his rack. "Did you see any whales?"

She got the feeling he was really asking whether she'd seen any transient orcas. She still wasn't sure she hadn't just imagined the black dorsal fin. "We saw Crossback and Bobbi, actually. I got to touch Bobbi this time."

David's lips turned up into a soft smile. "Nice. The transients must have left."

"It's been a while now and Rick hasn't seen them, so I'd say that's a safe bet."

She won the first game by over one hundred points and they started another. David took a significant lead this time. She had to exchange tiles several times to keep up. It pleased her to note that, depending on who got the better tiles, they seemed to play on the same level. They didn't talk much, instead communicating with facial expressions and body language in response to each other's plays.

"Done," Garren announced, not turning away from the monitor.

"Just a sec," David said to Cara, and headed over to check Garren's work. He scrolled down the computer screen. "I'm impressed with your layout skills."

Garren shut down the computer and followed David back to the Scrabble table.

"Thanks for offering your help," David told Garren. He swept a hand toward the Scrabble board. "Are you sure you don't want to play?"

"You're welcome. And no. You two have fun."

"I hope you don't feel like I stuck you with all the hard work," Cara said. "You're just way better than me at layout."

"You've done more than your share," Garren said. "Happy early birthday, Cara."

"Thanks. And good night," she said as he walked away.

"When's your birthday?" David asked, reclaiming his seat across from her.

"Tomorrow. I'm turning eighteen." She cringed when the number came out. It only seemed to emphasize her youth.

David offered no reaction as he made his next move on the board. "What do you have planned?"

She set down her next play and waited for him to add the points to her score. "Garren's coming over for the celebration my mom's putting together."

He raised his eyebrows at her.

So he wondered if she was dating Garren. He cared. Her heart threatened to burst from her chest as she shook her head in answer to his unspoken question.

He drew in a deep breath, then made his last play. She finished up the game with a win, though only by twenty-two points. He seemed to lose with too much grace, responding with his lopsided grin.

She narrowed her eyes at him. "You didn't let me win, did you?"

He shook his head and met her gaze. "I always give it my best, I swear. We're a good match."

A burst of energy sparked in her chest, where she imagined the tether extended toward him. She wondered if he intended the double meaning in his words.

He didn't look away for a few glorious seconds. Then he turned his eyes toward the table. "We should go now."

Outside, the sky had darkened, contrasting starkly with the parking lot's white overhead lamps. The air was cold, still, and silent. Even the seagulls were mute.

The quiet was comfortable at first. Until they reached her car. Spray-painted in thick, black letters across the driver's-side door was "S-L-U-T."

She stopped and stared at the word. Her stomach clenched and she clutched her midsection as if she'd been punched. David froze at her side and put a hand on her shoulder.

It took her a minute to get her feet to move again. They circled the car together. The passenger's side was a mirror image of the driver's side, punctuated by the long black scrape from Rick's bumper.

"Do you know of anyone who would do this?" David asked, his voice tight.

She shook her head, but her instincts told her Amber had done it. Amber wouldn't know about her feelings for David, but she'd made a competitive display the night before. Maybe she was still upset that Chris had dumped her years ago and had chosen to date Cara. Whatever the reason, Amber was as big of a pain in the ass as ever.

Cara's cheeks burned. She was too humiliated to look David in the eye. He might believe that about her, like half the students at Seaside, thanks to Chris. But she was a virgin, far from deserving of that judgment.

David's hand dropped from her shoulder. "I'll bet Amber did it. She feels threatened by you."

"Why?"

"When she saw a pretty girl waiting to spend time with me last night, it made her jealous. But like I told you before, I only took her out once."

He said she was pretty. His compliment registered in a tender spot within her, but she left it tucked away. Right now, she needed to deal with her vandalized car.

"I doubt the police could prove Amber did the damage," he said. "But I'd like to pay for the repairs."

"No. It's not your fault."

"Let me at least follow you home and explain this to your mom, then."

Her mom knew she was still hung up on David. It would only make matters worse to reveal that another girl who was interested in him, not to mention someone Cara used to go to high school with, was harassing them. But the prolonged time with David was something she couldn't refuse.

David held her car door open. She tossed her backpack on the passenger seat to hide the empty chip bags piled there.

"Don't walk alone at night, okay?" he asked as she buckled herself in.

"Okay." She wrapped her arms around herself, contemplating his protective words and relishing the memory of his arm around her, once again keeping her warm, safe, and secure.

"Everything look okay inside?"

She hoped it was too dark for him to see the plastic bag on the floor overflowing with empty soda bottles and fast-food wrappers. "Time for a cleaning, but nothing looks out of place," she said, her words rushed.

She grabbed her door handle and he removed his hand. After she yanked the door shut, she started the engine and waited for him to climb into his truck. He followed her out of the lot and kept a close distance behind her on the drive to her house.

Less than thrilled about driving her vandalized car, she didn't look at any passing drivers. She parked deep in and far to the side of the driveway, which was lined by bushes.

David parked on the street. They remained silent as she led him into the house and down the hall to the family room. Her mom jumped up off the love seat and stood straight as a soldier at attention. She drilled David with a straight-on, angry gaze.

Cara should have introduced him, but she hesitated too long, concentrating on her mom's rigid stance and hard stare.

"Sorry to bother you, Ms. Markwell. I'm David Wilson, the student teacher in Cara's journalism class."

"What's going on?" Her mom's jaw clenched as she looked to Cara to answer.

Cara couldn't find her voice to respond.

"Cara's car was vandalized," David said.

Her mom's shoulders relaxed, but her brows furrowed.

"Someone spray-painted . . . a hateful word on the driver and passenger sides," he said.

"Someone called me a slut, which is the opposite of the truth," Cara said, eager to defend her reputation.

"I think I know who did it," David said.

Her mom remained silent.

"I dated a girl—I took her out once and then told her I didn't want to see her anymore. She keeps calling and showing up—"

"What does that have to do with Cara or her car?"

"The girl came to the school last night to find me. She saw Cara there and felt threatened."

Cara recognized the strain in her mom's face, in the tightness around her lips.

"How old is this girl?" her mom asked.

"Twenty-one."

Her mom paused, then switched into her standard, problem-tackling mode. "We'll file a police report and an insurance claim for the car," she said to Cara. "As for this girl," she told David, "you should change your number if she's calling a lot. If she contacts you, you should make it clear that she's not to call you or come to your place of work. Threaten to get a restraining order if she doesn't listen. And you may very well need to follow through on getting one."

"Thanks for the advice," he said. "I'm hoping she'll back off. But I feel terrible about Cara's car. I'd like to pay for the repairs."

"We'll leave the details about the car to the police and the insurance company." Her mom motioned for them to follow her to the front door. "I'm serious when I say to ignore this girl," she told David. "Any reinforcement, positive or negative, can encourage her behavior." She especially emphasized her last three words.

Cara might have vandalized her car herself if she she'd known it would amount to her mom giving David professional advice to avoid contact with Amber. Cara's stomach twisted, but it was more of a happy, light feeling than a nauseating, anxious one. If her feelings for David weren't so intense, she'd be ashamed of how glad she was that his recent romantic prospect was a lunatic.

David said good night to her mom and offered another apology as he stepped onto the front porch.

"I need to grab my coat and backpack from my car," Cara said to her mom before she turned to David. "I'll walk you to your truck."

Cara didn't allow any time for her mom to object as she stepped outside and swung the front door shut.

At the end of the walkway, David held his hand out to her. She extended hers, which fit perfectly in his, as though it belonged there. Warmth radiated from her hand, up her arm, and through her chest. The thrumming energy between them intensified and the tether seemed to grow thicker and stronger.

David folded his other hand around hers. "I'm so sorry for involving you in my problems."

"You didn't do anything but help me."

He squeezed her hand before he let it go and walked off toward his truck.

"Good night, Cara." He didn't look at her again as he climbed into the truck's cab.

"Good night, David."

She watched him drive off, then slowly walked back to the house. Her mom didn't call for her when she stepped inside. She stopped in the family room doorway anyway.

Her mom looked at her head-on. "Is there anything else going on I should know about?"

"No."

"You know you can tell me if there is, right?"

"There's honestly nothing to tell." Cara sighed. She couldn't help but wish there were.

# TWENTY-ONE

On Cara's eighteenth birthday, Garren sat beside her in front of their lockers during lunch and pulled a special offering from his bag. He opened an ivory bakery box to display two cupcakes topped with whipped, snowy frosting and glittery, crystalline sprinkles.

"Happy birthday, Cara."

"Wow. They look fake." Her words almost sounded rude. But the cupcakes really did look too good to be real. She gave him a hug. "Thanks for thinking of me."

She lifted one of the treats from the box and unwrapped its delicate liner to uncover the soft, white fluffiness beneath. Her teeth sank into the moist dessert. The cake tingled on her tongue and the sweet frosting felt smooth against the roof of her mouth. This beat the apples, no question.

"Tell me about last night," Garren said before he bit into his cupcake.

He had to be asking about what happened with David, not about the vandalism to her car, or he would already have mentioned seeing it. She told him what had happened, explaining that David suspected that Amber was responsible and how he brought her home to talk to her mom.

"David's right. You shouldn't walk alone at night. You never know what someone might do."

She finished her cupcake and brushed off Garren's exaggerated concern along with the crumbs in her lap. "I thought you would've seen the damage to my car when you left the parking lot last night."

He didn't look at her as he added both their cupcake wrappers to the bakery box and placed the box back in his bag. "I'm not happy about it. I would have stopped it, if I could have."

---

The previous year, on Cara's seventeenth birthday, when Rachel had been her normal, affectionate, boisterous self, she'd given Cara balloons and a card and had made a fuss at school. Today, she didn't offer her so much as a glance. If demons really were plaguing Rachel, whatever Ms. Clark and her mom might have done to try to help her evidently hadn't worked. No matter what was going on with Rachel, though, Cara refused to let it ruin her eighteenth birthday.

The highlight of the school day was when David wished her a hearty "happy birthday" as she got up from her seat at the end of journalism class. His announcement roused a chorus of "happy birthday"s from Mr. Cutter and her classmates. She turned to smile at them, then walked over to where David stood at the front of the room.

"Have fun celebrating with Garren and your mom," he said. He sounded as if he wished he could come.

She wanted to tell him she wished he could come, too. But she just smiled and said, "Thanks." She looked him in the eyes and he held her gaze, sharing a brief moment of warmth with her.

In the student lot, Garren waited for her by her mom's Outback. Cara's car was in the shop, so her mom let her drive the station wagon.

But Garren wouldn't have known that she was driving it that day. Unless he saw her arrive in the morning . . .

Garren missed nothing. Maybe that should make her nervous. Yet, for some reason, she couldn't bring herself to feel spooked by him.

"Thanks for letting me join in your birthday celebration with your mom." He pulled her to him for a gentle hug. "I'll see you soon."

Early that evening, Garren arrived on Cara's doorstep holding eighteen white roses. The flowers weren't wrapped in tissue or cellophane, nor accented with baby's breath or other greenery. They were free of thorns, in perfect bloom, and not one petal, leaf, or stem revealed any flaws. The cool, smooth petals smelled sweet and rich, like the ideal rose fragrance perfumes and lotions failed to capture.

Cara's chin trembled. This was the sweetest gift any guy had ever given her. "Thank you. They're unbelievable." The roses appeared every bit as unreal as the apples and the cupcakes.

Garren kissed her cheek. She accepted the flowers and ushered him inside.

"Where did you get them?"

"Same place I get the apples."

"And that source remains a secret?"

"Yes. Sorry."

*No surprise there.* "Will you ever be able to tell me?"

He nodded. "Soon, hopefully."

Glad to get a promising answer, she didn't push.

In the kitchen, she arranged the roses in a vase of water. Garren carried the flowers for her through a short house tour until they reached her bedroom, where she had him set the vase on her desk. He only gave her room a cursory glance, as he did all the rooms in the house.

When they reached the family room, Cara's mom stood in front of the love seat. She'd taken the day off work to cook Cara's meal of choice—this year it was her grandmother's goulash—and to otherwise prepare for Cara's birthday celebration and for Garren's first visit.

Her mom greeted Garren with a tentative smile. "It's nice to finally meet you."

"Thanks for including me. I think it's special that you and Cara usually celebrate your birthdays together."

Her mom smiled broadly at him and took her seat. She continued to observe him as he sat beside Cara on the couch. Cara opened the stack of gifts her mom had piled on the coffee table: a much-needed new wallet to add to her backpack, an ebook reader loaded with several titles from her favorite authors, and a new outfit.

Garren's smile stretched widely across his face as Cara gushed over her gifts. She got up and hugged her mom, who pulled a small, white box from between the cushions of the love seat. Cara took the box and opened it to find a set of car keys resting on top of a light layer of tissue paper.

For a moment, she just stared at the keys. Then her mouth fell open and she snatched them up and rushed to the garage. Garren followed behind her mom.

Cara flipped the overhead light switch on. There, reminding her of a little bullet, sat an icy silver Honda Fit.

She clasped her hands together, then turned to give her mom another hug. "I definitely wasn't expecting this. Thank you!"

"You're welcome. With the police working on their investigation and the insurance company wanting me to wade through an abyss of paperwork, I figured we should just have the Civic painted and sell it."

Cara was thankful some good came out of the situation with her car anyway.

———

While Cara, Garren, and her mom ate goulash and cake and ice cream, her mom kept sneaking glances at Garren, whose attention seemed centered on his food. No doubt the analytical wheels were turning in her mom's psychologically oriented mind. Cara wanted to tell her to stop staring. But she knew her mom didn't mean to be rude. It was just her way.

"Are you up for a ride?" Cara asked Garren when he'd finished off the last of his cake.

She was anxious to drive her new car and to get out from under parental scrutiny. Though her mom obviously hadn't witnessed any of the signs of attraction she'd been looking for.

Garren rose from the table and picked up his plate. "Let me help clean up, and I'd love to go."

Her mom stood and held her hand out for his dish. "Thanks, but I'll handle it. You two go ahead."

Garren followed Cara back to her Fit. The car was a few years old, but the dealer had detailed it to perfection. They climbed onto the soft gray seats. Cara breathed in the freshly cleaned car smell, knowing it would soon be gone, overtaken by the scents of the sea.

The garage door opener from her Civic was already clipped to the sun visor. She pressed its button and the door lifted. Once she'd figured out the car's controls, she headed for the scenic byway.

Garren kept quiet as she drove. She started to speak, but he pointed at the windshield. Rolling her eyes, she pressed her lips together. She couldn't complain out loud. More than anyone else, Garren had a legitimate reason to consider her a bad driver.

Halfway to their destination, she noticed a red sedan behind them. She flashed back to the parking lot at Liberty Charters, that morning before she fell overboard, when a red Jetta had almost run into her Civic. It was dark out now, but Cara caught a few glimpses of the car under the streetlights they passed. The candy apple red shade was the same.

Cara glanced at Garren, her heart speeding faster than her Fit. He didn't appear to be looking in the side-view mirror or to have picked up on anything unusual. She pulled into a spot under a streetlight in the parking area above the beach she'd chosen.

The red car drove by slowly and light reflected off its rear. It was a Jetta, but it had California plates. The windows were tinted, so Cara couldn't see the driver, who drove on at a normal pace down the highway.

Garren came around to open her door. He still didn't give any sign he'd noticed the red car. They walked to the seawall and gazed down at the waves crashing against the rocks below. The chaotic water calmed her.

She was driving a new car no one would recognize. No one had intentionally followed them. She was just being paranoid.

# TWENTY-TWO

The next morning, after an hour of not being able to concentrate on either Scrabble or a book, Cara responded to an inner urge to walk to the beach. A bright ball of yellow sun burned in a vibrant blue sky. She made her way down the hill and, when she came to the sand, she had to look away from the glare of sunlight reflecting off the water's surface and focus farther down the coastline.

*So much for looking for the grays.*

Waves poured onto the wet sand below the drier strip where she walked. She concentrated on the soothing sound of the water trickling toward the shore. No wind blew, but crisp air nipped at her nose and cheeks.

A good number of people roamed the beach in front of Surfseekers Resort—families and couples, and groups of teens. One person sat as far away from the water as space would allow, in a batch of driftwood that had gathered against the high wall beneath the resort. Cara often climbed onto that piling to look for the grays.

She might not have taken a second look at the person on the driftwood, if the crop of dark hair hadn't caught her attention. The guy's elbows rested on his knees and he hid his face in his hands. Anticipation hummed in her belly.

Moving closer, she recognized the hair, as well as the lean frame and, finally, the hands. His fingers were thick and strong and she remembered they were soft to touch. His fingernails were always neatly clipped. Maybe it was a strange thing to find attractive. But as she stood directly in front of him, she knew the hands were David's.

The problem was, she didn't know what to say. He had to sense someone standing in front of him, yet he just sat there with his hands covering his face. If he could see between his fingers, he had to know it was her who stood before him.

He didn't greet her.

Panic poked at her. He might not want to associate with her outside of school, especially after all that had just happened with Amber and the vandalism to her car. But she couldn't walk away.

"You've come to my favorite beach," she said, glad her comment sounded soothing, yet not foolish.

His fingers slid down his face and he moved in slow motion as he sat up straighter. Whatever was bothering him, she wanted to sit next to him, to console him. But she didn't dare move any closer.

"It's my favorite beach, too." Weariness weighed down his words.

"What's wrong?" she couldn't help but ask. She didn't want him to think she was pretending not to notice his distress. They did enough pretending.

He scratched at his jaw. "I had an argument with my dad."

"Oh. I'm sorry. Do you want to talk about it?"

He raked his fingers through his hair, then rubbed his hands over his thighs. "My mom died a few years ago. I miss her, but it's worse for my dad. He gets lonely when I'm not around. He wants me to move home."

"And you don't want to leave?" *Please don't leave.*

"No . . ."

"Well, at least you know you'll sort things out with your dad eventually. Parents don't give up on their kids, right?"

His lopsided grin spread across his face. "Right."

She glanced at the spot next to him on the log, then back down the beach, not sure if she should stay or go.

"Where are you headed?" he asked.

"I was just taking a walk, trying to look for the grays. I'll probably go home now."

He stood and brushed sand from the back of his pants. "Do you mind if I walk with you?"

A huge grin broke out on her face before she toned it down into a close-lipped smile. "I'd like that."

Walking along the water's edge with the sun behind them, they were able to survey the water.

"I'm always looking for whales on the water now," he said, remaining close enough to her that passers-by would see them as a couple.

Cara fought the urge to lean into him. "Most of the time you'll be disappointed." *Unless you don't see transient orcas. Then you'll be glad.*

"It's still fun to look."

She caught a quick glimpse of his lopsided grin.

After a few anxious moments of silence, she said, "I'm looking forward to seeing the newspaper issue."

"Me, too. It'll be the first one I had a hand in."

"And probably the only one you'll get front-page photo coverage in."

He grimaced. "Did you really have to put my picture on the front page?"

"I did. And it's a great picture."

A new pink splotch appeared on his cheek.

They reached the stairs that led to the street nearest hers and she stopped. "I gotta head up now."

His eyes held hers, striking a spark of heat within her.

"Thanks," he said.

She wasn't sure what he was thanking her for. "Anytime," she said, worrying that another time might never come.

She thought he would leave then, but he placed his hands on either side of her face. His gaze dropped to her mouth and the heat in her chest flushed up to her lips. His face leaned toward hers and she closed her eyes as she waited for his kiss.

His soft lips touched her forehead. And then he was gone. She opened her eyes to see him jogging off down the beach.

# TWENTY-THREE

The first issue of the *Seaside Journal* came out on Halloween. David's photo appeared in color in the online edition and in black and white on the front page of the printed paper, alongside Cara's feature. Crossback's and Bobbi's photos, together with her update on her closest encounters with the grays to date, covered the bottom half of the page.

For the first time in her high school journalism career, the credits on the front page declared her the newspaper's editor. She'd wanted Garren's name printed as the layout editor, but he'd been adamant that the credit be given to the sophomore-in-training. She saved one copy of the printed newspaper in a hatbox on her closet shelf and kept another copy in her nightstand drawer.

Halloween night, Garren stood on Cara's doorstep in a black suit and tie. She'd requested that they dress in formal wear rather than costumes for the dance. A group of miniature ghosts, witches, angels, devils, princesses, and superheroes trailed behind Garren. Her mom greeted him and ushered him in before loading the kids up with candy.

Cara stood in the entryway wearing the new dress her mom had purchased for her: a black velour short-sleeved minidress, which she wore with a black bolero cover, black suede heels, and zirconia stud earrings, along with a coordinating bracelet and necklace. A small black clutch held her phone, money, and touch-up makeup. Earlier, she'd curled her hair, pinned most of it up, and let large tendrils fall. Her makeup job was thorough, complete with cranberry lipstick. The Rachel she used to know would have been proud of her effort.

Her mom handed her Garren's boutonniere, which consisted of a single white rose. Garren slipped a corsage on her wrist before she pinned his flower to the lapel of his suit. The rose she wore made the one she gave him look half dead.

She was curious to find out whether the rose in the corsage would have anywhere near the miraculous life span of the eighteen he'd given her for her birthday. After two weeks, it wasn't unheard of that the roses were still alive, but the flowers remained as pristine as the day she'd received them. Even though Garren seemed so opposed to the occult, her only guess was that he must have used some sort of "white" magick to affect the flowers. She couldn't bring the issue up around her mom, but she made a mental note to question Garren about it later that night.

Cara and Garren left while the trick-or-treaters demanded her mom's attention. Garren drove them down the byway to Above the Waves restaurant, overlooking the waters of Anchorage Bay.

Inside, a friendlier hostess than Lori led them to a window seat. Garren pulled Cara's chair out for her, and she sat and gazed down at the sea below. The dark water was lit by bright white mounted lights.

"The filet mignon and salmon both sound good," Garren said, perusing the menu.

Those were two of her top choices, too.

Their waitress arrived and Cara ordered a diet soda. Garren said he was fine with water. Cara felt comfortable ordering the filet mignon, since Garren had mentioned it, even though it was pricey. She had a feeling he'd insist on paying. He ordered the salmon.

The waitress batted her eyelashes at him.

He waved a hand toward Cara. "My date is the editor of her school paper. The first issue came out today. She did an excellent job on it."

The waitress paused uncomfortably before she congratulated Cara. As odd as it was for Garren to publicly praise her, a familiar flutter of appreciation tickled Cara's chest. Garren's royal treatment felt especially nice right now, considering Rachel had completely ignored her lately and David was off limits.

Cara and Garren arrived at the school for the latter part of the dance. Dozens of people in a mixture of formal wear and Halloween costumes crowded the gym. The dancers were speckled with bright lights that reflected off the silver-faceted orb hanging from the ceiling. Couples moved to the beat of the music pounding from large speakers on either side of the school's stage, which was curtained off and decorated with orange and black streamers and balloons. Other students gathered around the perimeter of the darkened gym.

Cara wound her arm through Garren's and he led her to the dance floor. At the few school dances she'd been to, she'd felt klutzy dancing and could hardly move her feet. Chris had held her too close and had tried to feel her up.

Garren held her at a proper half-arm's length, folded her hand around his, and placed his other hand on her back. They danced to the slower rhythm of a ballad and he leaned back and forth and side-to-side to guide her movements. Thrilled that she pulled off formal dancing for once, she couldn't stop smiling. Garren beamed at her.

The next time he twirled her around, she spotted a long table across the room, draped in black crepe paper and cornered off with glowing orange jack-o'-lanterns. David sat on a stool behind the table. His face was turned in her direction, but she couldn't read his expression in the dark.

Garren took a step back and lightly held her by her forearms. "I'll walk you over so you can say hello to David."

She shrugged apologetically. "Thanks. You're sure you don't mind?"

"Not at all."

Garren kept an arm around her waist as they made their way off the dance floor. David's deep green eyes lit up in the jack-o'-lanterns' candlelight. Cara met his gaze and felt the familiar warm tug pulling her closer to him.

"Got stuck with chaperone duty?" she asked him.

"It's always the rookie's job." He seemed to hone in on Garren's hand on her side.

"I'm going to visit the restroom. I'll be right back," Garren said.

"Take your time," David told him.

She looked at David's eyebrows rather than his eyes, hoping that would calm her nerves. It didn't. "It's good to see you." Pretending to push away tendrils of hair, she waved at her face to try to cool it down.

"You look great." He held out his hand.

Droplets of sweat broke out at her hairline, but she placed a dry hand in his. The tether's draw grew stronger. He bent toward her over the table, smiled slightly, and raised her hand to sniff the corsage on her wrist.

His smile faded. "Be good tonight." He brushed his thumb over the top of her hand before he let it go.

Her throat closed up, but she managed a flimsy smile and a nod. He flashed her his lopsided grin. All traces of the grin disappeared, however, when Garren came back to her side and wrapped his arm around her.

"We should go," Garren said, offering David a toned-down version of his dazzling smile.

Garren was right. If she stayed and continued to talk to David, people would notice the closer-than-normal interaction between them, if they hadn't already. She reluctantly said good-bye.

Glancing back over her shoulder, she saw that David was still watching her. He frowned. She frowned back, only turning away when Garren directed her attention to a dark corner. Two figures in black emerged and moved toward the exit.

"Rachel and Ethan are leaving," Garren said. "You could talk to Rachel."

Part of her wanted to. Another part of her recoiled at the thought. When she'd finally told Garren about the incident when she'd planned to drag Rachel to church, he hadn't been surprised. He reminded her, once again, that Rachel needed prayer to help her, but that she also needed to be receptive to it. So far, Rachel didn't seem open to any kind of interaction, except with Ethan.

"She's probably still mad at me."

"You could say *hi* to her, at least."

"How about we leave and say *good-bye* to her instead?"

Garren held his arm out to let her lead the way. They caught up to Rachel and Ethan under the glaring white overhead lights of the parking lot.

"Didn't you like the dance, Rachel?" Cara asked, speaking to her from behind.

The old Rachel would've been ecstatic about dances. Cara didn't get too close, uneasy about which Rachel might face her.

Rachel stopped, then spun around, her eyes dark and hazy. No anger shone in them. In fact, there wasn't any recognizable feeling in them. Ethan's eyes narrowed so much, they weren't visible.

Turning her nose up at Garren, Rachel said, "We're heading to a real party." Her tone was mocking, the same as it had been when Cara had brought Christmas cookies to her before Halloween. Rachel hooked her arm through Ethan's and they stalked off toward his black Chevy Malibu.

Garren led Cara to his truck and helped her into the cab, then shut her door and went around to climb in and start the engine.

A familiar candy apple red Jetta pulled up next to them, on Cara's side. Cara couldn't see the driver through the dark-tinted windows.

"You recognize that car," Garren said, his expression customarily calm and unreadable.

"I'm pretty sure I've seen it a couple of times—at Liberty Charters and driving behind us on my birthday."

"It's got the same California plates."

So Garren had checked out the car on the byway after all.

"It seems to be following Ethan," she said as the Jetta drove away and turned onto the street behind the Malibu.

"It looks that way."

Now that Rachel and Ethan were somehow associated with the

Jetta, Cara couldn't let this go. "Let's follow Ethan and Rachel to that party."

"We weren't invited."

"Rachel told us they were headed to a party. I can mistake that for an invitation, can't I?"

He shifted the truck into drive. "If you say so."

They exited the parking lot and sped up to get closer to the Jetta. Garren pulled over when the Malibu and Jetta turned down a side street.

"I'm only going to take you if you're sure you want to go," he said, evaluating her.

"I can get a better idea of what Rachel's messing around with if we crash the party. I want to go."

He put the truck back in drive. "Then I'll go with you."

"I wouldn't go in without you, I'll tell you that." But she didn't know if what she said was true. Anger swelled within her with each breath, mingling and competing with her fear.

Garren turned down the side road. Both the Malibu and the Jetta were parked on the right side of the street, in a row along with half a dozen other vehicles. Some teenagers or adults in costumes wandered down the opposite side of the road, but no one else was out.

The most activity on the block appeared to occur in a small, one-story house. Silhouettes dotted the curtains covering two lit windows on either side of the door, as well as another curtained-off window on the side of the house. Diffuse, flickering light shone from within.

Garren parked a block away. He helped Cara down from the truck's cab and tucked her arm through his. Their progress toward the house was slow, due to her nerves and high heels. Her knees shook when they finally walked up the few steps to the front porch, which was dark and barren of any Halloween decorations.

She knocked on the door and a blond Ethan look-alike answered. He grimaced at Garren.

"We're here to see Rachel," she said, standing tall and holding her chin high, though she had no idea if this guy even knew who Rachel was.

His eyes slithered over her. Her knees stopped smacking together and she tugged her bolero together over her chest. If she slapped the pervert, he might not let her in.

The guy's lips twisted into a mischievous grin. He glanced over his shoulder. "Rachel got started on a group thing. But you're welcome to wait with me until she's done." He licked his lips.

Garren tightened his grip on her arm. "She'll wait with me." He pulled her to his other side and pushed past the door guy.

If there had been much noise at the party before, it died down when they showed up. Black and orange taper candles burned in candelabras throughout the two visible rooms. The potent odor of sulfur hung in the air, mixed with scents of sweet and pungent herbs. The combination made Cara's stomach turn. She was indoors, yet she shivered at a chill in the air and rubbed her hands over her arms.

A dozen or more people crammed into the front living area. Some piled onto a black leather sofa and a matching club chair, others stood. Their outfits were casual or gothic ensembles in shades of black or gray.

Of the people in the front room, Cara recognized a good number of faces as former Seaside students who'd been seniors when she was a freshman. There were also a handful of current fellow students in the gathering, including a few girls from the popular clan. The others were quiet types, like Ethan. There was even a nurse Cara recognized from her recent visit to the hospital. The only greetings Cara and Garren received were blank stares.

All but a few people in the front room drank from metal chalices, like the one on Rachel's vanity, or from clear wineglasses or beer bottles. Endless bunches of glowing candles threw giant shadows everywhere. Distorted images on the walls made the house look twice as full.

At first, Cara was glad to spot Rachel's black cascade of hair in the next room. But when she and Garren moved around the side of the table where Rachel and Ethan sat, she saw they were part of a group surrounding a Ouija board. Their eyes remained closed as their fingers perched atop the game piece that resembled a white heart.

Lori, who had hostessed at the Cove, was the only person at the Ouija table with her eyes open. She dramatized each word she spoke. "It says, 'Get out.'"

A flash of long blonde hair registered in the corner of Cara's eye. Amber's curls brushed the top of a small table covered with tarot cards. A group of people lined up next to her post.

Amber's mouth broke out in an expectant grin and her shark-like eyes stabbed at Cara's. Involuntarily flinching and blinking, Cara was unable to look away until Lori's overbearing voice carried over.

"It keeps saying, 'Get out.'"

Rachel, Ethan, and their séance partners opened their eyes. They exchanged anxious murmurs as they watched the board. None of the participants touched the game piece, yet it moved in rapid circles, flew lengthwise across the table, crashed into the wall, and fell to the floor. Cara stared at it, her jaw hanging open in disbelief.

Looking as collected as ever, Garren grabbed the Ouija board from the table and broke it in half over his knee. It seemed like every head turned to look at him. He flung the two halves of the board to his sides.

Several people veered out of the way. Others left the house. Cara watched Garren, shocked. She'd never seen him act any way other than calmly.

Amber didn't so much as shift in her seat. Garren approached her and her mouth curled into a snarl. The group lined up for her scurried toward the edges of the room. With one hand, Garren overturned Amber's table, sending the tarot cards flying and fluttering to the ground.

Amber rose from her seat and her words came out in a guttural growl. "Get out."

Garren stepped up to her. "This won't be tolerated much longer."

Cara wasn't sure what to make of Garren's comment. And she was surprised that it sounded as if Garren and Amber knew each other.

Garren didn't wait for a response from Amber. Instead, he turned to the partygoers. "These are not games you're playing. You're not conjuring up harmless spirits. You're summoning demons that want to destroy you."

Rachel and Ethan moved to stand on either side of Amber, like bodyguards. The crowd Garren said Ethan hung out with obviously centered around Amber. And now, apparently, that crowd also included Rachel. Ethan's mouth set in a tight, thin line and Rachel's black eyes gleamed as she glared back and forth between Cara and Garren. Cara shrunk back from their sinister expressions.

Amber glided forth like royalty, in a full-length, black formal dress. Maybe she'd dressed up for the high school dance. Her car had been in the parking lot.

Garren moved to Cara's side as Amber advanced. Cara was tempted to cower behind him, but she forced herself to stay put. Amber stopped within inches of him and pointed at the door.

Her words were the same as before, but she sounded calmer and more confident. "Get out."

Garren ignored Amber and put a hand on Cara's shoulder. "I didn't mean to scare you, Cara."

Unable to speak, Cara shook her head at him. He was the only person present who didn't scare her.

A disgusted scowl shrouded Amber's face and her eyes burned in the candlelight, shifting from black glass to blue flames as they fixed on Cara. She held up her right fist and wrapped her left hand around it, as if trying to restrain herself from using it.

Adrenaline flushed through Cara's veins and her heart pounded painfully in her chest. Every muscle in her body tightened and she felt as prepared to fight as she was to flee.

Amber placed her hands on her hips. Her eyes had returned to their normal cobalt blue color. "You think you're so much better than me, don't you?" she asked Cara with a sneer.

"I'm definitely saner." Cara surprised herself with her bold, though true, words.

"And you think you're funny, too. Well, you won't be laughing for long. You made the wrong move when you stole Chris from me."

"I didn't steal Chris from you. And if you don't know, he dumped me, too."

"Of course he dumped you. But you did steal him. Though I have no idea *how*."

Amber's eyes focused on Cara's hair and face before they trailed over her dress and down to her shoes. Anger rose to a full boil within Cara, but she kept her mouth shut and her hands to herself.

"I got Chris back, you know, after he was finished with you. But you messed him up so badly I had to put a binding spell on him."

Chris had been messed up long before Cara had anything to do with him, but she thought better of saying so.

"The spell worked a little too well. He moved down to California to be with me. Then he became insanely jealous."

Cara doubted a spell had anything to do with it, but it served the witch right that Chris turned possessive on her.

"I couldn't reverse the spell. So he shot himself."

Cara's breath caught in her throat and she took an involuntary step backward. "How awful. Is he . . . ?"

"Dead? Yes. And you know who's to blame for that? You."

"What? I did nothing to Chris other than say 'no' when he only wanted one thing."

"You knew we were together," Amber said through clenched teeth.

The whole school had known Chris and Amber were together, *before* Chris broke up with Amber and asked Cara out. But Amber didn't look like the issue was open for discussion. And she was clearly out of her mind—and dangerous.

Amber cocked her head to the side. "The next move is mine. I'm only going to warn you once. Leave David to me."

---

Worried she might do or say something she'd regret, Cara rushed out of the house. Garren followed her and helped her down the stairs and to his truck. The shaking in her knees had grown exponentially since they'd arrived. She couldn't help checking over her shoulder to make sure no one had followed them.

On the ride home, after a few moments of loaded silence, she asked Garren, "Do you know Amber?"

"No. But I know about her involvement with sorcery. You must have noticed the heavy smell of sulfur in the house."

"There were so many candles burning in there, I wouldn't be surprised if the place burned down."

"The smell wasn't from candles. Sulfur is a sign of demons."

"Or matches."

"The smell was too strong to have come from matches."

"There were other gag-inducing smells in there, too."

"The herbs you smelled are used in witchcraft. And cold spots signal the presence of spirits." Uncommon worry lines branched across Garren's typically smooth forehead. "I hope you're not afraid of me now."

"I'm impressed, actually."

His face returned to its normal state of perfection. "Those people don't know the dangers they're dealing with. There is no such thing as harmless sorcery or white magick, not when entities are being called upon."

"To be honest, I always thought it would be fun to play with a Ouija board or tarot cards. I just never found an opportunity. But lots of people do. I have a hard time believing it's as risky as you're making it out to be."

"This situation is rare. The evil effects of sorcery are usually limited. But all the effects, when help is summoned, are the result of demonic influence."

"So, if magick done by summoning is always the effect of evil, then I take it you didn't work any of that sort of magick with the roses you gave me?"

"I did nothing to the roses."

"Then your source must have done something to them."

"Yes. But no magick was involved."

"And you can't tell me what your source did to the flowers?"

"No. Sorry."

*Of course.* She sighed and shook her head.

He got out of the truck and came around to open her door. "I hope I made some of those kids think about getting away from the dangers they're dabbling in."

He pulled her into a hug as he helped her down.

"You certainly got everyone's attention."

# TWENTY-FOUR

Halloween night, Cara woke often and thrashed about during nightmares filled with blonde witches, black-eyed demons, and sea monsters with giant white teeth. Seaside students had Friday off, but rather than staying in bed, she gave up the battle for rest while the sky was still black outside her bedroom window. She might be sleep-deprived, but she had big plans for the day.

After she showered, dressed, and blow-dried her hair, she did a light makeup job, trying to make it look like she hadn't spent much time on her appearance. When she knew her mom would be awake, she headed downstairs to the family room.

She sat in the armchair next to the love seat.

"What's wrong?" her mom asked, setting down her crossword puzzle and coffee cup.

Cara adopted a neutral reporter's tone and expression. "Rachel was hanging out with Mr. Wilson's stalker last night."

Her mom blinked and leaned back against the love seat with her hands clasped together in her lap. "Explain."

Cara relayed most of what had happened, starting with the red car following her and ending with crashing the party, leaving out the parts about Garren making a scene and Amber being the one who followed her. She didn't want to incriminate Garren and she also didn't want to emphasize that Amber was stalking both her and David.

Her mom pursed her lips before she spoke. "What I'm hearing is that the stalker Mr. Wilson dated is now targeting teenagers."

Cara wasn't sure what to say to that.

Her mom picked up her purse from the floor and pulled out her cell phone. "Liz wasn't impressed with the psychiatrist I suggested for Rachel. Maybe this will convince her to give him another chance."

A few seconds after her mom pressed a number on the cell, she said, "Hi, Liz. It's Mary. I'm sorry to bother you so early." After explaining all Cara had said, she promised to inform Ms. Clark of anything else they discovered. She ended by strongly suggesting that Rachel attend another session with a psychiatrist.

Her mom hung up and dropped her phone in her purse. "Liz appreciated us letting her know what Rachel's up to. But I don't want you doing any more detective duty. Stay away from that stalker, and that house."

"I will. I promise." She meant it. The promise seemed like an easy one to keep. Contact with Amber wasn't something she wanted to initiate. She got up to leave.

"Where are you going?" her mom asked, pointing a finger at the seat of the armchair.

Cara sat back down. "I want to talk to David about this."

Her mom's eyes widened. "David?"

Cara didn't realize she'd slipped until it was too late. She shrugged. "Fine. Mr. Wilson."

Her mom subjected her to an extralong sideway gaze. "Maybe I should also talk to David."

That wasn't a "yes." It might even have been a veiled threat. She choked back a comment about how she could have opted to talk to David without her mom's knowledge.

Her mom stared at her for what felt like forever. Cara kept a straight back and maintained eye contact. She didn't want to be defiant. But she would be, if necessary. This was important.

Her mom stressed each of her words. "I don't think your talking to Mr. Wilson is a good idea."

Cara pleaded with her mom with her eyes as well as her words. "Please let me talk to him?"

Her mom hesitated for several moments. Cara gave up waiting on a response and rushed upstairs to her room. Amber's threat sounded in her mind: *I'm only going to warn you once. Leave David to me.*

Cara grabbed her cell phone from her bag, sat on the edge of her bed, and tapped out a text to David:

This is Cara. I need to talk to you. Can we get together?

He called her back within seconds. "What's going on?" he asked in a rush.

"I need to talk to you about something that happened last night. Can you meet me at the beach by Surfseekers?"

"You're okay, right? Nothing happened to you?"

His protectiveness caused a familiar warmth to kindle in her chest. "I'm fine. Can you meet me at the bottom of the stairs?"

"I'll be there in fifteen minutes."

She bounded downstairs and nearly ran into her mom, who stood in the entryway at the bottom of the staircase. Cara slowed, but didn't stop.

"I'm not going to lie to you. I'm going to talk to David." Oops.

She did it again. "I need to know what he has to say," she added, before she slammed the door behind her.

Her mom's voice bellowed from behind it. "I expect to talk about it when you get back!"

<hr>

Less than ten minutes later, Cara stood at the bottom of the stairs by Surfseekers, surveying the water for any sign of whales. From the surface, the water appeared as barren of life as the beach. Soon, she spotted David running toward her, wearing dark gray running pants and a crimson, long-sleeved T-shirt. His short, dark hair blew back as he ran. When he made it over to her, he bent down with his hands on his knees and took a second to catch his breath.

He stood up straight and examined her face. He wouldn't be able to read much. Even she wasn't sure of everything she was feeling. She avoided eye contact.

"What happened?" he asked.

She walked toward the water. He followed after her. Concentrating on the cresting waves in the distance, she took deep breaths and tried to calm herself. A light breeze blew and hazy sunlight shone down from behind a thin cloud cover. The only sounds echoed from the rumble of the ocean and raucous seagulls.

Once he walked by her side, she said, "I've noticed a red Jetta has been following me for a while."

"Amber?"

"Yes."

He stopped, but she kept walking.

"I didn't know it was her at first. The car has California plates," she said more loudly, so he could hear from behind her.

He caught up to her and they reached the water's edge and walked alongside it.

"Last night, Garren and I saw the car and followed it to a house party."

His words were sharp. "Amber is crazy. Why would you follow her?"

"I wanted to make sure it was her. Also, she was following Ethan and Rachel."

She peeked over and saw his eyebrows bunch together.

"Rachel Clark?"

"Yeah, my once-upon-a-time best friend and her boyfriend. At the party, Rachel and Ethan were playing with a Ouija board. Amber hung out at a table covered with tarot cards."

He grimaced.

"Amber and I dated the same guy in high school. She accused me of stealing him from her."

This time, when he stopped, she faced him. His gaze dropped to the sand.

"She also warned me to leave you to her."

He still didn't look at her. "I had no idea Amber was involved with those types of things. But I'm especially not happy to hear she has a personal problem with you."

Cara might have figured he'd skip over the last part of what she'd said about Amber's warning. She locked her knees and clenched her fists in an attempt to hide her trembling legs and hands. "Amber was wearing a formal dress at the party. Did you see her at the dance?"

Now he looked up and met her gaze. "No, did you?"

"Only in the parking lot." She let the warm connection between them take hold. "I know I should wait to talk to you about this. But I need to know how you feel, if you're interested in Amber."

He didn't look away and opened his mouth like he planned to speak. But he remained silent. After a few tense moments, she heaved out a sigh and turned to walk away.

His voice was so quiet that, if there'd been a breeze, it would've carried his words away. "When I told Amber I didn't want to see her again, I said it was because I had feelings for someone else."

Cara turned back to him. "And she thinks I'm that someone else?"

His eyes met hers again and he held out his hand. She stared at it and stopped breathing. Then she took a deep breath, let it out, and placed her right hand in his. Warmth spread between them and the tether pulled taut. She watched as he raised her hand and placed it against his chest.

The swift, strong beating of his heart pounded under her fingertips. He dropped her hand and she lifted her eyes to his face again.

He looked as if he'd committed a crime. "I shouldn't be doing this," he said, and hung his head.

Not wanting to pressure him, she backed away. But he held her arm and stepped closer to her. His gaze dropped to her mouth.

She placed both her hands on his chest, then slid them around to run her fingers through the back of his hair. He tensed, but she tugged on his neck, and he leaned down. She bridged the final space between them, standing on her toes and letting her mouth meet his. His hands came to rest on the small of her back.

Lightly, she brushed her lips against his, then paused to look at him. A smile turned up one corner of his mouth. She took that as her go-ahead to kiss him the way she'd been dreaming about for months. At first, her mouth molded gently with his. He responded hesitantly. Then his breaths grew deeper and he drew her closer to him. Her lips covered his more fully and a warm wanting flooded her body.

He stopped to kiss her forehead, then held her against him. His chin rested on top of her head, just as it had when he'd held her on the *Lookout*. When he finally moved her back by the shoulders, he continued to hold on to her, but didn't smile.

"Please don't feel guilty about this," she said, placing her hands on his upper arms. "I can't explain the connection between us, but it's not wrong. I know it isn't."

He reached out and tucked a lock of hair behind her ear. His fingers brushed the side of her face. "That's why I feel guilty. Because I don't think it's wrong, either. But maybe I should."

She shook her head at him.

"Don't forget that I'm the creepy teacher in this situation."

"You are not creepy." She took his hands in hers and moved closer to him, until only their joined hands prevented their bodies from touching again. "And don't worry. We can keep this quiet." She hesitated before offering up a less desirable option. "Or we can wait until school's out, if you want. If you'll still be around."

He didn't answer, so she said, "I should get home."

He walked her there and didn't ask whether she planned to tell her mom about what had happened between them. She wasn't sure yet if she would.

No matter how David felt about what happened, she couldn't help but feel happy and guilty at the same time. She meant it when she said she didn't believe their involvement was wrong. But she felt selfish to want him so much that she'd put him in a position that could cost him his job and reputation.

Still, nothing could change the fact that she and David had admitted their feelings for each other.

---

In the kitchen nook, Cara's mom sat clutching a mug of coffee. She nodded for Cara to take a seat on the other bench. Cara wished she'd armed herself with a diet soda, at least to have something to do with her hands. But her mom's eyes fixed on her and she could tell she'd better start talking.

She rubbed her clammy hands on her jeans, then clasped them together on top of the table. "David and I admitted our feelings for each other."

Her mom raised her eyebrows and remained silent.

Cara sighed. *Better to just say it straight.* "We kissed."

Her mom set her coffee mug down and crossed her arms over her chest. "I can't believe he's allowing this to happen. He leaves me no choice but to report him to the school."

Cara moved her hands to her lap and squeezed them together under the table. She sucked in a ragged breath and struggled to keep the "don't you dare" look off her face. That type of reaction usually resulted in the opposite of her intended effect with her mom. Still, she thought her mom should appreciate that she was revealing any of this in the first place.

"I want to keep this private, but I'm telling you because I also want to be open and honest with you. I want to give this relationship a chance."

Her mom spoke as much with her hands as with her words. She

looked like she was trying to swipe something away. "You sound like an inexperienced, immature schoolgirl who believes that the first guy she feels romantically about is somehow her soul mate."

Cara reminded herself that her mom knew nothing about the connection she shared with David. All the same, it sure was convenient for her mom to suddenly forget about Chris. "He's not the first guy I've felt romantically about. And I'm not a fickle person. I don't believe David is either. Our feelings for each other are real."

"This could cost him his degree, Cara, his career. What you're doing—what he's doing—it's wrong."

Cara kept her tone light. "I don't believe it's wrong."

"This thing between you began with a life-threatening situation that intensified the chemistry between you. That chemistry led to infatuation."

"If it's infatuation, it'll fade with time and either develop into something more, or David and I will grow apart. Please give us the chance to find out."

Her mom abruptly stood. "Given the circumstances, it's wrong, Cara. And I'm sorry, but it's my job to put a stop to it."

# TWENTY-FIVE

Early Saturday morning, Cara opened her curtains to gunmetal gray clouds and waves that pitched sideways. Sherry confirmed that the whale-watching tours were canceled for the day.

Cara crawled back under the covers and tried to catch up on sleep. A few hours later, her phone buzzed and woke her from the memory of David's soft kiss. His number displayed on the screen.

She answered with a jovial, "Good morning."

"How are you feeling about what happened?" The worry in his words couldn't be written off as a warble in the phone reception.

"Happy. You?"

She kept her phone pressed to her ear, settled back against her headboard, and drew her knees up to her chest. Looking out her window at peaks of ocean waves, she prayed he had as much faith in their fledgling relationship as she did. But she knew she had to be prepared to put that relationship on hold. And to trust that Amber wouldn't be able to seduce him and steal him away from her.

"Did you tell your mom?"

The tether sagged when he didn't comment about how he felt. "Yeah, she wasn't supportive."

He let out his breath in a big whoosh. "Does she want to talk to me?"

"I didn't ask, but she didn't mention it, either."

He groaned.

"I hate to say this," she said, and truly, words couldn't describe how much she hated to say it, "but my mom threatened to talk to the school."

"She has every right to."

"I wouldn't have told her if I thought she'd say anything."

"It's okay. It's not your fault. And it's good for you to be honest with your mom."

"I understand if you think we should wait to see each other again."

"I think you need to take the weekend to seriously think about what you want."

"At this point, waiting seems like lying. But I won't put you in a bad position."

"Let me worry about my position."

She imagined the tether ripping away when she thought she might lose him. "I can't help but worry about you. About us. But whether we wait or not, I need you to know how I feel. This is what I want. I'm not going to change my mind."

"You need to know it's okay if you do."

Cara's mind whirled with all the unknowns surrounding how she and David would interact now. She'd never been more thankful for Garren's presence when he joined her on the wall during lunch on Monday. While the sunlight bathing her face helped calm her, the air was frigid and relaxation wasn't within reach.

Garren handed her an apple. "Sometimes things work out despite the obstacles," he said, accepting half of her cucumber and cream cheese sandwich and a bag of chips. "It's obvious that David has strong feelings for you."

"I know," she said, unable to infuse her words with enthusiasm.

She bit into her apple and chewed, obsessing over the fact that she'd stopped by David's classroom twice that morning and had only seen Mr. Cutter. She couldn't shake the guilt weighing on her. Her mom might already have called the administration and David might already have lost his internship.

More than ever, she appreciated the companionable quiet Garren always shared with her during lunch. When she finished her apple, he took the core just as her phone buzzed.

David had texted:

Want to get together to talk later?

She was grateful to get his message before lunch ended.

You didn't get fired did you?

No.

Where are you?

My place.

Can we talk there?

You're okay with that?

Of course. What's the address?

374 Jettison Avenue.

I'll come over after school.

See you soon then.

David's place was a little blue box of a cottage on a hill above the beach, less than a mile from Cara's house. The walk along the sand would be a nice one, but she chose to drive. Not wanting to take the chance someone might notice a student visiting a teacher, she parked two blocks away. Burying her face in the hood of her jacket, she hung her head, resenting having to hide and hating that she felt ashamed.

When David opened his front door, he met her gaze, and warmth poured through her. Their connection held, strong as ever.

"I take it you haven't changed your mind?" he asked.

"Not happening." She sounded much calmer than she felt.

Stepping closer, she held her hand out to him. He lifted it and kissed it.

She stood on her toes and gently pressed her lips to his. "Why weren't you at school today?"

"It's nothing to worry about." He kept hold of her hand.

She'd have to take his word for it—for now, at least. "So do I get a tour?" she asked and tugged him away from the door.

"The place is small, so it'll be a short one."

He led her by the hand to the middle of one big room, including the dining area just past the entry, the open kitchen on the left, and the living room to the right. White walls made the house look more spacious. Dark hardwood floors stretched throughout, uniting the spaces.

A nautical-themed rug spread out under a black leather couch and matching love seat set up in an L shape around a glass and wrought-iron coffee table. An entertainment center covered much of the right wall. French doors led to a back deck, and a small desk sat underneath a large, rectangular picture window that offered panoramic views of the coastline.

"Is this your decorating job?" she asked, surprised by how fully furnished the living area was.

"No, it came furnished. The desk's mine, though."

Through the window, Cara watched as beams of bright sunlight danced on the water. "The view is amazing."

"It's why I rented the place."

He guided her toward a hall at the right of the living room. His bedroom was to the left. She poked her head in, then stepped inside. He watched her from the doorway.

His bedroom décor consisted of numerous hues of blue. A thick, dark denim-colored comforter covered his queen-size bed, which was topped with two large pillows in light blue pillowcases. One pillow looked flattened by use, the other appeared untouched. The curtains hanging from his window matched the navy carpet and the walls were a bluish white.

She rounded back toward the door and he ushered her to the bathroom, which was white and basic and straight through the hallway entrance. Down the hall were three more doors, but he told her they were only linen and coat closets and a laundry area. He steered her back to the front room and wrapped his arms around her from behind as she gazed out the picture window.

Her whole body tingled at his touch. "It's cozy. I like it."

He gave her a final squeeze, then headed for a Scrabble game that sat on the dining table. She followed and he pulled out a chair for her. He went to the fridge and grabbed a diet soda bottle.

So he hadn't missed the empties in her old Civic. "Thanks," she said, accepting the bottle. She eyed the game board. "I haven't been practicing."

"Good." His warm breath tickled her ear before he kissed her cheek. "I have."

She wished she could keep things as light as when she first walked in his door, that they could just play Scrabble and enjoy each other. But her stomach twisted. "I don't feel like playing."

He didn't seem surprised. "Wanna talk?"

She nodded. This conversation wouldn't be fun, but her conscience wouldn't let her avoid it.

"We could go for a walk on the beach? Look for the grays?" he asked.

"People might see us."

"We can stick near the house, in case people walk by, if you're worried about it."

"Aren't you worried about it?"

"No."

She stood up from the table. "Sure."

He put a tentative hand on her back and they walked out the back door and down a short set of wooden deck stairs to his small yard. She held tight to his arm as they stepped down the steep grade that led to the sand.

He sat on a large, beached log and squinted up at her where she stood before him.

"I've been thinking, like you asked," she said, stepping closer to him to block the sun from shining in his eyes. "And I don't want to lose you."

"You won't." He took her hands, which instantly warmed in his.

"I can't let you lose your internship over me."

"I won't."

"I told you, my mom plans to talk to the school. I don't think I can talk her out of it."

"They can't get rid of me."

"How can you be so sure?"

"Because I quit."

"You quit? When?"

"Today."

She let out a sound that was part sigh and part groan, then collapsed beside him on the log. "So you quit because of me. That's almost worse."

He lifted her chin and ran his thumb across it. "I worried you'd blame yourself. But I seriously didn't quit because of you. I was wrong to think I wanted to teach high school."

She studied his face. "You're not just saying that so I won't feel bad?"

"Nope. So don't feel bad." He flashed her his lopsided grin.

"It always seemed to me like you enjoy teaching."

"I do. I just hoped for more enthusiasm from the students, I guess."

"I'm enthusiastic. And so is most of my journalism staff."

His green eyes brightened. "I know that. I'm talking about students in the English classes."

She nodded. "I understand what you mean. A lot of kids need to be motivated."

"And there are a lot of great teachers at Seaside who do a good job of that. But I don't want to play that role. I'd rather work with kids who are already interested in what I'm teaching."

"I get it. But what are you going to do instead, for now?" She leaned against him and watched the lurching sea. Her automatic whale radar didn't pick up on any activity in the water.

"My dad's still trying to get me to come home."

*Oh, no.*

"But I can find a job here for the rest of the year and start a new program for school next fall."

At least he seemed sincere about wanting to change his focus. And it didn't sound like he'd be moving out of town before she did. "I take it you haven't changed your mind, either, then?"

He planted a kiss on her cheek and cradled her close against his side. "Not happening."

---

Cara's mom didn't look up from the papers in her lap when Cara leaned against the family room doorframe.

"I heard the news." Her mom's lips pursed as she shuffled through her students' psychology assignments.

It took Cara a second to understand that her mom had called the school.

"You're glad David quit then, right?" Cara's voice rose with hope.

Her mom gave her a startled sideways gaze. "I didn't know he quit, only that he's no longer student teaching at the school."

"Well, that's why. He quit."

Her mom's face softened. "It's sad that he had to drop out of his program."

Cara shook her head. "He said he was wrong to think he wanted to teach high school."

"What's wrong is his involvement with you. He needs to drop *that*."

"Why?" Cara's tone belied a mix of anger and surprise, though she should have realized her mom wouldn't suddenly be supportive. "There's no reason for you to disapprove of our relationship now."

"Not true." Her mom pointed to the armchair.

"I'd rather not," Cara said, for the first time disobeying her mom's instruction.

Exhaling heavily, her mom set her assignments on the love seat and stood. "There's still an imbalance of power between you. I'm going to need to talk to him."

No way was she going to let her mom talk to David alone. "I'll set something up so the three of us can talk together."

"You need to quit seeing him."

Cara stood up straight and crossed her arms over her chest. "That's not going to happen."

Her mom put a hand on her hip. "I didn't mean to make it sound like I was giving you a choice."

"What are you going to do? Take away my allowance? My car? Kick me out? It won't do any good if you do."

Her mom frowned as if Cara was acting like an immature schoolgirl again. "I'm disappointed in you. You've never treated me with this kind of disrespect before."

Cara sighed and slumped against the doorframe. "I don't mean to disrespect you. Even though I'm eighteen now, I live in your house, so you're free to punish me. But I'm not going to let you destroy this relationship before it even has a chance."

Her mom's hand fell from her hip as she took a step closer. "I'll punish you if I have to. But all I'm trying to do is protect you."

"I'm trying to tell you that you don't have to."

"Yes. I do." A hint of defeat sounded in her mom's tone as she dropped back down on the love seat.

# TWENTY-SIX

"The new owners did a lot of modernizing in here," Cara said, the next day after school when she and David sat down for a late lunch at the Anchor, an oceanfront restaurant attached to Surfseekers Resort.

She admired the restaurant's remodeled interior in the daylight that streamed through the wall-to-wall windows. The new décor consisted of sheer sea-blue curtains and color-coordinated cylindrical glass light fixtures that hung over dark wood tables and chairs covering an expansive gray stone floor.

They were seated at a corner table with a view. Their waitress took their drink orders. Cara couldn't help glancing around to see if anyone they knew might see her and David together. Not that it should matter now, but the situation could be uncomfortable. She was thankful the half dozen diners around them were strangers.

Their waitress brought them their drinks and took their food orders.

When she left, David said, "I brought you here to give you a peek of the bar."

A blue neon sign above the alcove at the other end of the room read: THE HOLLOW. The view of the lounge area was partially blocked by a wall. Cara leaned closer to the window and caught sight of row after row of glass liquor bottles set in front of a sheet of mirrored glass. Blue lights, like the ones in the dining room, hung from the ceiling. Smaller, taller dark wood tables and chairs filled the area and another row of chairs pulled up close to the bar. A mounted TV broadcast a football game, but no patrons were visible.

"Why do you want me to see the bar?"

The bartender came into view. He was about David's age, though not as handsome.

"I bartended last summer. They hired me here yesterday when I applied for a position that's opening after Christmas. It's just a temporary thing."

Asking him to define *temporary* might seem too overbearing. She stirred her soda with her straw and took a sip. "The bar looks nice. I can't go in, of course." Which made her feel like a child.

"You aren't ashamed of me now that I'm a lowly bartender, are you?"

She let out a light laugh, relieved that he didn't seem to be thinking of her age. "Of course not."

Their eyes met and the warm, secure connection between them took hold.

"But you're going to have a lot of free time on your hands for a month or so," she said. "Are you going to leave, to visit your dad?"

"Yes."

She stared into her soda.

"On some weekends. And for Thanksgiving and Christmas."

She looked back up to see his lopsided grin.

"But I plan to spend all the free time I can with you."

The rapid flutter she always felt in her chest when he was near increased.

He rubbed the back of his neck. "My dad still wants me to move back home, though."

"Doesn't he know you got a job here?"

His jaw tightened. "He's not happy about it. He's paying my way through college, which is great of him. But he hangs it over my head like I owe him."

"Is he upset that you quit your internship program?"

"He was furious at first. But I explained things to him and he understands now that I need to make a change. He just doesn't want me staying here for the rest of the year."

The waitress carried over a tray and set down Cara's chowder and David's halibut.

They sampled their food and Cara waited for David to elaborate about his dad. He didn't.

She set her spoon in her bowl and laid a hand over David's on the table. "I don't want to cause problems between you and your dad," she said, though she also wanted to beg David not to leave.

He flipped his hand over and held hers. "And I don't want to cause problems between you and your mom."

"So what are we gonna do?"

"I don't want you to make any decisions based on me. Or my dad. Or your mom, even. You figure out what's best for you, and do that."

He squeezed her hand before he let it go.

A busboy cleared a nearby table. Cara hailed him over. He set his bucket of dishes on an empty table while she pulled her camera from her bag.

She held the camera out to him. "Would you mind taking a picture?"

He took the camera and worked out the right buttons to push while Cara sat close to David, with the view of the water through the windows in the background. The busboy took a few shots and handed the camera back. Cara thanked him and kissed David's cheek.

"It's definitely nice not to have to hide," David said as she returned to her seat.

"Unfortunately, there's still my mom to deal with," she said and drained her soda. She hated to have to share bad news, but she couldn't keep things from him. "She called the school to talk to you yesterday and they told her you weren't student teaching there anymore."

"I hope you told her I'd be glad to talk to her."

"I told her I thought the three of us should talk."

"I could invite her over."

"I'm not sure we should tell her where you live." She was only half joking.

His laugh was short and stilted. "Why? What do you think she'll do to me?"

"I'd just prefer she not know where to find us."

He frowned at her. "She *is* your mom, Cara."

"I know. I just think she needs more time to get used to our relationship."

"I say we make dinner for her one night this week. I owe it to her to hear her out. So do you."

"I'd think you'd be in better spirits after kicking my behind in Scrabble like that," David teased that evening as he settled next to her on the couch. He handed her a bottle of soda and they sat back to watch wave after wave of white surf roll from the black sea onto the beach below.

Cara toyed with the cap on her bottle. "I want to ask you something."

"Ask me anything," he said, wrapping an arm around her shoulder.

"Is Amber so crazy about you because you slept with her?"

He pulled back and looked at her, but she kept her eyes on her soda.

"I didn't sleep with her. I barely know her."

"Didn't you want her?"

"No."

Cara wasn't so sure about that. Amber was certainly sexy.

"Really, no." He squeezed her shoulder. "I sensed something was wrong with her from the beginning.

*That* Cara could believe.

"And I don't sleep around."

And *that* was all she needed to hear.

She set her soda on the coffee table, turned toward him, and placed her hands on his chest. He froze, then let her ease him back until he was lying down on the couch. His eyes grew huge as she straddled him, and when she held his forearms down, they flexed under her hands.

Gazing into his wide green eyes, she bent her head down toward his. Any doubts about the strength of his feelings for her faded away with the warmth that enveloped her. She wanted nothing more than to be with him, to be intimate in a way she was sure would feel right, with someone she trusted to treat her right.

Having little experience, she expected to feel uncomfortable taking the lead. Yet she didn't. Touching David felt natural.

Her lips met his and her hair draped over the sides of their faces. Invisible stubble on his cheeks and chin scraped lightly against her face, tickling her as she took in the soft smoothness of his lips. Her hands traveled over his abdomen and chest and her whole body throbbed when she pressed tightly against him.

He barely returned her kisses at first. Soon, though, his mouth moved firmly against hers. She didn't relent with the intensity of her touch until he throbbed beneath her, too.

Passion rushed at her in waves. Then the small, clear voice in her head warned, *"Wait."* She didn't want to wait. It was as if desire opened its jaws within her and demanded to be fed. Still, this didn't feel right, like she thought it would. Not right now.

At the same time she heard the warning in her head, David wrapped his fingers around her wrists. He sat up and held her away from him, but continued to hold on to her for a moment before he let her go.

He took in a deep breath and exhaled heavily. "We should wait."

"Why?" she asked, breathless. She pulled back, grabbed her soda from the coffee table, and worked on slowing her breaths before she took a long swig.

He rubbed his face and raked his fingers through his hair, then motioned for her to come to him. She set her soda back down and moved closer.

He held her lightly, by the shoulders. "This might sound selfish, but I think I'm the one who's most at risk in this relationship."

"How so? You can't lose your job now."

"What's between us is special. You can't have much to compare it to. You might start wondering if there's something you're missing."

Her pulse raced. She shook her head. Nothing could compete with their connection.

He rubbed her upper arms, then dropped his hands to his thighs. "I haven't been close to a . . . girl . . . since my mom died. I don't think I could take it if I lost you, too. It would be a mistake to rush things."

She brushed his hair back, then cupped his cheek with her hand. "You won't."

He didn't look convinced.

"But I understand that it could be a mistake to move too fast."

He rested his forehead against hers.

"Waiting will be hard," she said, and sighed.

He kissed her lips, then her nose. "Hard, but worth it."

---

"I'm guessing you were with David?" her mom asked, blocking Cara's entrance into the house when she got home just before ten.

"You guessed correctly."

Her mom dragged her by the arm to the family room and dumped her in the armchair. "I told you I don't want you to see him. And I warned you I would punish you if you didn't obey me."

Cara counted to five in her head, willing herself not to lash out. "I still think you should respect my decision."

"I can't do that. I'm going to have to ask you to stay home when you're not in school. When I'm not here, I'll call the home phone to check on you."

Cara had no intention of letting her mom lock her away from

David. But she'd already done and said enough to make her mom angry. "I'll stay home, if you'll agree to have dinner with David and me this Friday."

Her mom dropped down on the love seat. "Fine. We'll have him over for dinner so I can talk to him."

"No. David and I will cook dinner at his place."

Her mom's eyes blazed. "On one condition."

Cara waited.

"You drive there with me and come home with me."

Cara was quick to nod. Her mom could just as easily have said "no."

"Until then," her mom said, lips twitching, "I want you home."

# TWENTY-SEVEN

Cara followed her mom's orders and drove straight home after school on Wednesday. David remained unaware of her imprisonment. She invited him to come over to her house during the evening hours while her mom was teaching a night class.

When he arrived, Cara led him upstairs to her bedroom and held the door open. He took a peek inside, then stepped back into the hallway.

She placed a hand on her hip. "Scared of something?"

He snickered and slipped through the door, then moved over to the wall covered with blown-up whale photos. "Crossback and Bobbi?"

"Mostly."

He turned to study the framed pictures of her and Rachel that topped her dresser. Then he peered out the window at the white-caps reflecting in the darkness. "You have a pretty nice view."

"It's not as close-up as yours, but I'm not complaining. To be honest, though, I spend most of my time looking at a computer screen."

His gaze fell to her laptop. "Me, too."

Stepping over to her desk, he sniffed the roses Garren had given her, then scanned the assortment of books and CDs lined up on the hutch. "You have diverse taste."

"Thanks." Her top picks were on display for him. Mounds of other books and CDs were stacked in boxes in her closet.

He looked up at her one framed painting and asked, "Is that the beach by Surfseekers?"

"Yep—my favorite."

"Mine, too, if you remember."

"Of course I do."

He flashed her his lopsided smile before he moved over to her bed and sat on the edge, facing the window. A tendon in his jaw popped. His gaze had returned to the eighteen white roses in the vase on her desk. She'd replaced the water in the vase twice, but the flowers were still in immaculate condition, nearly a month after she'd received them.

"Let me guess," he said. "Those are from Garren."

The roses from Garren weren't something she meant to hide from David. She just didn't know how to tell him they were a birthday gift without sounding like she was lying, or loony. Her mom had questioned her about the fresh flowers a few days before and gave Cara a distrustful sideways gaze when she'd told her they were the same roses Garren had given her for her birthday. Her mom understandably suspected they were from David.

David's attention shifted to the photo of the two of them at the Anchor she'd printed, framed, and displayed on her nightstand. His expression brightened.

She walked over to where he sat on the bed. "Yes, the roses are from Garren. I know they seem like a romantic gift. But it's not like that." Her fingers played in his soft, dark hair. "At first, even I couldn't believe I wasn't attracted to Garren. But we're honestly only friends."

David looked over at the roses again. "It's not natural for a guy who's just friends with a girl to treat her the way Garren treats you."

"I promise, you have nothing to be jealous about. Really, Garren seems strangely asexual."

David huffed out a chuckle.

She tilted his chin up with her fingers, so he'd look her in the eye. "You trust that I don't have the same feelings for Garren that I have for you, don't you?"

He paused until warmth pulsed through the tether between them.

When he nodded, she kissed him deeply on the mouth, then lightly on the forehead. "Then please believe that Garren isn't after me."

David shook his head, sure she was being gullible.

"The only guy I've had feelings for other than you was Chris, the guy Amber and I both dated. But I didn't feel anywhere near as strongly for him as I do for you." She continued to lightly run her fingers through David's short hair. "I'm glad I was never intimate with him. He was a jerk. And I was a fool."

David pulled her down with him as he lay back on the bed. He rested her on top of him. "You weren't a fool."

Too quickly, he set her on her side. They faced each other with their heads propped on their hands. He placed his other hand on her hip and she stroked his arm through the smooth cotton of his shirt.

"It's hard to know who you can trust. We all get it wrong

sometimes." He brushed her cheek with his fingers. "And then sometimes we get it right."

"Speaking of getting it wrong," she said, her gaze dropping to his chest. "Is Amber still bugging you?"

"She calls and she came over a few times, but I've been able to get rid of her."

"It's my fault she's after you."

"It's not your fault. But I don't like it that she's upset with you for reasons I can't control. I wish you'd told me about Chris sooner."

"Chris isn't a happy memory."

He smoothed her hair out of her face. "I understand that, but after Amber showed up at the school and your car got vandalized, even though I knew she was dangerous, I didn't know she was after you personally."

"Amber doesn't scare me." *Much.*

"She damaged your car. And she threatened you at her Halloween party. Also, Seaside's administrative assistant quit—suddenly—and Principal Roberts told me that Amber had something to do with that. He wouldn't give me specifics and he wouldn't tell me why he didn't hire Amber. But I could tell he was worried about what she's capable of. I'm worried, too. About you."

It wouldn't be a surprise if Amber had a record. She was a stalker. No doubt she'd earned a restraining order or two. "Tell me how you and Amber met."

A teasing grin touched his lips. "You started it."

"Me? What did I do?"

"After I met you, I couldn't get you off my mind. When I found out you were a high school student, I did my best to try to forget you, but I couldn't." He stared at a strand of her hair as he ran his fingers through it. "I got lonely. One night I went out to try to meet someone else. I went to the Hollow, but there were only couples in the bar. Then Amber walked in. It seemed like fate that she showed up."

"Only now you know better."

"I knew better then, too, really. We talked and she wanted to come to my place or have me over to hers. I didn't want that, so I told her I'd take her out another time."

"And you kept your word."

"Yes." He pulled her closer to him. "But I went home and thought of you."

She resisted the urge to move even closer. "Did you tell her you'd see her again after the last time you took her out?"

"No. She said she sensed something was bothering me, and I told her I was trying to get over feelings for someone else and that it wouldn't be fair to pretend I was interested in her."

"What did she say to that?"

"She said she'd wait for me to get over it."

Cara couldn't help thinking that Amber could visit the Hollow any time she wanted when David was working there. "Did you tell her not to bother?"

"I should have told her that from the start. But I didn't flat-out tell her to leave me alone until that night she showed up at the school before our layout session."

At least he'd finally gotten around to telling Amber to forget it. Not that she'd listened.

"When you went to the Cove and had the chowder again, were you with Amber?" That unanswered question had been haunting her since the day she'd interviewed him.

"No, I went alone. I knew it would remind me of you."

Heat flushed through her.

Things were going too well with David to let Amber interfere anymore. "Can we talk about something else?"

He placed his hand back on her hip. "Just promise me you'll stay away from Amber, especially when I'm gone for Thanksgiving."

"You say that like I want to hang out with her or something."

His bicep bulged under her hand. "Is it just going to be you and your mom celebrating here on Thanksgiving?"

"No. Garren's coming over."

David propped himself up higher and looked down at her.

She sighed. "As a friend."

"Doesn't the guy have a family of his own?"

"I'm not sure, actually. He insists on keeping everything about his life private."

David fell onto his back. "That seems odd. And convenient."

"He might have a sad life." She rubbed David's arm. "Let's be nice."

"We can consider the dinner we have with your mom this Friday a pre-Thanksgiving meal."

She laid her head on his chest. "There you go. That would be nice."

# TWENTY-EIGHT

When Cara came home from school on Thursday, she avoided her mom by locking herself in her room. Rather than telling David she'd been forbidden to see him, she said she had plans. In truth, the only plan she had was to play Scrabble in her jail cell. Her mom called up to her, asking her to come down to help cook dinner. She yelled back that she didn't feel well.

The next day, Cara didn't ask her mom's permission before she headed to David's place after school. She and David prepared dinner in silence. He put potatoes in the oven to bake and seasoned steaks to broil. She prepared her favorite avocado salad. When she finished, she left without a word between them, just a short kiss. He had to be at least as nervous as she was about her mom coming over.

At home, Cara found her mom on the love seat, still in the skirt suit she'd worn to teach that morning.

"Where have you been?" her mom asked with a stern sideways gaze.

"I told you David and I were going to cook dinner for the three of us tonight. It's almost done. Are you ready to go?"

Her mom pushed up from the love seat, grabbed her purse, and left Cara to follow her to the door. "I'm driving."

The silence in the Outback was heavier than the silence had been in David's kitchen. At David's place, Cara and her mom climbed his front steps, and Cara rang the doorbell. David welcomed them in and took their coats. He invited her mom to sit on the couch to take in the view while he brought her a cup of coffee.

Cara and David set the table. When they'd filled three plates with food, David laid them out. Cara called her mom over.

Her mom didn't touch her food and turned to David with a tight-lipped smile. "I'm going to be frank when I say that I expect you to do the right thing and end your involvement with my daughter."

David stopped slicing his steak and met her mom's gaze. "I've been careful to avoid doing the wrong thing."

Her mom shook her head. "You might not be Cara's teacher any-more, but an imbalance of power still exists between you two, even if it's only on a subconscious level."

Her mom paused, then continued when David's gaze dropped to his plate. "Cara is too young to handle a mature relationship. And you must know she's leaving this summer. Which leads me to be-lieve you're less than serious about a relationship with her anyway. I hope you'll spare her feelings."

David didn't comment. He looked to Cara, whose heart dropped to her stomach. She'd expected her mom to observe her and David and see that they related well. Instead, her mom had unleashed harsh words that Cara couldn't take back. Worse, before now, Cara had never really considered the possibility that David might think of their relationship as short term.

Her mom stood from the table. "Thank you for inviting me over."

David stood to face her mom with a stiff smile. "You're welcome. I respect your opinions."

David's forced smile fell into a frown when Cara stood. He didn't look her in the eye.

She was still too stunned by her mom's blunt comments to say anything other than, "I'm sorry, David."

Her mom took her by the arm and led her out the door.

———

On Saturday, Cara fought an urge to head to David's place. She worried her mom had succeeded in turning him off to their relationship. Or that he truly only planned to date her until she moved away.

A breakup like that would be too much to take. It would almost be better not to date him at all. But she couldn't bear that thought. She told herself she was being paranoid again. David would call her later.

She waited until she heard the drone of the garage door opening and closing before she went downstairs. Never again would she obey her mom's command to stay cooped up at home. Not after last night.

Half a banana was all she could stomach for breakfast. She climbed into her Fit and drove to Liberty Charters under a drizzling, gray sky.

Captain Rick's truck was the only vehicle in the lot. Cara was glad to see his shiny new rear bumper. He'd insisted on replacing it at his own cost, saying he didn't want her insurance premiums to go up. Her real father might have abandoned her, but Rick was a first-rate substitute.

The bell above the office door jingled as she stepped inside the office. Her mind carried back to when she'd first met David. She recalled his deep, soft voice, his lopsided smile, his intent green eyes as they'd searched hers when they'd both touched Crossback, his urgent tone in the water when he'd told her to hold on to him and not let go. The memories made her want to cry at the same time that they made her smile.

Sherry sat at her desk, her lips pressed together and down in the kind of frown you'd see on a child whose dog had died. Rick stood behind her with a hand on her shoulder.

"What's wrong?" Cara asked.

Rick squeezed the bill of his hat. "I called off the rest of the tours for today, kiddo. Those transient orcas went after Bobbi."

It felt as though something cold and hard had struck Cara's chest. In her mind's eye, giant white teeth flashed beneath a shiny black snout.

"Those transients are still here?" Cara asked.

Rick nodded.

Cara looked pointedly at Sherry. "Is Bobbi hurt?"

"We're not sure," Sherry said. "We've been communicating with other boats that are still out there, but the attack has been going on for over an hour now."

"Over an *hour?*"

"It takes time for the transients to exhaust the grays," Rick said.

"And to drown the babies," Sherry added, her frown deepening.

This additional tsunami of worry built up within Cara and rolled out in a flood of tears.

Rick came to her side and patted her back. "Don't cry. I'm sure Crossback's fighting hard to keep Bobbi safe and to guide him to shallow water."

Cara blotted the tears away from the corners of her eyes and sniffed. "Can we help stop the attack?"

"Not unless you want to become a part of it," Sherry said.

"We can't just sit here and do nothing. Maybe being out there to support Crossback and Bobbi would help?"

"I know you love those grays," Rick said. "But after what happened with the transients and the zodiac, I'm not keen on going out there when they're being aggressive."

Cara pouted.

"All right," he said, and groaned. "If you really want to be there for them, I'll take you out."

She didn't let on that she was still paralyzed with fear at the thought of being on the water with the transients and that her fear quadrupled when she imagined them in attack mode. She tacked on a semismile.

"But if those transients so much as look at the boat, we're getting out of there," Rick told her.

*That was good to hear.* "There's hope that Crossback and Bobbi will both be fine, right?"

Rick's attempt at a smile failed. "There's always hope."

<hr>

The *Lookout* jetted across the water, slapping against the waves beneath it. Cara pulled her hood over her head. Tiny drops of rain pricked at her face until Rick slowed the boat.

They'd reached a spot over a mile offshore, where a patch of frothing seawater came into view. The glistening black-and-white bodies of two transients stirred up the water as they rammed into Crossback's side. Cara froze at the sight of the tall, triangular dorsal fins.

Rick brought the zodiac as close as he safely could to the edge of the scene. He positioned the boat within the semicircle formed by other observers. His face remained drawn as he snapped several pictures. Cara fell to her knees and gripped the side tube.

The killers retreated and their dorsals submerged, then broke the surface again as they rushed back toward Crossback's gray-and-white, mottled body. Guarding Bobbi, whose shorter, darker length hugged close behind his mother, the large, gray whale remained where she was. The two transients struck Crossback's side, headfirst, so hard that her giant body partially lifted out of the water.

As the killers charged again, Crossback slapped at them with her tail flukes. Her third blow connected with the head of the transient that nearly reached Bobbi. The killer backed away, but the second transient lunged at Crossback. Its enormous, pointed teeth clamped onto her flipper and pulled her away from her baby. The first transient joined in the effort, sinking its teeth into Crossback's other flipper. Red streams flowed from the tips of both Crossback's fins when the killers left her where they'd towed her, several yards from Bobbi.

One transient moved to the sidelines to join three smaller orcas. The killer that had taken a break headed back for Bobbi.

"It looks like two of the adults are doing the hunting," Rick said, then pointed at the other group of transients. "Those other three young ones are learning by observing."

Cara didn't care for Rick's educational commentary at the moment.

Crossback swam back for Bobbi, but a transient had already reached him. The killer rammed into his little body. Bobbi flew out of the water and landed with a loud splash. The killer made its way back to the baby and pounced on top of him, forcing him underwater.

Tears streamed down Cara's face, mixing with rain. She couldn't find her voice to call out to the grays.

From behind her, Rick put a hand on her shoulder. "You don't have to watch this, kiddo."

"You call them transients," she said, her voice breaking. "They're killers."

"It's all part of nature. And the grays are called *devilfish*, you know, for their fierce defense. Crossback's not giving up."

Cara rested her forearms on the side tube and clasped her hands together.

*Please*, she pleaded. *Help Bobbi and Crossback survive this.*

Both killers jumped on Bobbi now.

"Crossback, hurry!" Cara shouted.

Crossback sped toward the killers and used her tail flukes to land crushing blows to their backs as they tried to drown her baby.

In the short time Cara and Rick had been watching, the battle had moved closer to land.

"It looks like the transients are giving up," Rick said.

Unfortunately, it could be too late. Crossback buoyed Bobbi up on her belly, but the baby's limp body slid off his injured mother and sank beneath the surface. Crossback disappeared behind him.

Rick was right about the fighting being over, though. The adult killers headed back to join the juveniles, then zig-zagged off toward deeper waters. Cara breathed into her hands with relief. All the way back to Liberty Charters, she continued to pray that Crossback and Bobbi would recover.

# TWENTY-NINE

Cara was still reeling from the transient attack on Crossback and Bobbi that night when David's number displayed on her cell phone screen. The heaviest portion of her sorrow lifted and the rough edges of uneasiness that had grated at her gut for most of the afternoon smoothed over.

But the heaviness and roughness returned to a greater degree when he said, "I'm at home, in Richland. I've been thinking, and your mom made some good points."

Cara winced at this news almost as much as she had when she'd seen Bobbi's limp body after his attack. She prayed David hadn't gone home for good. No words came to her.

After an uncomfortable pause, David continued. "We should talk Monday night when I get back. Call me around six, if you can."

Thank God he was coming back. She wanted to tell him how great it was to hear his voice—even though he sounded miserable—how worried she was about their relationship and how much she wanted to fight for it, how scared she was for Crossback and Bobbi.

"Sure," was all she managed.

"Good night, then." His quiet words sounded sad and apologetic, like a final good-bye.

Garren answered Cara's call on the first ring Sunday morning. He agreed to go out with her and Rick to look for Crossback and Bobbi. An hour later, he met her in the lot in front of Liberty Charters.

"Such a sad face," he said, greeting her in all his perfection as she stepped out of her Fit.

No sun shone through a thick cloud cover overhead, but she fished her sunglasses out of her backpack and put them on. No rain fell, either, yet she covered her head with her hood. Knowing Garren, he'd already guessed she was hiding evidence of not having showered and having cried herself to sleep the night before.

"I'm worried about Crossback and Bobbi," she said.

"And something happened with David."

She nodded and hung her head. Garren held his arms out and she fell into them. He hugged her close, then secured her against his side and guided her toward the office. As she detailed her phone conversation with David the night before, her voice faltered, and she sniffed back her tears.

They paused outside the office door.

"You think David changed his mind about your relationship."

"I'm worried he might have."

"Worry is normal. Your relationship is new and miscommunication is common. Be careful not to jump to conclusions."

She was trying not to. But that was yet another thing that was easier said than done.

Out on the water, the common whale sighting grounds teemed with grays, many that interacted with the *Lookout* more than usual.

The whales swam alongside the boat and glided underneath it. Several spyhopped nearby.

But there was no sign of the transients. Or Crossback and Bobbi. Cara worried the other grays were trying to convey a message—a morbid one.

———

Cara wished she didn't have the day off school for Veterans Day. The distraction might have helped. As it was, she fretted all day, alternating between wanting 6:00 p.m. to come quickly and not wanting it to arrive at all. When the time came and she dialed David's number, his answering "Hello" sounded neutral, unreadable.

"You're home?" she asked, hoping he knew she meant at the beach house and not his dad's.

"Yeah."

She still couldn't read his tone.

"Do you want me to come over so we can talk?" she asked.

"Why don't we meet at the bottom of the stairs by Surfseekers?"

It couldn't be a good sign that he didn't want her to come over. Like the last time she talked to him, all she managed to say was, "Sure."

A half hour later, David waited at the bottom of the stairs with his back to her as he faced the dark, raging sea. Orange-tinted lights mounted on the resort wall to the right highlighted the stretch of beach before them. The smell of a nearby bonfire sweetened the air and waves swished softly on the sand.

"How was your trip?" she asked when she stood directly behind him. She wanted to touch him, but didn't feel comfortable enough, or desperate enough, yet.

He whirled around as if she'd taken him by surprise. His gaze fell to his shoe and he dug its toe in the sand. "Thanks for meeting me."

"Why would you thank me for meeting you?" She put a hand on his upper arm.

He didn't back away, but also didn't respond to her touch.

"What's going on, David?"

"I wanted to tell you that I respect your mom's opinions, and I understand that it could be hard for you to express those things yourself."

"What are you saying? You think I agree with what my mom said to you?"

His expression remained guarded. "You didn't disagree with anything she said."

"You didn't disagree with anything she said, either," she said, her tone more snippy than she intended.

"So you don't agree with her?" He looked into her eyes.

She took a deep breath and slowly let it out as their warm connection reestablished itself. "Not at all. Do you?"

He looked down for a moment, then back up at her. "No. But your mom cares about you. And she believes what she said. I respect that."

"Do you respect her opinions more than you care about us?"

He hesitated. "I don't want to push things if us being together is too much for you."

She shook her head. "The only thing that would be too much for me would be if there were no *us*."

Her eyes chased his as they traveled over her face. Finally, his gaze settled on hers.

"I have a confession to make," he said.

She didn't know how to take his casual tone. Her heart constricted.

"I have plans to move to Seattle this summer."

If he could see her face as well as she could see his in the orange glow of the resort lights, he had to notice when her mouth dropped open.

"You're moving to Seattle, too?"

"Yep." His lips bunched up, as if he was trying not to laugh at her dumbfounded reaction.

Warm waves of relief flowed through the tether between them and thawed her frosty heart. "Since when?"

He stepped closer to her. "I hadn't planned to get involved with you during the school year." He tapped her nose with his finger. "At first, I decided to wait until the summer to see if you were still interested. I knew you'd be leaving for college, so I figured if I moved to Seattle, I'd have time to try to win you over."

She couldn't believe she was hearing such magical—no—*providential* words.

"I enrolled in some classes at the UW. Hopefully I'll be able to teach college."

She smiled up at him and he shared his lopsided grin with her.

"I'm glad you're happy. I was waiting to tell you because I worried you might think it was a bit much."

She wrapped her arms around his waist and laid her head against his chest. "It is. Much more than I could've hoped for."

---

The next day, Cara's mom insisted on driving her to school and picking her up.

After school, Cara climbed into the passenger seat of the Outback. "You're not taking my car away for good, are you?"

"I just wanted to make sure you were available after school so we could do some shopping, get a bite to eat, and talk. Not that you don't deserve to have your car taken away. You haven't done as I said when I told you to stay home when you weren't in school."

"After the way you treated David, I'm not going to serve your prison sentence, no matter what you do to me."

They drove down to the outlet mall, surrounded by strained silence. Her mom brought her back to the store they'd shopped at before her first date with David. Cara acted as a clothes hanger while her mom selected items from the racks.

"Do you like this top?" her mom asked, holding up a blouse.

"It's nice."

Her mom added the shirt to Cara's load. Cara felt a twinge of guilt when she realized that all the outfits her mom had selected were for her. She might be grounded, but she was still being spoiled.

"I'm assuming you want to talk about David?" Cara asked.

Her mom sifted through another rack of blouses. "We could start with that."

"He told me last night he's moving to Seattle this summer, to be near me. He'll be taking classes at the UW. He wants to teach college."

Her mom grasped the bar of the rack in front of her. "It remains to be seen whether he'll follow through with that plan."

Cara shook her head, though her mom didn't see it. "I guess only time will convince you that his feelings for me are sincere."

Less than an hour later, Cara and her mom walked into the Cove and waited by the hostess stand. Kathy walked over, balancing a tray, and nodded for them to follow her.

"Sorry, ladies. We're short a hostess at the moment. But there are plenty of window seats to choose from."

Cara wondered if Lori was the hostess who either quit or got fired. Her mom followed her to the same table Cara and David had sat at on their first date. Kathy set her tray down by another window seat and served one of the few groups of customers in the restaurant.

Pointing down at Seagoer's Cove, Cara said, "David and I fell overboard right outside that rock wall."

Her mom looked down at the water, but remained quiet.

Kathy appeared with a soda for Cara and a cup of coffee for her mom. "I've got the chowder coming," she said.

"Is Lori still working here?" Cara asked Kathy, whose face scrunched up with disapproval.

"I shouldn't gossip, but I hope you're not hanging out with that girl. She's mixed up in some bad things. We had to let her go."

Cara's mom nodded as if she understood. Probably, her mom thought Kathy meant Lori was doing drugs. Maybe Kathy did mean that. But Cara knew what Lori was really messing around with. Not that her mom would believe any of that.

Kathy headed off to the kitchen.

"So what is it you wanted to talk to me about?" Cara asked her mom.

"I'm going to a conference in Seattle next month. I want you to come with me. We can check out the UW campus again and look into getting you a room at the dorms."

"I want to get an apartment. And I can do that hunting online. I don't need to get specific until spring."

"I'd still like you to come with me."

Cara sipped her soda. "If you're trying to keep me away from David, taking me away to a conference with you isn't going to work any more than trying to lock me up at home."

Her mom pegged her with a pleading sideways gaze.

"Not that it's any of your business, but if it makes you feel better, David and I aren't sleeping together," Cara said.

Her mom's eyes widened.

"And that was David's decision."

Leaning back against her chair, her mom studied her, then said, "I hope I don't regret this, but I'm going to give you the benefit of the doubt and trust you to be smart."

Cara smiled, grabbed her mom's hand, and squeezed it.

"So be smart," her mom ordered.

# THIRTY

Cara had counted on Ms. Clark to find a way to help Rachel. But come Thanksgiving break, Rachel remained as comatose and glued to Ethan as ever. Fortunately, Garren was coming over for Thanksgiving dinner, so Cara would have a chance to ask him for help. God willing, whatever he came up with would work.

That year, Cara was reminded of the holidays back when her grandparents had been around. Once again, a male figure was present during Thanksgiving dinner, to carve the turkey and serve the trimmings after the women spent most of the day cooking. Except Garren also helped in the kitchen.

He seemed to enjoy the preparations. Several times, Cara caught him pausing to inhale the succulent scents of turkey baked with butter-drenched onion, celery, and bread stuffing. He smiled at Cara as if he were the most thankful person in the world.

Before they ate, Cara, her mom, and Garren sat at the dinner table and expressed their gratitude for each other. Cara mentioned her thankfulness for her mom and Garren, as well as for David, and for her mom's making an effort to accept their relationship. Her mom gave thanks for Cara. Garren gave thanks to God.

Cara wanted to ask about Garren's family, but didn't want to put a damper on the joy he seemed to be feeling celebrating with her and her mom. After eating a heaping plateful of turkey and the trimmings, he still found room for the pumpkin pie and whipped cream Cara's mom served for dessert. Still, he beat Cara's mom to the majority of the cleanup. Cara offered to help, but her mom shooed her out of the kitchen.

"This is my chance to get to know Garren better," her mom said, carting off their glasses.

At the kitchen sink, Garren smiled and shrugged as he rinsed their dinner plates.

Cara removed the linens from the table and wondered how David's Thanksgiving celebration was going with his dad. It troubled her to think they were missing David's mom and this might be a sad holiday for them. David had promised to call every night he was gone. She kept her phone close, anxious to talk to him.

Once Garren and her mom finished up in the kitchen, Garren offered to take Cara for a walk on the beach. He drove them down to the same spot Cara took him on her birthday. They bundled up against the cold, fastening their jackets and pulling on their hoods.

Salty sea air mixed with sand scraped at Cara's face as Garren helped her down from his truck. Strangely, the wind died down entirely as they walked. She stopped to look at him. The darkness of the night and his hood cloaked the details of his face.

"You've been right about so many things when it comes to Rachel," Cara said. "I'm hoping you can help me come up with a plan to help her."

He lowered his hood and smiled at her. "Of course. If you can arrange for us to see Rachel, I know an expert on demonic possession."

"An expert on demons?"

"An exorcist."

She should have foreseen this kind of thing coming from Garren. "I can't tell Ms. Clark we're bringing someone over to do an *exorcism*." She couldn't control her incredulous tone.

"An exorcism can also be referred to as a blessing."

Cara thought about that for a few moments as they strolled across the sand. "I guess I could tell her we're coming over to do an *intervention*—that we want to say some prayers and offer Rachel a blessing?"

"Sounds about right."

Glad to have a somewhat solid plan in place, Cara reflected on Thanksgiving dinner. "My mom wanted to see what you thought about my relationship with David, didn't she? That's why she wouldn't let me help in the kitchen."

It irked Cara to think her mom still thought she might be interested in Garren. She kicked at the sand as they walked. "What did she say?"

"She seemed to think I was secretly in love with you."

"No way. She's a psychologist. She should be able to tell you're not."

"I think she did think I was in love with you before I talked to her. I told her we're close, but not romantically involved. I didn't mention your relationship with David."

"Speaking of David. Things like your spending Thanksgiving with me, and the flowers for my birthday, they're making him pretty jealous."

"It's good for him."

"It's not so great for me, always having to insist that we're just friends."

"It'll be good for you, too," he said, taking her hand and holding it as they walked, "when David learns to get over it."

Cara checked her phone when she got back from her walk with Garren and was disappointed to see she'd missed a text from David:

*My dad and I had an early dinner. Call me whenever you're done celebrating. Miss you.*

She dialed his number. He answered on the first ring, in a whisper.

"My dad's sleeping in the next room and the walls are thin. Sorry I have to be so quiet."

Even hearing a trace of his voice caused her chest to swell with warmth.

"Sorry I missed your text. How was your Thanksgiving?"

"It's always tough without my mom, but my dad's glad to have me here."

"It's good that you're spending time with your dad. I'm sure that would make your mom happy."

"I'm sure you're right." She was glad to hear a smile in his voice.

"I can't wait to see you."

"I'll only be gone for the weekend. And I'll call you again tomorrow." His last words were slightly louder. "I can't tell you how much I miss you."

"I miss you more."

Friday morning, Cara sat on her bed staring at her cell phone, rehearsing what she'd say to Ms. Clark. Finally, she dialed her cell number.

"Cara?" Ms. Clark answered, surprised to hear from her.

"Hi, Ms. Clark. Hope you had a happy Thanksgiving. How's Rachel?"

Ms. Clark sighed. "Thanks, sweetie. Rachel's still not herself. Spends all her time with Ethan." Resignation sounded in her tone.

"I'm hoping you won't mind if I come over with a couple of friends for an . . . intervention? We'll say some prayers, do a blessing?"

Ms. Clark's tone sounded more upbeat. "What a sweet idea. I'm not sure Rachel will react well to it. But I'll try to make sure she's here when you come."

"Does this Sunday work? Later in the afternoon, when you're home from church, maybe?"

"Yes. Let's pray it will help."

———

Cara pulled up to the Clarks' bungalow Sunday afternoon and parked behind Rachel's Corolla. Garren stood next to his truck, accompanied by a man wearing a purple religious robe who held a small, brown, leather-bound book to his chest. As Cara got out of her car and approached them, she saw that the man had a light dusting of silver in his short, dark hair. So he was likely older than he first appeared.

Garren gestured to the distinguished-looking man. "Cara, this is Archbishop Egan. Archbishop Egan, Cara Markwell."

Cara couldn't fathom how Garren got an *archbishop* to come to Rachel's house. Maybe this was part of the job description, but it seemed like it should be a lot more difficult to enlist the in-home help of such a high-ranking clergyman.

"You made the right choice to seek help for your friend, Cara," the archbishop told her with a slight bow of his head.

*We'll see*, she thought, before she said, "Thanks for coming."

She led Garren and the archbishop to the front porch and rang the bell.

Ms. Clark's jaw dropped when she opened the door and saw the archbishop.

"We're here to offer a blessing for Rachel," the archbishop said with a gentle smile.

Ms. Clark's look of open-mouthed shock faded at the word *blessing*.

"Thanks for letting us come," Cara said, and placed a hand on Garren's arm. "This is Garren. He's a friend from school."

Ms. Clark nodded, put a finger to her lips to warn them to keep quiet, and let them in. They followed her down the hall toward Rachel's room. Their procession reminded Cara of a convoy heading to an execution.

Ms. Clark opened the door to Rachel's room. Sitting up in bed, Rachel stared at her vanity. She briefly glanced at the archbishop.

Then she looked at Garren, and her eyes glinted like black onyx. "What is *he* doing here?"

The voice wasn't Rachel's. It reminded Cara of how Amber's voice had sounded low and guttural when she'd issued a warning to "get out" at her occult party. Cara gripped Garren's arm and stepped behind him. Garren didn't say anything, but laid a hand over Cara's.

"Don't talk to the demon," Archbishop Egan said, tucking the book he held in his robe pocket. "It will only deceive."

He lifted one end of the stole that hung around his neck and moved toward Rachel, whose face tightened. Her lips pressed together.

"*Ecce crucem Domini,*" the archbishop said as he made the sign of the cross over Rachel, then himself, Ms. Clark, and Cara and Garren. Touching the printed cross on the edge of his stole to Rachel's neck, he placed his other hand on his head.

Cara couldn't believe Rachel was letting the archbishop touch her. But Rachel seemed almost paralyzed by his actions. Her body went rigid and her eyes grew wide.

The archbishop dropped the stole and fetched a bottle of yellow oil from his pocket. He uncorked it, shook some onto his finger, and made the sign of the cross on Rachel's forehead. She hissed at him.

"*Sit nominis ti signo famulus tuus munitus,*" the archbishop said, then exchanged the oil for the book in his pocket. He opened it and continued to speak in the same unfamiliar language Cara assumed was Latin.

Ms. Clark stood on the side of Rachel's bed, wringing her hands.

Cara remained behind Garren and squeezed his arm. "Isn't there anything we can do to help?"

"We can pray, if you want."

"Out loud?"

"Yes."

"What should we say?"

"We can say a deliverance prayer. Repeat after me."

"*Lord, we pray that you bind the spirits, powers, and forces of darkness, the netherworld, and the evil forces of nature. Take authority over all the curses, hexes, demonic activity, and spells at work here and break them.*"

Each word from both Archbishop Egan's and Garren's mouths resonated loudly, clearly, and deliberately. Cara's words sounded weaker, but she didn't stop, even when Rachel's head whipped from side to side as if she, or the demon, was saying "NO."

"What is your name, demon?" the archbishop asked, in English now. He drew near Rachel again and Cara thought for a second he might kiss her. Instead, he blew air in her face.

Rachel's head stilled and it looked as though her lips were in a battle over whether to remain open or closed. Through her clenched teeth came the name "Succ—or—ben—oth."

After finishing their current recitation of the deliverance prayer, Cara and Garren stopped praying. Cara shuddered to think that not only did a demon possess her friend, but it also had a *name*.

"The demon of jealousy," Garren whispered in Cara's ear.

She couldn't bring herself to feel surprised that Garren knew about the demon.

The chilling voice, more menacing now, burst forth from Rachel. "We'll still get her."

A wave of revulsion passed over Cara. She didn't understand why, but she was sure Rachel's eyes fell on her when the demon finished its last statement. Cara clung tightly to Garren's arm.

The archbishop resumed speaking in Latin. Rachel heaved. A gush of white, pasty liquid, dotted with clumps of what looked like small bunches of leaves, poured from her mouth and splashed onto her comforter. A wide, wicked grin, like the one Cara had seen on Amber at the occult party, spread across Rachel's face. She broke out in a fit of manic laughter before her black eyes turned back to a more normal, milk chocolate color.

Vomit dribbled down Rachel's chin and the laughter subsided. Rachel yawned, her mouth stretched open wide, and she exhaled heavily. Her eyes closed and she fell down on her side on the bed. She remained unmoving, apparently asleep.

Ms. Clark sat on the bed beside Rachel and wiped Rachel's face with a tissue. Her voice cracked as she asked the archbishop, "Is she going to be okay?"

"Yes," Archbishop Egan said, closing the book in his hands. "Sleeping is common after a demon leaves."

Cara moved to the archbishop's side. "What did the demon mean when it said, 'We'll still get her'?" she asked him.

"Most likely that it will come back, and bring others with it, if Rachel isn't prayerful and doesn't stay away from sorcery," the archbishop said, to both Cara and Ms. Clark.

Ms. Clark looked at Rachel, who slept peacefully on her bed, then at the archbishop. "I need to talk to you about helping another person Rachel's close to, who I'm certain is also possessed. But I'll do everything I can to make sure Rachel stays away from the occult activities she's been involved with."

The archbishop put a hand on Ms. Clark's shoulder. "I have faith Rachel will do what she needs to in order to avoid another, probably worse, attack."

Cara prayed fervently for that same faith.

Ms. Clark ushered everyone out of Rachel's room and thanked them for coming. When Ms. Clark asked the archbishop to follow her to the living room, Garren nodded to him and followed Cara, who stumbled down the hall and out the door. Outside, Garren stopped next to her Fit.

"I cannot believe what just happened," she said, stopping to face Garren and finding comfort in his complete calmness. "How did you get an *archbishop* to come perform an exorcism?"

"I called him. He's a servant of God."

Garren's words sounded so reverent that Cara wondered if maybe he was considering training to be a priest, if that might be the ever-elusive reason he didn't seem attracted to anyone.

"You know so much about all this," she said. "Are you planning to become a priest?"

"No. But I'm always ready to help in the battle against evil."

And now he sounded like a superhero.

"Do you really believe the exorcism and our prayers worked to help Rachel?"

"Yes."

"And do you have faith, like the archbishop, that Rachel will be able to avoid another demonic attack?"

"I hope she will. She'll know what to avoid now. It's certainly something to pray about."

Prayer. How strange that something she'd never thought about much before, but had been doing a lot more of lately, could be so powerful.

# THIRTY-ONE

Cara drove home after Rachel's exorcism, still in a state of shock. Her mind refused to accept what had just happened, though she couldn't deny that Garren had been right, as usual. Through her windshield, the sun winked at her as it sunk lower in the sky.

The cleansing, soothing spray of a hot shower was the best therapy she could think of. She parked on the street and gripped the wheel while she struggled to understand what had just happened. Rachel's demon had been banished and couldn't cause any more harm, she kept reminding herself. So there was no reason to be frightened. She hoped.

An eerie silence and a gloomy gray filled the interior of the house. Cara shook off the discomfort that fell over her like a cloak.

Her mom was probably still at the outlet mall taking advantage of the after-holiday sales. Cara flipped on every light she passed as she made her way upstairs to the main bathroom. Her cell phone didn't show any new activity. She frowned, wishing she could hear the comforting sound of David's voice.

In the bathroom, she turned on the showerhead, undressed, and stepped under the hot spray. Her mind numbed as she concentrated on the water massaging her skin and pattering against the shower floor. Shampooing her hair and lathering her body with soap, she let the water pound her until her tightly wound muscles relaxed.

Feeling as clean and calm as possible, considering what she'd witnessed, she stepped out of the stall and wrapped up in a towel. The house remained silent. She moved slowly down the hall and opened her bedroom door. Something caused her to hold back. A heaviness hung in the air, as if the space had been violated not long ago.

She scanned the room's interior. The photo of her and David at the Anchor was missing from her nightstand. The hairs on her forearms stood straight up, like hackles on a cat's back.

Tightening the towel around her body, she entered her room. She crept over to her nightstand and opened the drawer. David's photo from her new teacher feature stared up at her. But the photo of her and David at the Anchor wasn't there.

Her eyes were drawn to the flowers in the vase on her desk. The roses sagged and were brown and shriveled. Beside them, crumpled in a similar state of decay, was the rose in the corsage Garren had given her. She shut her nightstand drawer and sucked in a quick breath.

The roses had been as fresh as ever this morning. And they weren't just dying, either. They looked bone-dry dead. She walked over and touched one. It crumbled to dust on her desk.

Next to the rose dust lay a small sachet. She didn't want to touch it, but curiosity took over, so she picked it up with the tips of her fingers and twirled it. Fine black powder bulged behind a thin, translucent casing. Black thread sealed the contents. She sniffed at it. Burnt paper and sulfur created a nauseating scent, combined with a sweet floral smell she recognized as jasmine.

The sulfur reminded her of what she'd come to think of as the sorcery house. Amber had to be responsible. Somehow the witch had broken into her home.

Fury filled her as she thrust her limbs into a top and jeans and jammed her feet into her sneakers. She shoved the sachet in her pocket, grabbed her keys, and stomped off to her car.

Firing up the Fit's engine, she recalled her promises to stay away from Amber. She'd fully intended to keep them. But as far as she was concerned, they were no longer valid after this break-in.

If Amber thought Cara was going to play the coward, she was wrong. This had gone too far. The harassment had to stop.

Amber might not live at the sorcery house, but Cara would bet that she did. She drove in that direction, and sure enough, when she passed by, the Jetta sat parked outside. Her heart thumped hard and fast at the sight of the car.

The sky had shifted from a rich blue to a deep black. The house's curtains were drawn shut. Light only shone through the south-side window. It was steady, like an overhead.

Swigging on a diet soda, Cara tried to suppress the fear churning in her belly. Her discomfort only increased with the bubbles. She'd lost all the courage she drummed up on the drive over as soon as she laid eyes on the Jetta. Still, she refused to go home like a weakling.

She parked her Fit a few blocks away and snuck over to hide in the neighbor's bushes. The path to Amber's lit side window was straight and no one appeared to be looking out from inside any nearby houses. Cara hunched over as she ran toward the window. Then she stood with her back against the house's siding. Her heart hammered so hard, she imagined Amber would hear it from inside and discover her.

The curtains obscured the side view into the house, but there was a gap where the two curtains met that she might be able to see through. She crouched underneath the window frame. Several slow, full breaths failed to settle her nerves.

Giving up on her efforts to calm herself, she lifted her head to peer through the slit in the curtains. The view of the inside was clearer than she expected. She leaned closer to the window for a better look, but ducked every few seconds, expecting Amber's face to pop up on the other side of the window at any moment.

Against the far wall of what Cara remembered as the game room, figurines had been placed at the back of a small table, a depiction of a naked man with horns on the left side, a naked woman on the right. Between the figurines sat a tall, fat, white candle. In the center of the table was a silver-toned ball covered with holes with a chain dangling from the top. On either side of the ball were two shorter, wide, red candles.

Taller taper candles were set in holders in front of the red candles. The candle on the left was gold, the one on the right was black. White block letters ran up the sides of these candles and a photograph rested against each one. The images came from the picture missing from Cara's room. Amber had torn it in two and covered Cara's eyes with red Xs and David's with red hearts. One candle read: CARA, the other: DAVID.

Cara slowly backed away from the window.

Amber's voice sounded in her left ear. "It was easier than I expected to lure you here." The witch whispered her words.

Cara whipped around and looked directly into Amber's beautiful, wicked face. Every nerve in her body zinged to life. Her back flattened against the house.

The only direction she could move to get away was sideways. She tried to slide toward the house's edge. As she moved, the rough wooden siding snagged her shirt and cut the skin on her back.

Amber cocked her head to the side. "I have something for you." She held up an envelope, as if wielding a weapon.

Cara stopped her sideways squirming. Whatever it was Amber had to offer—something like a note, by the looks of it—Cara would be glad to take it and flee. She prayed this could end that simply.

Even in the dark, she saw the witch's blue eyes blacken. The potent odor of vanilla, oranges, and cloves, along with an undercurrent of sulfur, gusted up Cara's nostrils, disorienting her.

In the next instant, Garren's silhouette appeared over Amber's shoulder. Cara drew in a shocked breath.

Garren's tone was firm. "Go, Cara."

At the sound of Garren's voice, Amber's black, rock-hard eyes widened.

Cara didn't need to be told to leave. Everything in her warned her to run fast and far away. But even if Amber hadn't been blocking her, she felt glued to the house.

Amber clutched the envelope she held to her chest and spun around to face Garren. He jerked his head to the side, encouraging Cara to run around the witch. Cara's invisible bonds broke and she bolted past Amber and fled down the street.

Cara looked back as long as she could without fear of tripping. Garren turned and ran in her direction. She didn't wait for him. By the time she reached her car, her breath came in ragged bursts.

Garren made it to her side and patted her back. "You'll be all right."

She gulped in breaths of air and nodded. "How did you know where to find me?"

"I saw you leaving your house and followed you."

She wondered for a second if maybe he was a stalker after all. At the moment she didn't really care. She had a feeling he'd saved her from something much worse.

"It wasn't wise of you to go to that house."

"Amber broke into my house and left some weird spell in my room. I can't let her get away with that." Cara retrieved the sachet from her pocket. Her hand trembled as she held it up.

Garren pinched it with the tips of his fingers and looked at it like he wanted to spit on it.

She popped the locks on her Fit and jumped into the driver's seat. Garren let himself in on the passenger side. She immediately pressed the button to lock the car doors.

"This won't hurt you," Garren said, dangling the sachet. "It's part of a divisive or breakup spell, which would only work on a weak relationship."

Relieved, she snatched the sachet back and dropped it in an empty cupholder. She'd show it to David when he came back to town.

"Still, confronting a witch isn't wise," Garren said, his tone thick with warning.

"I know that. Now."

"My truck's around the corner."

She turned down the side street he pointed toward and pulled up behind his Silverado. "Why is Amber scared of you?" she asked.

He glanced up at the roof of the car before he looked her in the eye. "I know the weaknesses when it comes to sorcery. As long as you make smarter choices than you did tonight, I have faith that I can protect you."

Garren, her protector. David would love that. She truly appreciated Garren's help and concern, though. She was sick of everyone telling her to be smart, but she hated to imagine what Amber might have done to her if Garren hadn't shown up at just the right moment. And she couldn't blame Garren for being upset that she almost got caught in the web Amber weaved. Cara was mad, too—at both Amber and herself.

At least for now, Cara accepted Garren's flaky answer. She gave him a hug and grudgingly let him out of her car. As soon as he stepped out, she relocked her car doors. She drove behind him back to the main road and was touched that he'd gone out of his way and drove all the way to her house. He waited until she was inside before he took off.

Cara quietly locked the front door, then checked the back door and the door in the kitchen that led to the garage, where the Outback sat in the dark. All of the doors were locked, as they had been when Amber somehow got into the house earlier. A fresh flow of adrenaline rushed through her. She leaned against the kitchen counter, silently counted to ten, and willed her pounding heart to slow its pace.

Amber definitely showed signs of being under demonic influence, like the guttural voice at her Halloween party and the sharklike eyes. Cold ripples of fear continued to slide up Cara's spine. Determined not to let the witch get to her, she tiptoed up the stairs. No light shone under her mom's door.

In her room, the time on her alarm clock read 11:23. She turned on the light, changed into a nightshirt, and grabbed her phone. Propping her pillow against her headboard and checking her cell, she saw David had texted her. How stupid of her to waste time she could be spending talking to him messing around with Amber.

His text told her he was spending another night in Richland. She sagged against her pillow. She was sad enough missing him for this long. Waiting another day would be torture.

Whatever time she got his message, he wanted her to call him. She dialed his cell number and, like the night before, he answered in a whisper.

"I'm sorry I didn't text you earlier today. I wanted to come back and see you, but my dad had other plans."

She doubted David would believe the craziness she'd been through that day. He'd also probably be mad about what she'd done. And the last thing she wanted him thinking about before he went to sleep was Amber. So she told him about Crossback and Bobbi, how there had still been no sight of them.

"Those are special whales. I'm sure they'll show up. Have faith."

That was another one of those easier-said-than-done things, but she was working on it.

She'd wait until Tuesday to tell him about Rachel's exorcism and to lay Amber's latest lunacy on him.

# THIRTY-TWO

Now that the weather had turned wintry, Cara and Garren were forced indoors during lunch. They sat on the floor in front of Cara's locker on the first Monday in December. Cara pulled Amber's sachet from her backpack.

"Tell me again why Amber left this for me?"

"Amber must have been trying to cause a breakup between you and David," Garren said. "She would have written out a spell, read the incantation out loud, burned the paper she wrote it on, and then added the ashes to the sachet to leave for you."

"I found it next to the roses you gave me for my birthday."

He avoided her gaze.

"I know you always say you can't tell me where you got the flowers. But they were as dry as dust. Can you tell me what that's all about?"

He looked up, and the locker behind him clanged as the back of his head hit it. Then he turned to look at her. "The roses were tainted by the presence of evil."

She wasn't surprised to get a cryptic answer from him. "The presence of a demon?"

"Yes."

"I figured Amber must be under demonic influence. I see some of the same signs in her that I saw in Rachel."

He nodded.

"I saw other stuff through Amber's window that must have been part of another spell she cast," she said, and explained the candles, photos, and figurines. "Do I need to be worried about this occult crap?" She was joking. Sort of.

He didn't look amused. "What we need to worry about is that Amber won't stop."

"What else do you think she'll do?"

"I saw she had an envelope she was going to give you last night."

"Yeah." Cara snickered. "Instead of a gun or a knife, or even her fists, she pulls an envelope on me."

"Guns and knives and fists aren't the only weapons that can do damage. Whatever you do, if Amber gives you an envelope, don't open it."

"What do you think would be in it? Anthrax?"

He didn't join in her joking. "Another spell. One that might work. I'm not kidding when I say not to open any envelopes." He raised his chin slightly, in response to whatever he saw over her shoulder, and stood.

Cara shifted around at the sound of footsteps smacking across the linoleum. Rachel and Ethan towered over her. She leapt to her feet and stepped close beside Garren.

Rachel held up her hands. "Relax. I'm back. See?" She swung in a circle with her arms out, palms up, displaying a white long-sleeved tee, jeans, and sneakers that were characteristic of the best friend Cara hadn't seen in months.

Rachel's brown eyes once again resembled warm caramel rather than murky puddles of mud or cold, black glass. Her huge grin stretched across her face, then fell into an exaggerated frown. "I know sorry doesn't cut it. But I honestly didn't know what I was fooling around with."

"Neither did I," Ethan said, speaking to Cara for the first time ever.

Rachel rolled her eyes.

Cara looked closely at Ethan. He'd gone back to his old hoodie, jeans, and sneakers look. A hint of pink touched his cheeks and his hair looked thicker and shinier. The biggest difference, though, was that his eyes were no longer narrowed. They were bright and open, a light shade of hazel.

"After you left my house, my mom had Ethan come over and the archbishop performed another exorcism. Ethan insisted on apologizing to you in person." Rachel never looked at Ethan as she spoke.

"I really am sorry—" Ethan said.

Rachel cut him off. "Thanks for helping me," she said to Cara. "You, too, Garren." She offered him an apologetic smile, then hung her head.

"You're welcome," Garren said without a trace of anything but complete sincerity in his voice or on his face.

"Amber had been feeding me potions and cursed objects with binding spells placed on them since last summer," Ethan said. "I fed the same things to Rachel."

"Why did you get mixed up with Amber in the first place?" Cara asked him.

"She came up to me one day last summer and asked me to go have coffee with her. I couldn't believe some hot, older chick was interested in me. She must have started giving me potions that day. I would have done anything for her from then on." He glanced at Rachel, but she stepped farther away from him and closer to Cara.

"Were you and Amber a couple?" Cara asked him.

"Nah. She moved to California after graduation, then came back to Liberty after her boyfriend committed suicide. I don't think she'd gotten over that."

*And still hadn't.*

"I was actually after you to begin with," Ethan said, to Cara.

Cara maintained a neutral expression.

"Amber wanted me to feed you those binding potions. So I thought I'd try to get to you through Rachel."

Rachel placed a hand on her hip. "In other words, you *used* me," she said to Ethan, glaring at him.

Ethan gritted his teeth at Rachel's words. "Rachel doesn't believe it," he said to Cara, "but even though I'm sorry about what happened, I'm glad I got a chance to find out how awesome she is."

Rachel shook her head. "You *poisoned* me. Enough said."

"Only because Amber poisoned *me*," Ethan countered, but Rachel didn't respond.

"How does Amber feel about you two dropping out of her . . . coven, or whatever?" Cara asked.

"Neither of us have talked to her. I doubt she knows anything has changed," Ethan said.

Cara held up the sachet. "Amber left this in my room. She also tried to give me an envelope. If she's trying to cast spells on me, does that mean I'm under demonic influence, too?"

"No. You're not," Garren said. "But you could fall victim to a curse."

Rachel nodded at Garren's words.

"How do you know so much about witchcraft?" Ethan asked Garren.

"I've been around it," Garren said.

Garren had made it clear he was opposed to sorcery. His comment made Cara wonder if his family might be involved in those types of things. That might explain why he didn't like to talk about his personal life.

Rachel pointed to the sachet still hanging from Cara's fingertips. "That's from a breakup spell Amber cast for you and David, right? Not you and Garren?"

"Yes, for me and David," Cara said defensively and dumped the sachet back in her bag.

Rachel wound a strand of hair around her finger. "I guess that wouldn't be considered a student-teacher scandal at this point. Not that people in this town won't still talk." She turned to Garren. "But I just have to say that I don't get it. You're the hottest guy at Seaside. You could have your pick of any girl, probably along the whole coastline, yet you hang out with Cara, who's hot for teacher. What's up with that?"

"David isn't my teacher anymore," Cara stressed.

Garren put his arm around Cara's shoulder. "Cara needed a friend."

Rachel's mouth opened, then closed, and her hand fell from her hair. "I guess she did." She pulled Cara into a hug. "I'm sorry I wasn't there for you."

Cara returned the hug and patted Rachel's back. "I'd say being under demonic influence is a pretty good excuse."

# THIRTY-THREE

It felt more like a year had passed than a week by the time Cara drove to David's place after school on Tuesday. He opened the door for her and his lopsided grin brought on a grin of her own. She dropped her backpack on the floor as he pulled her inside and into his arms.

On the dining table, there sat what looked like a box of roses. This was one arena in which David did *not* want to compete with Garren. David let her go, walked over to the table, and picked up the box. His right hand covered the writing on the top as he carried it over to her.

"You didn't have to get me flowers."

He removed his hand to reveal the inscription beneath. Stenciled on top of the box was CRAFTY CONFECTIONS.

"These are chocolate roses. I'm hoping the way to your heart is more through your taste buds than your nose."

"A-ha." She picked up one of the flowers and took a bite of a petal. The chocolate tasted smooth, rich, and sweet. Sweeter still was the thought David had put into getting the gift for her.

She kissed his cheek, broke off the rest of the petal she bit into, and slipped it into his mouth. "I love them. Thank you."

He put an arm around her waist and steered her over to the couch. They sat, and he set the box on the coffee table. "I never asked you on the phone if Garren enjoyed your Thanksgiving celebration."

She had little reason to, but she felt a pang of guilt. "Would it bother you if I told you Garren and I held hands when we walked on the beach after Thanksgiving dinner?"

"Before or after you confessed your undying love for each other?"

She checked his expression to see if it matched his light tone. It did. "You're really not jealous?"

He put out his hand. She placed hers in his and savored the full force of the warmth she'd missed between them.

"I gave up on any jealousy I felt toward Garren as soon as I saw the look on your face when I told you I was moving to Seattle."

She kissed his hand. "That's good to hear." Feeding him a leaf, she asked, "How's your dad?"

David hid his chocolate-filled mouth behind his fist. "He's okay. Still lonely, though. And he still wants me to come home."

"For the rest of the year?"

"For good."

She struggled to maintain a smile. "You didn't change your plans, did you?"

"No, but I wish my dad would let it go." He got up and walked to the fridge. "Want a soda?"

"Sure. Thanks."

He opened the bottle for her and handed it over. When he didn't say anything more about his dad, she took a swig of the soda, set it down with the rest of her rose on the coffee table, and got up to grab her backpack from the entryway.

Sachet in hand, she came back to sit on the couch. She detailed her encounter with Amber at the sorcery house. David's fists clenched atop his thighs as she spoke. She decided not to mention the envelope or Garren rescuing her. Even if David had gotten over his jealousy, he still wouldn't like it that Garren followed her. Also, she didn't want to admit that Amber frightened her. She saved the news about Rachel and Ethan for last, only explaining that they'd been disciples of Amber's, but were now back to their old selves.

"So Rachel and Ethan were part of some coven Amber organized?"

"Sort of. The consensus is that they were under demonic influence."

His brows pulled together. *"Demonic influence?"*

She nodded.

"And you believe this?"

She wanted to share the whole truth with him, but his doubtful tone told her he wasn't ready to hear it. She bit her lip and shrugged noncommittally.

He took the sachet from her and flipped it over in his hand. "And Amber thinks this nonsense is going to break us up?"

"I think so."

"Do you believe *that?*"

Garren had said breakup spells only worked on weak relationships. She wanted nothing more than to believe her bond with David was strong. "No."

"Then let's ignore this. Well, let's ignore everything except the fact that Amber broke into your house. I take it you didn't call the police?"

She shook her head. "I didn't tell my mom about it, either. She doesn't need a new reason to oppose our relationship." She took the

# THIRTY-FOUR

Rick canceled the whale-watching tours the following Saturday due to inclement weather. He told Cara he hadn't seen Crossback and Bobbi or the transient orcas since the attack. Cara said her prayers that the grays were alive and recovering and the transients would finally leave.

The outlet mall struck Cara as the safest place to confide in her mom—the shopping junkie—about Amber.

"Raspberry's my favorite, but sometimes the scent's too strong," her mom said, sniffing at a body lotion. She passed it to Cara. "This one's nice. Smell for yourself."

Cara took the bottle and sniffed, then gave her mom a big smile. "Love it."

Her mom took the bottle and gave Cara a knowing sideways gaze. "That's more enthusiasm than I'd expect from you over a lotion. What gives?"

Cara grabbed another lotion from the shelf, flipped it open, quickly sniffed at it, then began opening and closing the cap. "Remember the day after Halloween when I told you a red Jetta followed me?"

Her mom gave up searching the shelves and looked Cara straight in the eye. "You found out who it was?"

sachet and dropped it in her backpack. "And I can't prove that Amber broke into my house or that she left anything in my room."

His words were firm. "You need to tell both your mom and the police about this, regardless of what anyone else thinks of our relationship."

She sighed. "Okay, but I seriously doubt the police will be able to find any evidence that Amber broke into my house, just like they couldn't find any evidence that she damaged my car."

"At least they'll know she's up to something. And I want you to take your mom's advice about Amber. Don't encourage her anymore."

She opened her mouth in protest. "Amber's the one harassing *me*."

"I know," he said, cuddling her close to his side. "But your mom said that any reinforcement can encourage her behavior. So no more going to her house, for one. Agreed?"

Groaning, Cara watched the thrashing waves in the distance. Amber didn't need any extra motivation. "Agreed."

Cara sighed. "I knew who it was then, too. I just worried that if I told you it would make you more upset about David."

Her mom's lips pursed. "I take it the person was David's stalker?"

Cara nodded. "There's more, though."

Her mom pointed a finger at the shelf behind Cara, instructing her to set down the lotion. "Let's finish this discussion at the deli."

At the other end of the mall, Cara and her mom sat at a small, corner table in Liberty Deli, picking at croissants.

Her mom's tight-lipped expression replaced her smiley shopping one. "Go on."

Cara pulled a flake from her croissant and let it disintegrate on her tongue. "The person who's been harassing me—David's stalker—is a girl who was a senior at Seaside when I was a freshman."

"So you know her?"

"Yeah. Her name's Amber Miller. We both dated Chris Adams when I was a freshman, and she's angry with me because she thinks I stole him from her. I didn't. But now she's trying to steal David from me."

Her mom frowned at her. "I wish you would've shared this with me sooner. I thought it was bad enough that this girl was associated with David. But it sounds like you're her true target."

Cara gritted her teeth. "There's more to tell, I'm sorry to say."

Deep lines creased her mom's forehead.

"Remember how I told you Amber's mixed up with occult stuff like Ouija boards and tarot cards?"

Her mom looked like she was holding back from rolling her eyes as she slowly nodded.

"Amber practices witchcraft. She's been trying to cast breakup spells on David and me. I wouldn't worry about it, except that she broke into our house the other day and left a spell in my room."

Her mom dropped her croissant, brushed off her hands, and clasped them in front of her on the table. "I hope you understand that all this witchcraft and spell nonsense is ridiculous."

Cara didn't respond.

"What's *not* ridiculous is that you say this girl broke into our house. What exactly did she leave in your room?"

Obviously, her mom wasn't going to accept that the occult activities Amber was initiating were dangerous, any more than David had.

Cara grabbed her backpack, pulled out the sachet, and held it up. "I found this on my desk after you and I had both been gone for the day, when you were at the after-Thanksgiving sales." *And I'd been watching Rachel get delivered from a demon.*

Her mom barely gave the sachet a second look. She smashed the rest of her croissant in her napkin and stood. Cara dropped the sachet in her backpack and followed her mom to the garbage to throw their napkins away, then out to the parking lot.

"What does David have to say about all this?" her mom asked as she popped the station wagon's locks.

"He thought it was important for me to tell both you and the police. But I doubt the police will be able to prove that Amber's done anything to harass me."

"David's right," her mom said as they climbed into the Outback. "We need to file another report, like we did for your car. We need to build a case against this girl. Stalkers rarely give up."

# THIRTY-FIVE

Cara helped David clean up after they'd eaten a stir-fry dinner at his place the following Saturday. He went to get their coats. It was earlier than usual for her to head home on a weekend night, even though she always made it a point to get home at a decent hour to encourage her mom's growing acceptance of their relationship. But David had to get up early for his first ocean fishing trip. And her mom was leaving town the next morning for her conference in Seattle.

Cara and David pulled on their hoods and wrapped their arms around each other. Cold, briny air surrounded them as they walked the beach toward Cara's house.

"I hope you don't think it would bother me if you went out sometimes, to the bar or wherever, instead of always hanging out with me," she said.

David's arm hugged tighter around her waist. She looked sideways and caught his lopsided grin.

"Is that what you think I want to do? Escort you home so I can run off to party?"

She bumped him with her hip. "Of course not. But if that's ever what you feel like doing, I want you to know I wouldn't mind."

"That's sweet." He tucked his face under her hood and kissed her cheek. "But I'm not into that scene. Besides, I have a fishing trip scheduled at the crack of dawn."

"I don't envy you that," she said, chuckling. "I'll stick to my not-so-awfully-early whale-watching trip."

"I hope you see Crossback and Bobbi tomorrow."

She hoped so, too.

He walked her up the stairs from the beach to the street and then the few blocks to her house. They reached her front porch and she tensed when he held her to him. Her mom might see.

David showed no signs of worry. He gave her a lingering kiss. "I'll miss you tomorrow. I should be back by early afternoon. Wanna play Scrabble?"

She relaxed in his arms. "Call me when you get back."

"Why don't you hang out at my place when you get back from your tour? Enjoy the view."

"I do enjoy the view."

He gazed down at her with a look that warmed her whole being and erased any fears she had of his ever leaving her.

"Take this, then." He released his hold on her, reached into his back pocket, and held up a key. "This is my only spare. It's yours."

The next morning, behind Cara's curtains, no threatening clouds loomed in the dingy sky. The sea, however, was a torrent of tossing waves. She'd awoken at dawn, though still later than her mom, who'd left early enough to squeeze in a full day of shopping in Seattle. She dressed quickly and grabbed a banana and a granola bar before she climbed into the Fit to head to Liberty Charters.

Before she started the engine, her cell phone rang. It was Sherry. All tours were canceled for the day due to a storm moving in. The larger fishing boats went out, but David might come home early if the captains decided to play it safe.

She chose to walk the beach to David's place. The stretch of ocean was as beautiful as ever, but the sea roared as forceful winds pushed at it. Waves broke and rolled sideways. Veering around the large chunks of seafoam that dotted the beach made her feel like she was on an obstacle course.

She struggled against the winds that pushed at her as they did the waves. Her hood covered her head and she kept her sunglasses on to keep the sand that whipped up out of her hair and eyes. The smell of seaweed swirled in the air and thick, gray clouds rolled in. Good thing the walk wasn't long. No doubt conditions would be rough for David's fishing boat.

Relief from the elements came only when she stood in the shelter of David's portico. She turned the key he gave her in the lock on the front door and a peaceful sense of belonging overcame her. She stepped inside, shut and locked the door behind her, and pulled back her hood to look out the picture window.

The view from David's place always mesmerized her. The panorama was close-up and clear compared to the muted portrayal in the painting in her room or the longer-distance views of the ocean from her house. At the moment, the picture window revealed a more tumultuous scene than usual.

Coupled with the leather scent of the sofas, David's house smelled like a combination of his muskiness and the sea. Those aromas communicated comfort to Cara. They represented her David.

The edge of a Post-it note curled up from the Scrabble box on the dining room table. She walked over, pulled it off, and read, "I miss you." She hugged the note to her chest before she tucked it in her bag. In the kitchen, she opened the fridge. Another note was stuck to a six-pack of diet soda bottles. Again, the note read, "I miss you." She added it to her bag with the first note.

By the time she'd searched the whole house, she'd collected seven notes, all conveying the same message. The last five Post-its were stuck to the French doors to the deck, the big sofa, the TV, David's bedroom pillow, and the bathroom mirror.

After she collected the last note in the bathroom, the front door creaked open. She froze in the hallway. Her skin prickled.

David could have come home early due to a canceled fishing trip. But the person who entered didn't make any noise. Cara was more than a little frightened by who she thought it was.

The hallway was hidden from the living room area, so she was able to quietly sneak down to the coat closet. She thanked God the door didn't make a sound when she opened it and shut herself inside. Not that it would matter if she hid. If it was Amber and if she knew Cara was here, the witch would easily find her in this little shoebox of a house.

Slinking as far back as possible in the small closet, she considered her options for protection. Her backpack hung from her shoulder, but she didn't carry any type of weapon. She unzipped her pack and fumbled for her cell phone in the dark. Her fingers closed around it and she held it up and turned it on. The lit screen allowed her enough visibility to see that the closet's contents included only coats, other outerwear, and footwear.

A heavy pair of boots was the only tool she could find for defense. At least she could call 911. If she had time for that.

The *click-clack* of thin heels came to a stop in the hallway and Cara shut off her phone. Again, darkness surrounded her. She prayed repeatedly that Amber was just here to be her crazy stalker self, to snoop around David's place.

Seconds later, the heels click-clacked again. They were headed her way. Abruptly, the clacking halted, and the hinges on the linen closet door next to her squealed as the door opened.

A couple of metal items tapped against each other before the linen closet door closed again. Cara scooted farther back in the closet, held her breath, and waited for the door that shielded her to swing open.

The heels clacked in the opposite direction. Cara let out a silent sigh. David's home phone rang then, and the clacking stopped.

After three rings, a man's voice blared from a speaker on an older-model answering machine. "David? It's Dad. Are you home?" There was a slight pause. "I hope you're not wasting your time with that girl. I meant it when I said you need to come home. Call me."

The line went dead and a dial tone sounded before the answering machine cut off.

Amber made a grunting sound that might have been a laugh. Then her heels started clacking again. Her footsteps sounded like they were landing on the linoleum in the bathroom. The mirrored vanity cabinet doors squeaked open. Seconds later, the medicine cabinet doors closed with a magnetic *click* and the lower cabinets shut with a thud.

The clacking heels returned to the hardwood in the hallway. Cara again thanked God when the footfalls headed toward David's room, rather than toward her.

Pressing her ear against the door, Cara made out the sound of fabric ripping and Amber's muffled voice. Unless she was imagining it, she could swear she also heard another, lower-pitched voice. She couldn't make out any words.

Holding up her cell phone, she turned on the screen. With a shaky hand, she switched the phone to call mode and poked her pointer finger at the key pad. She hit the 9, but missed the 1. On her second attempt, she clenched her fist tighter and jabbed her finger at the numbers. Her call connected.

"Liberty County 911. What's the exact location of your emergency?"

As if she could speak at the moment. Amber might hear her. And it seemed like a reasonable assumption to think that the authorities could track her by GPS.

Cupping her hand around her mouth, she whispered, "374 Jettison Avenue." She drew the phone away from her ear and listened for any sign that Amber was coming for her.

Amber's voice carried down the hall from David's bedroom. It sounded like she was chanting.

"What's the emergency?" the operator asked.

Again, Cara whispered. "Someone broke into my boyfriend's house."

"Are you at your boyfriend's house now?"

"Yes."

"What's the phone number you're calling from?"

Not understanding how that information could be important enough for her to risk being discovered, she almost didn't answer. But Amber's muffled chanting continued, so she quickly relayed her cell phone number.

"What's your full name?"

"Cara Markwell."

"Are you the only one in the house?"

Other than the intruder. "Yes."

"Are there any weapons in the house?"

Not in the closet, unfortunately. "Not that I know of."

"Okay. Can you tell me exactly what happened?"

Probably not, without the witch hearing.

Amber's chanting had stopped. Heels clacked in the hallway again.

"Ma'am?" the operator asked.

Cara heard fingers tapping on a keyboard on the other end of the line. "Wait," she whispered.

"I'm dispatching police officers to your location. Don't hang up," the operator told her.

The smack of heels sounded against the hardwood. The footfalls faded in the living room, when Amber must have walked on the laydown rug, then picked up again before the front door clunked shut.

Cara's words streamed out in one pent-up breath. "She just left."

"She? So you got a look at the intruder?"

"No, but I heard high heels. I'm sure it was Amber Miller. I filed a report with Officer Taft last week after she broke into my house."

Cara's whole body trembled now as it burned off the excess adrenaline that surged within her, ready to serve her if she chose to run or battle. But she hadn't had the courage to confront Amber. And now she didn't know if she would even be able to leave the closet.

More keyboard tapping sounded on the other end of the phone connection. "Can you tell me exactly what happened?"

Cara was explaining what had occurred since Amber arrived when three loud raps struck the front door.

"Someone's here."

"It's the officers I dispatched. Go ahead and open the door for them. Stay on the line until I tell you to disconnect."

Cara burst out of the stuffy closet and bolted for the front door. Through the peephole, she saw two uniformed officers, a man and a woman. Another cruiser pulled up in front of the house just as Cara opened the door a crack and peeked around it.

"The intruder just left," she told the officers who stood on the porch.

Officer Taft stepped out of his police car and strode up the walkway. "I'll handle this. You two clear the house," he told the other officers, who entered and began a walk-through.

"You're with the officers?" the operator asked.

"Yes. Thank you."

"You can hang up now. I'm disconnecting."

# THIRTY-SIX

Cara shoved her phone in her backpack and breathed a sigh of relief when Officer Taft stopped outside the front door.

"Hello, Cara."

She opened the door wider for him to enter.

He remained on the porch. "This isn't the address we have for you from your last report."

"This is my boyfriend's house."

"We'll need to talk to him. Is he here?"

"No."

"Where was he during the alleged break-in?"

*Alleged* sounded accusatory, but she chalked it up to standard procedure.

"He's out fishing."

The other officers came back through the living room, exited the house, and told Officer Taft all was clear.

He excused them and turned to Cara. "Until we talk to the person who lives here, you'll need to keep off the property."

Again, this was likely protocol, but it felt abrupt.

The other officers took off in their cruiser.

"Let me lock up," Cara said, and dug her keychain out of her backpack.

"Where did you get the key to the house?" Officer Taft asked as Cara twisted it in the doorknob.

She suppressed a huff. He could be at least a tad more sympathetic after what she'd just been through. "David gave it to me."

"Your boyfriend? The one who lives here?"

"Yes." She turned to face him.

He pulled out a small notepad and a pen. "What's his full name?"

"David Wilson."

He jotted that down. Noting her unstable steps, he stowed the notebook in his pocket and took hold of her elbow to help her down the stairs. "Why don't you have a seat in my car?"

She held back for a second. Sitting in a police car sounded more like punishment than protection.

"Unless you'd rather sit in your own vehicle?" he asked as they continued toward the street. The air had stilled, but the threatening storm clouds remained.

"I walked here."

He appraised her as he opened the passenger side of his cruiser. "Let me give you a ride home, then."

She slipped into the passenger seat and looked up at him as he asked, "What were you doing here while your boyfriend was out fishing?"

His face looked as neutral as his tone.

"David thought I'd like to enjoy the view until he got back."

Officer Taft didn't comment. He shut her door and walked around to the driver's side. She glanced around at the intimidating array of electronics in the car, as well as the steel-mesh and bulletproof partition between the front and back, and especially the huge rifle mounted just behind and between the two front seats. Following Officer Taft's lead, she fastened her seat belt.

As he started the engine and pulled away from the curb, he asked, "Did you get a look at the intruder today?"

"No. But like I told the 911 operator, I heard high heels. I'm sure it was Amber, the girl I filed a report about last week."

He readjusted his grip on the steering wheel. "Why don't you tell me exactly what happened?"

Cara described all she'd heard.

Officer Taft remained silent until he parked in front of her house. "We'll need to contact Mr. Wilson."

She nodded and unbuckled her seat belt. David was the one who'd insisted she involve the police. It was good that he'd get to hear about Amber's antics from the authorities this time.

"I'll be in touch if we need anything more from you."

She thanked him and stepped out of the car.

"Thanks for your cooperation," he said as she closed the cruiser door.

He watched her as she walked up the walkway to her house and opened the front door. She turned to wave at him, but he drove off without another look in her direction.

# THIRTY-SEVEN

Cara locked her front door, leaned against it, and called David. His voicemail message came on. Her shoulders relaxed. Even his recorded voice soothed her.

After the beep she said, "Call me when you can. I'm at my house. I'd love for you to come over here tonight. You need to have your locks changed."

David called soon after, in a panic. "What happened? Why didn't you stay at my place?"

"I'll tell you about it when you get here."

Despite her fearful memories from that morning, she'd calmed down since then and didn't want to upset David. But she also didn't plan to hang out at his place alone again. Ever.

"I'll come over after I wash up."

His other line buzzed.

"I'll be waiting," she said. "And I missed you, too."

David showed up on Cara's doorstep a couple of hours later, fresh from washing up after his fishing trip. Wearing a tight smile, he ran his hand through his wet hair.

She took his arm and pulled him inside. "Did Amber do something at your place?" she asked as she led him upstairs to the entertainment room.

He stopped in the middle of the room. "Nothing that I noticed. I got a phone call from an Officer Taft."

She sat him down with her on the futon. "He came to your house after Amber's break-in and drove me home. He's the same officer I talked to last week."

"How did Amber get into my house?"

"I don't know." Cara had never figured out how Amber had gotten into her house, either. "Maybe I forgot to lock the front door."

David exhaled long and hard. "Officer Taft told me Amber has also reported you for harassing her and for trying to break into her house."

Cara leaned back and gawked at him. "She did *what?*"

"She filed reports against you. The police wondered if you might be fabricating things."

"They think I'm lying?"

He held her hand. "No, I don't think they really think that. Not after I set them straight, anyway."

Cara wasn't so sure. Amber might have cast some spells at the police station.

David tugged her hand.

She gritted her teeth.

His expression turned serious. "Don't let Amber's games get you down. She doesn't deserve our attention."

"Amen to that." She sighed and mussed his hair. "Want to watch a movie?"

"Sure," he said and leaned back against the futon.

"What flavor?"

"Your choice."

From the lower cabinet of the armoire against the opposite wall, she selected a thriller and inserted it in the player. She brought David the remote and he set it down on the futon. He took both her hands in his, which felt like soft heating pads.

"Did you hear my dad's message?" he asked.

She nodded.

"I hope you won't dislike him for it."

"I didn't completely understand it, actually."

"Remember when you found me on the beach by Surfseekers, after my dad and I had an argument?"

"Yeah?"

"That argument was about you."

She tried to make sense of that. "We weren't together then."

"I'd told my dad about my feelings for you. He wasn't happy to hear it. And at this point, I think he's worried I'll run off with you and he'll hardly ever see me again."

"He knows you're moving to Seattle, right?"

"Yeah. But he's still trying to control me financially."

"You can always get financial aid if you need to. And Seattle isn't far from the Tri-Cities. You'll be able to visit your dad as often as you want to."

"He thinks he and I will both be happier if I stay in Richland. But that's not what I want. He needs to get used to the idea that I'm moving on with my life. That's the only way he can move on with his."

His last statement spoke to her. "You could say the same thing about my mom."

"I could see that," he said, and shared his lopsided grin with her. "Once again, we prove to be a good match."

She waved him up to help her let the futon down into a full-size mattress. "No sign of Crossback or Bobbi out there today?"

He frowned. "No, but we weren't near their feeding grounds long." She frowned back.

"Don't worry," he said, and lay down on his back on the futon mattress. "I just know they'll show up."

He turned on his side and used the remote to work on starting the movie. She held up her finger for him to wait for her, then went to the linen closet to grab a pillow for him. On the way back, she stopped in her room to grab her own pillow.

As the movie started, she set the pillows on the futon and curled up against David's side. Her hand traveled up his chest. She felt a few hairs poking out of his shirt, near his neck, and couldn't resist the urge to touch them.

She reached under his tee. He tensed when she touched his abdomen, then relaxed when her hand moved up and her fingers ran over his chest. Though minimal, the hair intrigued her. She tugged his flannel top and T-shirt up, but he pulled them back down.

"I'll behave." She sat up and pouted down at him. "Please?"

He groaned, sat up, and pulled the shirts over his head. "Let's have you keep your top on though, okay?" He smiled, but his tone was serious.

He lay back down, with his head turned sideways to watch the movie. She let his soft hairs caress her cheek. His clean, minty muskiness smelled stronger than ever, and yearnings she still needed to gain better control over built up within her.

Practice helped. She breathed in his fragrance and continued to explore with her hand, not paying any attention to the television screen. Her head rose and dipped down with the rise and fall of his breaths.

She must have fallen asleep, because when she opened her eyes, he was sitting next to her, palming her forehead.

"Cara? You're shivering. Are you all right?"

He'd set her head on her pillow and wrapped her in the quilt from her room. She couldn't stop shaking and a dull pain throbbed in the middle of her forehead. When she moved, her stomach clenched, and she worried she might throw up.

"I don't feel so good." The heat turned up inside her.

"You must have caught something."

She held her limp arms out to hug him. He leaned down to embrace her and kissed the top of her head.

"Please stay with me," she said, clinging to him.

"Do you want to move to your bed?"

"Can we please sleep in my mom's room?"

"Your *mom's* room?"

"It's closer to a bathroom."

He only hesitated for a second. "Right."

He carried her down the hall with her pillow and quilt. In the master bedroom, he settled her on her mom's bed, tucked her pillow under her head, and rearranged the covers. She shoved off the quilt, wriggled out of her jeans, and rolled into a ball on her side. He curled his body around hers.

She woke later, needing to vomit. Her stomach heaved and a stream of bile seared her throat and dribbled onto her pillowcase. David sat up to help her, but she eased his hand off her waist, flung her pillow at the bedroom door, and rushed to the master bathroom.

The feeling that she needed to throw up passed as she knelt in front of the toilet. She pushed herself up and went back to the master bedroom. David sat up in the bed. She waved for him to stay there, grabbed her vomit-soiled pillow from the floor by the door, and staggered down the hall to her bedroom.

When she flicked on her bedroom light switch, the brightness blinded her. Shooting pain stabbed her in the middle of the forehead and her stomach gurgled. She feared she'd have to rush back to the bathroom.

Walking across the room, she swayed on her feet. She opened the closet door and continued to clutch the doorknob when she tossed her pillow in the hamper. A couple of deep breaths eased her nausea. She flipped the light off on her way out of her room and stood still again in the hall until her eyes adjusted to the dark.

Her dizziness passed. She made a quick stop in the main bathroom to brush her teeth.

Back in her mom's room, she grabbed one of the pillows propped against the bed's headboard and lay down with her head on it. David cuddled close to her side and draped his arm across her waist. Now she felt fine. In fact, she was certain she'd never felt better.

Cara woke to something soft brushing her cheek. Sitting by her side, David stared down at her and ran his fingers along her face.

"How are you feeling?" he asked.

"Much better." She sat up and smoothed her messy hair. "You're not leaving, are you?"

"You have school in an hour."

"But I've been sick."

"You don't feel well enough to go?"

"I guess I do. But I'd rather stay with you."

He shook his head and stood. "I'm not going to have your mom find out you skipped school to hang out with me while she was out of town. If you feel well enough to go, you should go."

Cara grimaced, swung her legs over the side of the bed, and got up. "Fine, I'll go."

# THIRTY-EIGHT

Before first period, Cara stood outside her trig classroom and texted David:

> I'm hoping you'll come to my place again after school?

David still hadn't texted her back when lunch hour came. She dumped the textbooks that filled her backpack in her locker and sat down with Garren and Rachel. She'd neglected to bring a lunch. Thankfully, ever-reliable Garren hadn't forgotten her apple and Rachel was willing to share her pita bread and hummus.

"What's got you so upset?" Rachel asked, watching Cara's hands as she juggled her apple and her phone.

"David spent the night with me for the first time last night."

Rachel glanced at Garren. "Um, that sounds like a conversation we should save for a private moment?"

Cara shook her head and checked her phone for any new messages. Nothing. "It's not like that. I felt sick. He took care of me."

"Then what's the problem?" Rachel asked.

"I texted him this morning and he hasn't gotten back to me."

Garren steadied her hand that fumbled with her cell. "Maybe he's sick now, too, and isn't paying attention to his phone."

"Maybe," Cara conceded. But something felt off to her, something more than David possibly feeling sick.

After lunch, she ditched school and drove to David's house. His truck sat in its usual spot in the driveway. She parked on the street out front and hurried up his front steps, then paused on the porch. The door could be unlocked, and his house key hung on the key chain in her pocket, but she was arriving unannounced.

She knocked. No answer. The door was locked, so she used the key. Inside, she was surrounded by silence. The curtains were drawn over the picture window, draping the interior in a dreary darkness.

She slowly made her way across the living room and drew the curtains open. Milky white light from an overcast sky poured over David, where he lay huddled under a blanket on the couch. His face was pale, except for the shadows under his eyes. He shivered like she had the night before.

Sitting on the edge of the couch beside him, she placed her hand on his forehead. A sheen of cool sweat covered his skin. He let out a soft sigh. She removed her hand, sat up straight, and looked down at him. He didn't look at her.

"I texted you and got worried when I didn't hear back. You look like I felt last night. But I bet you'll get over this quick, like I did."

He didn't comment.

"Did you eat or drink anything today?"

Still, he didn't respond. She went to the fridge and pushed aside diet soda bottles and milk and orange juice cartons to pull out a sports drink. Uncapping it, she brought it over to him.

"Sit up and take a few sips of this."

He pulled himself up, accepted the bottle, and took a small sip. She sat next to him.

He still didn't look at her. "You should be at school." His voice was a weak monotone.

"My mom can't blame you for my cutting a few classes. I'm a senior and I get good grades. Besides, I was sick last night. And you took care of me. Now you need someone to take care of you."

He took a bigger sip of the sports drink. "I'm fine. You should be in school." He set the drink bottle on the coffee table, pushed himself up off the couch, and hobbled to the bathroom.

She heard him retching and wanted to go comfort him, but his uncharacteristic behavior toward her since she'd arrived left her uncertain how to react.

His torture ended and tap water splashed in the bathroom sink. The water shut off and he came back to collapse in a sitting position against the arm of the couch. She covered him with a blanket. He shoved it off.

"I need to apologize to you," he said, not looking at her.

The tether between them grew frigid. "Apologize?"

"I was wrong to get involved with a high school student."

Now the tether became a heavy, icy weight attached to her chest. "What are you saying?"

She touched his hand. A fraction of warmth seeped through. His eyebrows pulled together and, for a second, he looked like he didn't remember what he meant to say.

He pulled away from her touch and shook his head. "I didn't mean to hurt you. I'm sorry. Please leave."

Standing, she stared down at him, speechless. Her frozen heart fused with the tether. Any minute now he would start to make some sense. He couldn't have just told her that what had happened between them was a mistake.

She desperately clung to the possibility that his sickness was disorienting him. He got up and limped off toward his bedroom. In a zombielike state, she walked out, dropped into the driver's seat of her car, and left him.

Near a little-known access point at Boulder Beach, she parked on a side street and let her tears flow freely. Exhaustion overcame her. She pushed her arms into the sleeves of her jacket, then pulled the heavy wool blanket from the emergency kit in the back of her Fit.

Garren had persuaded her to create the kit, in case a natural disaster occurred when she moved to Seattle, like the major earthquake that was decades overdue. The ensemble scared Cara more than relieved her because it suggested tragedy in waiting. But now she was grateful for it.

In a similar way, the temperate weather conditions reminded her of the calm before a storm. Stillness hung in the air, making her feel like she was stuck in limbo.

On the beach, she chose a spot not far from the stairs. An automatic brief scan of the ocean's relatively still surface didn't reveal any whale activity. She spread the blanket on the sand and crumpled down on it, using her backpack as a pillow. Hugging her knees, she balled up on her side.

She hoped sleep would come easy, so she could avoid rehashing what had just happened. When she thought of how quickly and easily David broke off their relationship, she was reminded of Chris doing the same thing, and her father leaving her mom. Her air supply seemed to cut off. But she couldn't accept that David, the mature, loving guy who had risked his career and his reputation to be with her in the first place, the only guy she'd ever felt a *providential* connection with, would suddenly stop caring for her.

Amber had to be involved. Still, whatever the reason for David's behavior, Cara couldn't deny that he'd rejected her. She curled up in a tighter ball on the blanket and tried to let the sea hypnotize her. A fresh stream of tears tracked down her face. She closed her eyes and the murmur of the ocean lulled her to sleep.

Her eyes blinked open sometime later and she caught a glimpse of a towering, black dorsal fin cutting through the water, not far from shore. Pushing up onto her knees, she saw the transient orca's snout lift, as if it was acknowledging her, before it dove underwater and lobtailed, slapping its tail flukes against the surface of the water.

Cara glared out to sea, angered that the transients hadn't left, not wanting to dwell on what they'd done to Crossback and Bobbi, and especially not wanting to accept that there was nothing she could do about any of it.

At home, she couldn't remember the drive back to her house or how she'd made it to her bedroom, she'd been mired in such a fog of despair. Her pillow was missing from her bed, so she went to her mom's room to grab another one. She picked up the pillow David had used and pressed it to her face. The scents of his muskiness and his mint shampoo brought on a fresh crop of tears. She took the pillow to her room and buried herself under her covers with it.

The next morning, Cara woke at 4:00 a.m. and the horrible reality of the previous day threatened to suffocate her. The tether felt irreversibly frozen. She squeezed her eyes shut and lay still until sleep mercifully fell over her again.

When she next woke, it was to her alarm clock beeping an hour before school began. The clear, quiet voice in her head told her to go to her classes. School actually sounded like the perfect distraction. Only, she doubted she could make it through the day without breaking down.

There might not be anything she could do to change David's mind about breaking up with her. But she held on to the hope that he'd only rejected her because Amber had cast some spell on him. In that case, Cara just needed to find a way to break it.

She washed the tear-stained streaks from her face, brushed her hair, and got dressed. Food didn't seem appealing, so she skipped breakfast and headed out. When she turned the Fit down David's block, she stomped on the brake pedal. His truck sat in the driveway, as she'd anticipated. What she didn't expect to see against the curb in front of his place was a red Jetta.

She pulled over and parked a few doors away, then ran down the street and up David's steps to beat on his door. There was no answer. She twisted the doorknob, but it was locked. So she flipped through her keys, slipped the one David had given her into the lock, and let herself in.

Stepping into the entryway, her eyes fell on Amber, who stood in front of the couch, clothed from head to toe in body-hugging black. Cara stood, paralyzed, for several moments before she forced her feet to move and carry her over to face the witch.

From where he sat on the couch, David spoke to Amber. "Take it easy on her."

Amber cocked her head to the side. Her hands clutched her hips and her lips twisted into a familiar, mocking grin as she looked Cara over.

Cara's pulse raced so fast she worried she'd pass out. "What are you doing here?"

Amber might as well have slapped Cara across the face when she looked to David to answer Cara's question.

"I need to commit to a more appropriate relationship," he said, his eyes never leaving Amber. "I never gave Amber a fair chance."

Cara couldn't imagine how Amber could've stolen David away so easily, spell or not, particularly in the short time between yesterday and this morning. She reminded herself again how Garren said breakup spells only worked on weak relationships. The bond between her and David had seemed so strong.

She wished she had enough control over her emotions and her voice to yell at Amber. Instead, sadness, anger, and fear worked together to choke her and her words came out in a whisper. "What did you do to him?"

"So sorry if your feelings are hurt," Amber said, slinking onto the sofa beside David. She placed a hand on his thigh. "I told you to leave David alone. You should have listened. Now go home and get some rest. You don't look so good."

David's dazed eyes remained on Amber. He knew the witch had cast breakup spells to attempt to destroy their relationship—like the sachet spell—even if he didn't believe those spells could be effective. If Cara could only remind him, convince him of what Amber must be doing, he might snap out of it.

"David, look at me," she said. The tears she sniffed back amplified her pleading tone.

His cloudy eyes looked past her. She reached out to touch his hand. Before she could make contact with him, Amber grabbed her wrist, shot up from the couch, and dragged her by the arm to the front door.

Amber jerked the door open and twisted Cara's arm behind her back, nearly lifting her off her feet. With a flick of her wrist, Amber flung her onto the porch.

As Amber slammed the door, she cautioned, "I told you I would only warn you once."

# THIRTY-NINE

For the second time that day, Cara felt a strong inner urge to go to school. A public meltdown still felt inevitable, though. So she drove down to the same spot at Boulder Beach she'd visited the day before. No whales today, which was a relief. Another episode of a transient taunting her might send her over the edge. She spread out her blanket, lay down, and let the ebb and flow of the surf numb her.

A loud smack sounded in her ears at the same time that a heavy blow landed on top of her skull. White spots bloomed against black behind her eyes and a piercing pain erupted at the top of her head. A warm trickle spread down her scalp. She reached up to feel the spot. Her fingers tangled in a mass of wet, sticky hair.

Someone strong flipped her onto her stomach and she screamed for help as a cloth wrapped around her eyes and was tied behind her pounding head. Still screaming, she jerked over onto her back. Her attacker sat on top of her. She blindly kicked at the air.

Rough cloth gagged her, cutting off her screams. Then gloved hands grabbed her arms and pulled them together in front of her. Fabric crossed back and forth between her wrists. Her legs were bound at the ankles.

A pair of slender arms lifted her effortlessly and carried her like a baby across the sand and up a set of stairs. She strained to wrestle free, but the tiny arms held her solidly. Her tongue pushed and pulled at the gag in her mouth until she loosened it enough to breathe more easily.

Her sense of smell improved. Amber's fragrance wafted all around her. The strong combination of vanilla, oranges, and cloves mixed with sulfur and something like moss.

They ascended the stairs and Cara's weight transferred from one of Amber's petite arms to the other. On level ground, Cara was slung over Amber's shoulder. A key twisted in metal and a *pop* sounded as a trunk opened. Cara tumbled onto a prickly carpet that grazed her cheek. A final rush of salty air blew in before the trunk door banged shut. The odors of dirt and what smelled like spoiled meat closed in on her.

She couldn't figure how it was possible for Amber to have carried her so far and to have shifted her around with such little effort. Then she recalled Amber's unnatural strength when she flung her out of David's house.

The driver's door opened and closed, the car's engine started, and they began moving. Cara tried to gather her scattered thoughts. A reenactment show came to mind. She remembered an episode she'd seen about a woman who was captured and thrown into a trunk. The woman had kicked out a taillight and waved her hand out the opening to attract attention. She was saved by an onlooker's tipoff to police.

Cara was not only bound, but also blindfolded. The odds of her finding the taillight, kicking it out, and getting both of her feet or hands through the small space were slim. But she had to try something. Because whatever torture Amber planned for her, it surely wouldn't be pleasant.

It was difficult to shift to another position in such a cramped space. She hadn't even accomplished that when the car came to a stop. The trunk flew open and cool air blew in, clearing away the stifling scents of decay she'd been boxed in with. Amber lifted her out of the trunk and once again cradled and carried her as if she were weightless.

A door creaked open and swung shut behind them. Inside, Cara was overcome by more foul odors. The scents of lit matches and burnt wax assaulted her. She also thought she recognized sage by the smell of dried leaves.

The scents muddled together. This had to be the sorcery house. Her stomach pitched and she heaved against the cloth that gagged her.

She'd anticipated being shut up in a closet, or worse. Instead, she was settled on top of a soft mattress. Cord wrapped over her waist and chest, thighs, and ankles, and cinched her against the bed. With that restraint in place, she started to give up any hope of escape.

The cloth in her mouth was yanked out and her sense of smell went into overdrive. The room she lay in reeked of dirty feet. Amber's gloved hands squeezed her mouth open and a few objects fell on her tongue. Two poked like thick little twigs, one felt smooth. The taste was sickeningly sweet.

Knowing anything Amber gave her must be harmful, she held the items between her teeth so they wouldn't dissolve on her tongue. Something rustled on the other side of the room. She turned her head and spit the objects out. They slid down her cheek and behind her neck. She turned her face upward again as the rustling stopped.

Amber shoved the cloth gag back in Cara's mouth. Cara thrashed against her restraints, but couldn't break free. A buzz of panic built up inside her and she centered her attention on it, hoping to use her fear and a sense of self-preservation to help her remain strong.

A fresh, sharp pain shot across her scalp as fabric swiped across the spot on her head where she'd been hit. Amber left the room, shut the door, and began chanting something Cara couldn't decipher. Or maybe she was talking to someone else—a man, by the sound of it. Just like she had at David's house, Cara was sure she heard two distinct voices.

The door opened again and the mattress beneath Cara lifted and flopped back into place. Again, the door closed. The last sounds she heard were the squeal of the front door as it opened and a banging as it slammed shut.

As Cara jerked her legs against her bindings, one of her sneakers slipped off. She used her sock-covered foot to pry off her other shoe and peeled her socks off with her toes. The ties around her ankles felt looser. She moved her feet up and down in a sawing motion. The rough denim of her jeans chafed at her calves and the skin on her ankles burned with every movement of her legs.

She thrust her weight upward and to the left, hoping to slide the mattress onto the floor. It flung up and wobbled, threatening to flip over. If it did, it could smother her. She made a shorter thrust with her legs instead. The mattress made a sideways jump.

As she continued to maneuver sideways with smaller movements, sweat broke out on her forehead and upper lip and she panted for breath. She figured she'd managed to shift the bottom of the mattress at least halfway off the boxspring. But her escape was taking too long. Amber might come back and catch her.

Sawing with her legs again, faster this time, she ignored the pain that felt like razor blades slicing against her skin. Her heels dug into the mattress, trying to make room between her ankles and the cord cutting into them. She yanked her feet apart once, twice, three times, and finally was able to pull half of her left foot out of the cord. Her toes crushed together, but she continued to pull up with her foot until she thought the bones there would break.

Her foot burst free. She lifted it and threw her free leg sideways, then drove it downward. The mattress bent at the bottom and slid off the boxspring at an angle, so the corner came to rest on the floor. She continued to press down with her leg, until her toes brushed the spongy carpet. One more stretch and both her feet set down firmly. The bindings across her legs, waist and chest slackened enough with the mattress's new angle that she was able to squirm out of them.

She used her bound hands to pull the gag from her mouth, but she couldn't reach the knot behind her head to remove her blindfold. Like she had with her legs, she sawed with her forearms, but the fabric around her wrists was stubborn. She used her teeth to loosen the knot.

Once her hands were separated, she removed her blindfold. Her eyes quickly adjusted to the room's dim gray light. She was fully free.

Leaning down to grab her shoes, she spotted something that looked like a dead bird on the box spring. Her stomach constricted just looking at it. She held her breath to stave off the dirty sock smell in the room and moved toward the window.

Through a part in the drapes, she saw a dishwater sky dumping rivers of rain. No one was in sight, but her view of the street was blocked so she didn't know whether the Jetta might be parked there. For all she knew, Amber could have returned.

Cara needed to be quiet. But after she unlocked the window, she found that it was stuck and she had to wrench up on it. The wood groaned loudly and the frame only budged a couple of inches. She had no choice but to bang up on it with her palms. There was a loud cracking sound, and finally the window slid open.

Amber hadn't burst through the bedroom door, thank God, so she must still be gone—probably at David's. Shaking the thought from her mind, Cara jumped out into the side yard and sucked in deep breaths of fresh air as she ran from the house. Her feet were bare, her shoes clasped in her hands.

A safe distance away, she realized her feet were freezing. She sat on a curb and slipped on her soaked sneakers. Several drivers twisted around to peer at her, but no one stopped.

She remembered her car was still at the beach. And Amber had her backpack, which held her keys. She sprinted home.

# FORTY

Parked in a row in front of Cara's house were Garren's Silverado, Rachel's Corolla, and Ethan's Malibu. The front door was locked, so Cara rang the bell.

Rachel flung the door open, grasped Cara by the shoulders, and turned her from side to side, inspecting her. "What happened to you? And where's your car?"

Cara couldn't respond as she adjusted to the added shock that her house wasn't empty. Rachel pulled her into a hard hug and shut and locked the front door behind them.

Garren appeared at Cara's side. She leaned against him and he supported her weight and steered her into the family room. Rachel wrapped a throw blanket around her shoulders and sat her down on the couch. Garren sat on one side of her, Rachel sat on the other. Ethan was seated in her mom's spot on the love seat.

"The school got a hold of your mom when you missed classes, so she called looking for you. I told her I didn't know where you were," Rachel said. Her expression grew pained when she continued. "She said she talked to David and he told her he broke up with you."

Cara closed her eyes to brace herself against the misery those words brought on and nodded, not sure if she could explain the ordeal she'd been through.

"Your mom's on her way home from Seattle. My mom's working, but she excused me from school so I could try to find you."

Cara opened her eyes and sorted through her scrambled mind. "Amber found me at the beach and tried to knock me out. Then she took me to her house and tied me up." She touched the top of her head and winced. The resulting, searing pain reminded her of her capture. "I escaped. I should call the police. But last time I reported Amber they thought I was making things up."

"I wouldn't doubt that Amber spread some of her magick over at Liberty PD," Ethan said.

Rachel stood in front of Ethan and blocked his view of Cara.

"Amber filed complaints against me," Cara said.

"Does she know you got away?" Rachel asked.

"I don't think so. She left." Cara blinked back the tears that pooled in her eyes. "She's probably at David's. He said he was going to give a relationship with her a chance."

"She must have cast a spell on him," Rachel said.

"That's what I was hoping," Cara said and looked to Garren. "But you said breakup spells only work on weak relationships."

"The spell on David wouldn't have been a divisive or breakup spell," Garren said.

"It would have been an infatuation or binding spell," Rachel added.

*Like the spell Amber cast on Chris. Before he killed himself. The spell Amber said she couldn't reverse.*

Both hope and horror surged through Cara. She brushed tears from her eyes and imagined the cold, heavy tether lightening and warming as she struggled to remain optimistic that David might return to his normal self, that he could be saved.

"What do we need to do to break the spell?" Cara asked.

Ethan looked like he wanted to speak up, but Rachel silenced him with a threatening look.

Cara looked to Garren.

"We need to put an end to all the spells, including the ones Amber cast on you," Garren said. "The first thing we need to do is find the objects she placed spells on, so we can destroy them during a deliverance ritual."

"What if she cast spells we don't know about?" Cara asked. "And what if she put away the items from the breakup spell I saw at her house?"

"You don't need to worry about the breakup spells," Garren said. "Those spells weren't effective. It's the other spells Amber cast on you that we need to worry about."

"What other spells?" Cara asked.

Garren's eyes flashed a fierce blue. "Destruction spells."

Cara's stomach felt like it dropped to her feet when realization hit. "Amber's trying to kill me?"

"The spells can be broken," Garren said, his eyes softening as hers grew wider.

"She'd have to leave objects for death curses somewhere near you. We're thinking she left something here at your house," Rachel said. "In your pillow or under your mattress, and that's why you were sick the other night."

Cara thought back to how she'd felt feverish and nauseated. She'd been using her pillow. After she'd vomited on it, she'd left it in her hamper. "I think you're right about the pillow. I stopped using mine the night I was sick and then I felt better. I'll go get it."

She jumped up and wobbled on her feet as her head spun.

Holding her elbow, Garren helped her up the stairs. He waited in the hallway while she went to her room and grabbed her pillow from the hamper in her closet.

As she turned to leave, she spotted an envelope on her desk, in the same spot Amber had left the sachet. Creases covered the outside and lumps formed where hard objects poked from within. Cara picked it up and something lightweight slid around inside. Her fingers made out a connection of hard, thin, curved objects.

She remembered Garren's warning not to open any envelopes. But the urge was strong. Lifting it to the light, she couldn't see through it to make out any distinct shapes.

"I'll take those, if you want, before they make you sick." Garren stood at the door.

Dizziness caused Cara to sway as she walked over to him to give him the pillow and envelope. He stepped forward to meet her, took the items, and held her arm to help her down the hall and stairs.

In the family room, Ethan remained on the love seat while Rachel paced in front of the couch. Garren sat down with Cara.

She stared at her normal-looking though stained pillow. "Can you show me what Amber did?" she asked Garren.

He nodded and pulled off Cara's pillow case. There was a jagged tear in the pillow's lining that was crudely sewn back up with thick, white thread. When Garren ripped the pillow open, Cara's stomach rolled.

The object closely resembled the thing that looked like a dead bird under the mattress at Amber's house. Dark hair and feathers wound around a white swatch of fabric that appeared to be smeared with dried blood. Small pieces of wood, beads, and black thread surrounded the fabric.

"Spells are placed on objects that include personal belongings, so a certain person will fall victim to the spell's purpose," Garren said. "Usually, the person gets sick first. Then the spell takes a stronger hold."

He touched the hair first. "This is yours."

Next, he fingered the white fabric. "This is probably from a piece of your underwear."

Finally, he pointed to the dried smear. "And this is most likely your blood."

Cara grimaced at him. "How would Amber get my blood?"

"There are ways. Having a victim's blood to work with makes a spell much more effective."

Cara touched her head, where she'd been hit and Amber had swiped at it, and winced at the sting. "Amber put something under the mattress she tied me to that looked just like this. She also tried to feed me something like pills or twigs, but I spit them out."

Ethan chimed in. "She must have been trying to sedate you, to make sure you'd be exposed to the cursed object long enough. Did the stuff she fed you smell funny?"

"The whole room smelled like stinky feet. Whatever she fed me tasted sweet." Cara grew more nauseated by the second, just thinking of all the disgusting smells she'd been subjected to. Her stomach made a miniheave. She closed her mouth and swallowed.

"That would be the herb valerian," Ethan said.

Rachel's mouth bunched up with irritation while he spoke, like she was holding back from telling him to shut up.

"Valerian works like a sedative," Ethan continued. "Amber probably gave you something stronger, too. Good thing you spit it out."

Cara turned back to Garren. "Amber took my bag, and my car

keys are in it. I didn't look for it before I left, but there should be a window open on the side of the house. Would you go over there and look for it for me? As long as she's still gone?"

Garren stood. "Of course. I'll get the other object she placed there, too. Ethan can come with me and we'll try to find your backpack so we can get your car."

Cara hoped Amber hadn't taken her bag somewhere else. Or that she hadn't gone back to the house and grabbed it. It wouldn't be a good thing if the witch found her missing.

"What if Amber comes looking for me?" Cara asked.

"We obviously won't let her in," Rachel said.

"She hasn't needed an invitation before," Cara said. "And locks don't seem to stop her."

"I forgot," Rachel said. "Amber said spells for breaking into places are simple ones. She never taught me any of them, though."

"Me, neither," Ethan said, shrugging.

Cara turned to Garren. Her eyes were drawn to the white package still clasped in his fist. "Can you show me what's in the envelope?" she asked him.

Garren's jaw tightened. "Quickly." He peeled it open and pulled out what looked like a necklace made of small, curved sticks.

Cara leaned closer for a better look, but her stomach seized up, warning her not to get too close to the thing. The object resembled a rosary. From the bottom, rather than a crucifix, there hung what looked like an upside-down cross. The centerpiece was a small skull with fangs.

"What is that?" Cara asked.

"It's devoted to a death curse Amber intended for you," Garren said.

Cara's stomach flopped. "What's it made out of?"

"Snake bones."

She looked at Garren with pleading eyes. "Can you help me break the death spells?"

Garren's jaw loosened and his lips turned up into a soft smile. "A deliverance ritual should take care of all the spells." He slid the ominous necklace back in the envelope.

Cara wondered what a deliverance ritual was exactly, but her concern shifted to David. "Amber must have put something in David's pillow, too. We need to get it."

Ethan rose from the love seat. "Amber's not going to let you see David."

"I can wait until she leaves his place," Cara said.

"What makes you think David will give you his pillow?" Ethan asked.

Cara faltered, but maintained her resolve. "I have to try to help him."

"The best thing would be to exorcize Amber's demon," Garren said.

"Amber summoned the demon to get revenge against Cara," Rachel said. "She's not going to let us perform an exorcism on her."

"The demon of vengeance," Garren said, as if he were referring to a familiar enemy. "A powerful one. It would have a good deal of control over Amber if she summoned it. There's no guarantee it could be exorcised."

Ethan rubbed his jaw, thinking. "If Cara can get David to go with her to the beach, I'll bet I can get Amber to follow."

Cara's hope soared.

"Whatever happens," Garren said, his focus on Cara, "we need to perform the deliverance ritual and destroy the cursed objects to ensure that Amber's spells are broken."

"How do we perform the ritual?" Cara asked.

"I'll explain it to you later." He waved Ethan over to follow him. "We shouldn't waste any time."

# FORTY-ONE

The front door closed behind Garren and Ethan and Rachel ran over to lock it. She came back, sat next to Cara on the couch, and lightly picked at her blood-crusted, matted-down hair. "You should get cleaned up while we wait for the guys to come back."

Cara shook her head. A shower sounded too leisurely at a time like this.

"There's nothing we can do until they get back anyway," Rachel said. "If Amber comes, I'll call the cops. They can catch her in the act if she tries to break in."

*Good luck with that.*

"Your mom should be home soon, too. If she gets here before you're done, I'll let her know what's happening."

*That oughta be good.*

"Otherwise, I'll have my mom call her."

*Even better.*

It would be next to impossible to make Cara's mom believe all the supernatural craziness going on in Liberty.

Giving in to the temptation of a shower, Cara took a quick one, gently washing the blood from her hair and ignoring the sting of her scalp and the burning around her ankles. When she was dressed, she sat against her headboard with her laptop and did a search for "deliverance prayers." The first result sounded like the same prayer Garren had taught her during Rachel's exorcism. She printed three copies, folded them into small squares, and shoved them in her pocket.

She made it downstairs just before Garren and Ethan returned.

Garren held out an apple for her. "You look hungry."

She'd skipped breakfast and should be starving, but she didn't have an appetite. The apples Garren gave her were too good to turn down, though. She accepted his offering and took a bite. Sweet and delicious as ever, she could swear one bite of the fruit infused her with energy.

"I found the cursed object Amber left for you at her house," Garren told her.

"Amber hadn't been back?" she asked.

"It didn't look like it," Garren answered. "Your backpack was in the corner of the room you were left in." He slung it off his shoulder and handed it to her. "Ethan drove your car back from Boulder Beach."

She set her backpack down. "How did you know what beach I went to?"

"It's the most secluded," Garren said.

He knew her too well.

"It's also a good spot for the deliverance ritual," he continued.

"When do we need to do that?" she asked.

"As soon as possible. Here's the plan. I'll get Archbishop Egan to help get the things we need. Ethan can wait until you and Rachel leave David's house. Then he can try to get Amber to come with him to the beach. I'll be waiting there with the supplies and the archbishop," Garren told her.

Cara smirked. "What are you gonna do, teleport the archbishop there?"

Garren shook his head and chuckled. "He's vacationing here. He wanted to make sure everything went smoothly with the exorcisms."

"Oh." *How conveniently generous of him.* "So do you think there's hope for exorcising Amber's demon?"

"There's always hope," Garren said, rubbing her shoulder.

That sentiment had become the theme of her life lately.

"Good," Rachel said, moving away from Ethan, who had inched closer to her. "So Garren's got the supplies and the exorcist." She looked at Cara with a pained expression. "I just don't think we're going to be able to get David away from Amber."

Cara ignored Rachel's skepticism. "If Amber's there, we'll wait until she leaves."

"What if she doesn't leave?" Rachel asked.

"She'll want to check to make sure I'm dying or dead, won't she?"

Rachel frowned. "I guess you're right. But we don't know how long she'll wait before she does that."

"We'll worry about that when we get to David's place," Cara said. Her tone made it clear she wouldn't accept an alternative plan.

Rachel sighed with resignation and stood before Cara with her hands clasped together in mock prayer. "Will you let me drive your new car?"

Cara grinned and grabbed her backpack. Ethan came over, dangling her keychain from his pinky finger.

Cara grabbed the keys and tossed them to Rachel. "Drive safe."

The elements echoed Cara's outrage. Heavy wind blew sideways and shards of rain slashed at her face as she and Rachel dashed to the driveway to climb into the Fit. Waves beating on the shore sounded from blocks away.

Smacking the Fit's dashboard, Rachel let out her own angst, frustrating herself as she tried to figure out how to work the car's windshield wipers. Cara gave her a quick rundown of the Fit's controls.

Rachel parked a block away from David's place, in an empty driveway. Cara figured the homeowner was at work and wouldn't return for at least a couple of hours. The spot allowed her and Rachel to keep an eye on David's house, while hopefully remaining inconspicuous. Ethan parked another half block away.

The tether cooled and hardened at the sight of the red Jetta parked on the street. After waiting on Amber for twenty minutes, Rachel started drumming her fingertips against the steering wheel. Rachel could act impatient all she wanted, but Cara planned to wait all day and night for an opportunity to help David, for a chance to salvage their relationship.

Another ten minutes ticked by. Finally, Amber appeared on David's porch, looking like a supermodel in her skin-tight, slinky black clothes. She skipped down the stairs, slipped into her car, and drove off.

The Jetta disappeared around a corner. Cara raced down the street and up David's front porch steps. She knocked on the door, and when David answered, he looked into her eyes. The still-icy tether began to melt.

He looked almost like his normal, handsome self. His cheeks flushed with color again and he was dressed in a pair of jeans and a charcoal-colored sweater. But his eyes were clouded over and she only felt a mild warmth when he looked at her.

She held out her hand. He stood back, then shook it. There was a flash of confusion, just like the last time she'd visited him. A shot of warmth coursed through her.

"Can I come in?" she asked and plastered on a fake smile.

His shoulders relaxed and he opened the door wide for her to enter. When he dropped her hand and closed the door behind them, he stiffened again. "What can I do for you?"

Keeping a semblance of a smile on her face was difficult. She didn't know how to explain anything that was going on without sounding like she was out of her mind. Tears might work, but she didn't want to manipulate him like Amber was doing. Nor did she want any more of his pity.

"I want to show you something in your pillow."

"Excuse me?"

She looked over at the couch where he'd rested when he was sick. His bedding was still there. She rushed over and grabbed his pillow, then brought it over and pulled off the case to display the telltale gash sewn up with thick thread. He stared at it and backed several steps away from her.

This wasn't working out the way she'd hoped. And time could run out. Her cell phone was tucked in her pocket, in vibrate mode. If Rachel texted to warn her Amber was back, she needed to get out of there, to take the pillow with her and destroy it. That was the only way to get David back—the real David—the one she'd come to know and love.

She tore open his pillow and pulled out the offensive object inside. It was similar to the thing at Amber's house and the one

Garren had taken from her pillow, only a combination of dark hair intertwined with blonde hair poked out of this one. The cloth was navy, the thread was red, and there didn't appear to be any blood anywhere.

David eyed the object, slack-jawed, then looked at her with accusing eyes, as if she were the one who had planted the horrendous thing. She shook her head, but his rigid demeanor told her he wasn't going to believe her if she told him Amber did this. Shoving the rough object back in the pillow's filling took some effort. She was glad when it was out of sight.

He backed up another step. "I understand that I hurt you, and I'm sorry. But you can't go around making up stories, following Amber around, and pulling pranks like this to try to get my attention."

So now he believed Amber's lies, just like the police did.

Cara swallowed her protests and tucked his pillow under her arm. "Please let me take this. And please don't tell Amber."

Her cell phone buzzed in her pocket. She was too late. Amber had figured out she'd disappeared more quickly than Cara had anticipated. The witch would walk in the door any second. And at this point, Amber's attempts to stop her might be more direct.

Cara grabbed David's hand to beg him to listen to her. Warmth flowed back and forth through the tether and his eyes cleared as he looked at her.

Footsteps clapped across the front porch. Time had run out.

She clung to David's hand. "Please, come with me."

He didn't resist when she dragged him toward the French doors to the deck. The front door swung open just as they closed the back doors behind them. Hunching over, they ran down the deck stairs, hurried around the side yard through the tall sea grass, and fled down the street.

They crawled into the back of the Fit. Rachel started the engine, and Cara threw David's pillow in the front passenger seat. She glanced back toward David's house. Ethan ran up the front steps.

Rachel turned onto the highway. David moved closer to Cara in the compact rear seat. He used his free hand to rub his forehead, then reached out to run his fingers through her hair.

His face fell. "What did I do?"

"You don't remember dumping me?" she asked with sarcastic brightness.

He flinched. "I do now. I'm so sorry—"

This apology she was grateful for. She cut him off with a soft kiss. His fingers wove into her hair and he kissed her back as if he might never get the chance again.

She eased back and tightened her grip on his hand. "The spell only seems to break when we touch. So hold on to me. Don't let go."

"Is that what's happening? I'm under a *spell*?"

"We're on our way to break it. Permanently," she said.

He caressed her cheek and warmth flooded her as his clear green eyes held hers. The last remnants of ice melted from the tether. He pulled her head down to rest on his chest.

Rachel's eyes smiled at Cara in the rearview mirror. Cara sighed, for the moment completely at peace. David was back to himself and was with her, where he belonged. She wouldn't lose him again. This deliverance ritual had to work.

# FORTY-TWO

Above Boulder Beach, gray clouds concealed the sun as it continued its slow descent toward the horizon. The rain had stopped and the wind had died down. A few yards from the water, Garren and Archbishop Egan—who again wore his purple robe—stood behind a large metal drum.

Garren hailed them over. Rachel ran to him. He handed her the pillows containing the cursed objects and hung the mockery of a rosary from her left wrist. She tossed the objects in the drum. Then Garren handed her a bottle of holy water and a can of kerosene and she poured both over the items.

David stopped close to the stairs and tugged on Cara's hand to hold her back. His brows furrowed as he surveyed the scene farther down the beach.

"We need to perform a ritual to break Amber's spells. She placed spells on objects she put in the pillows," Cara explained.

"Why are there two pillows?"

"Amber placed spells on me, too. Destruction spells."

"*Destruction* spells?"

"Like death spells. To get rid of me."

He squeezed her hand and pulled her closer. "Well, thank God those spells didn't work."

Garren walked over to them.

"They might have," Cara said. "I just happened to use the wrong pillow, not open an envelope, and escape from Amber's house when she tied me up."

David spoke through his teeth. "How do we stop her?"

Garren stepped to Cara's side. "Now that Rachel poured holy water and kerosene over the objects, we'll need to pray over them, burn them, and scatter the ashes in running water."

Rachel approached and David whispered in Cara's ear. "What is Garren, a witch hunter?"

"I don't know," Cara whispered back. "But he knows what's going on here. Believe me."

She turned to Garren. "Should we wait and see if Ethan's able to get Amber to come?"

"No. We should get started."

Cara reached into her pocket with her free hand and retrieved the copies of the deliverance prayer she'd printed. She handed one to Rachel.

"I have three copies of the deliverance prayer you taught me," Cara told Garren. "We can recite it if Amber shows up. If that would help?"

"Prayer always helps," Garren said before he headed back toward the water where Archbishop Egan waited by the drum.

A car door slammed on the road above. Ethan followed Amber as she scurried down the stairs to the sand. A large tote hung from her arm. Cara couldn't help but worry what Amber might have stashed there. The witch headed for David and stopped less than a foot in front of him.

Wind kicked up and Amber's vanilla, orange, and clove scent mingled with a stench like rotting garbage. Cara gagged.

"David, please don't tell me you're listening to any foolishness from these kids." She sounded like a parent scolding a child.

David eased Cara behind him. "I won't let you hurt her."

Amber's gaze shot down to the water and shifted between Garren and Archbishop Egan. "What's going on here?" she asked Ethan, her eyes narrowing with suspicion.

Ethan grabbed one of Amber's wrists and Rachel grabbed the other. With her super strength, Amber nearly jerked free. But Rachel and Ethan managed, barely, to hold her.

Another car door slammed. Amber's head whipped around toward the sound. Cara's mom and Ms. Clark descended the stairs.

Her mom looked wary as she drew near and she gave a wide berth to Rachel and Ethan as they struggled with Amber.

The witch had the nerve to address her mom. "These kids are making up stories about magic spells."

"What's going on here, Cara?" Her mom turned to her, concerned, then glared at David as though she'd like to kill him.

Cara didn't know how to respond.

"Amber's lying," David said, holding Cara's hand tight. "She's the one making up stories and messing around with spells."

Her mom's confused and disturbed look reminded Cara that Rachel had said her mom had spoken to David. In addition to the news of their breakup, he must also have shared Amber's lies with her mom, but related them as truths. Now he was backtracking, which wouldn't make sense under normal circumstances.

Rachel backed David up. "Stop lying, Amber! You used your spells to control Ethan and me and to force David to be with you. And you're trying to kill Cara."

A shocked look came over Cara's mom's face.

Amber shot Rachel a condescending smirk. "That's ridiculous." She continued to try to pull free, but Rachel and Ethan struggled and held on tight.

Archbishop Egan left the drum and moved up the beach toward Amber with a bottle of holy water and a silver tool that resembled a long baby rattle. Amber's eyes locked on the bottle. The archbishop made the sign of the cross over himself, then Amber, and then over all present. He immersed the tool in the holy water and sprinkled it all around.

Amber growled.

Cara's mom watched Amber, open-mouthed. Ms. Clark whispered in her ear.

Speaking in Latin, the archbishop repeated the words he'd first said during Rachel's exorcism. "*Ecce crucem Domini.*" He raised his stole.

Amber again jerked against Rachel's and Ethan's holds when the archbishop touched her neck with the garment. A strong, biting cold wind picked up and held the archbishop back.

He pushed against the resistance and said, "*Sit nominis ti signo famulus tuus munitus.*"

The wind died down. The archbishop dipped his tool in the bottle again and sprayed Amber's face with holy water.

Amber screeched and her lips curled back over her teeth.

From his robe pocket, the archbishop retrieved a small book and he continued with his Latin prayers.

Amber's facial muscles and hands twitched and her body contorted backward at a severe and awkward angle, until her long blonde hair brushed against the backs of her calves. Rachel and Ethan maintained their holds, but were tossed about with Amber's odd movements.

Amber thrust upright again and her body went rigid. Her eyes rolled down in their sockets until only the whites were visible. Amber's arms flung to the sides and Rachel and Ethan were thrown several yards across the sand.

Ms. Clark clutched Cara's mom's arm and the two hurried over to check on Rachel.

"Give me your name, demon," Archbishop Egan ordered.

Amber's teeth clenched. Her body remained rigid.

"Your name," Garren commanded. His tone was one Cara had only heard him use once before, with Amber, at the Halloween party, when he'd said, *This won't be tolerated much longer.*

The demon choked on the sounds escaping Amber's lips. "Air—eee—ock."

The stifling scent of sulfur hit Cara and she shivered at a burst of cold in the air, though the wind hadn't picked up again. David hugged her to his side.

Rachel and Ethan scuttled over and Cara handed Ethan a copy of the deliverance prayer. Rachel pulled the copy Cara had given her from her pocket and both Rachel and Ethan began to pray.

*"Lord, we pray that you bind the spirits, powers, and forces of darkness, the netherworld, and the evil forces of nature. Take authority over all the curses, hexes, demonic activity, and spells at work here and break them."*

Cara's mom rushed over and grabbed Cara's arm, to try to drag her away. Cara wouldn't budge. She gently pried her mom's hand off.

During that moment of distraction, Amber moved. Her hand shot out and wrapped around David's forearm. David lost his hold on Cara and his eyes clouded over. Moving to Amber's side, he looked around him, as if surprised by his surroundings.

Cara left her copy of the deliverance prayer in her pocket and ignored Ms. Clark pulling her mom aside. Instead, she moved forward and grabbed David's hand to pull him out of Amber's grasp. But the demon's hold was unbreakable.

David looked down at Cara and the filmy cover receded from his eyes. He gritted his teeth and put his own effort into trying to pull his hand free. It was impossible.

The Latin and deliverance prayers continued.

Amber's eyes closed and a low, inhuman chuckle erupted from within her. The demon spoke in a deep, amplified voice. "Leave, you imbeciles!"

Garren called Rachel and Ethan over to where he stood by the metal drum. He motioned for Rachel to strike a match and set the items inside ablaze. A burst of flames shot up, making the sea behind them look like liquid metal. As the vile objects in the drum burned, dark gray plumes of acrid smoke swirled up toward the lighter gray sky.

As Garren watched over the fire, Rachel and Ethan again recited the deliverance prayer. The archbishop stayed close to Amber and continued to chant in Latin, as he once again made the sign of the cross.

Amber let go of David.

Cara towed him backward. He laced his fingers through hers. She held on tight.

Amber's eyes remained closed when the demon turned Amber's

head in Cara's direction. A wicked smile spread across Amber's face. Rivers of ice rippled through Cara's veins and tore at the edges of the tether.

The demon reached into the bag that hung from Amber's arm and withdrew a knife with a long blade covered in etchings similar to those Cara had seen on the knife in Rachel's room. It aimed the point of the blade at Cara and stabbed three times, as if to taunt her. David pulled Cara behind him.

Then the demon flipped the knife, presenting the handle to both Cara and David, and aiming the blade at Amber's body. Reaching around David, Cara grabbed for the handle, but overreached, and her forefinger sank into the sharp blade. The cut barely stung, yet when she took the knife and held it with the blade pointing downward, blood from the wound dripped down it.

Amber's arms spread wide in a quasi-sacrificial invitation. "Do you not want revenge?" the demon asked with a sinister laugh.

Cara strained to get her words out. "No one. Is going to kill. Anyone."

David gingerly pulled the knife from Cara's grasp. He used his other hand to squeeze her cut finger, applying pressure to stop the bleeding.

The demon grinned and lunged, jerking David forward and once again breaking his connection with Cara.

"Amber?" David said, his face stricken with a look of confusion and despair. "What happened to Amber?" He stared at the demon, who turned Amber's face to him with that wicked smile, then looked past him to smirk at Cara.

Cara tried to move toward David, but her mom was there, pulling her back.

"Let me go, Mom," Cara said, her words firm. Her mom maintained her hold. "Please," Cara added. Her mom slowly loosened her grip. Ms. Clark appealed to Cara's mom. "Cara knows what she's doing. If you want to help stop the demon, then let's pray."

Rachel joined them and held up her copy of the deliverance prayer. Reluctantly, Cara's mom turned her eyes to the paper and began to recite the prayer.

Suddenly, David changed his hold on the knife. At first, Cara thought she'd have to stop him from stabbing Amber. Then she noticed how the knife's blade angled toward his body.

He was going to stab himself.

Cara dove for him, hoping to knock him off balance. But Amber's hand locked around her wrist like a shackle, holding her in place. Cara yanked and twisted and pulled, but couldn't break free.

David's eyes closed and he raised the blade above his head, the point still angled toward him.

"David, stop and look at me!" Cara yelled.

His eyes opened in response to Cara's cry, but he didn't meet her gaze, only hesitating for a moment before focusing on Amber again. The knife poised precariously above his head.

Archbishop Egan reached into his robe pocket and pulled out the holy water bottle. He yanked off the stopper and splashed the contents in Amber's face.

The demon howled and flinched back, dropping both Cara's and David's arms. Cara rushed over to David and placed her hands on either side of his face.

The moment she touched him, his eyes widened, cleared, and met hers. She silently prayed that the spell hadn't taken too strong of a hold, that David would come back to his senses. Energy flowed through the tether and he stared down at her in horror.

The knife dropped to the sand. The demon clutched at Amber's face and bared her teeth at Archbishop Egan. It snatched up the knife and dove at Cara and David, knocking them to the ground.

As they fell, Cara threw her arms around David, covering him. Fear bubbled up within her, but her scream wouldn't come. Pressing closer to David, she turned to look up at the sharp point of the blade that hovered above her.

A voice in her head urged her to let go, to run to her mom, to let the demon kill David. Trying to sacrifice herself would only result in the demon killing both of them. But she loved him. That was all the motivation she needed.

Cara's thoughts raced. There had to be a way to escape this. Maybe she could somehow roll them both free, in the last moment before the knife plunged down. If the bad stuff could really happen, the miraculous stuff could happen, too.

Then she remembered Amber's superhuman strength and all the air rushed out of her. Her only hope was that the demon would be satisfied with fulfilling the mission it was summoned for and would spare David.

There would be pain, she realized. Her head spun with thoughts of how severe the suffering would be and how long she would have to endure until death released her. She buried her face in David's neck, gritted her teeth, and braced herself.

The demon snorted, and Cara knew the blade was falling.

Then David kicked out, knocking the demon off balance, and rolled so that he was shielding Cara from the knife, which now aimed at his back. "Cara, *run!*" His eyes pleaded with hers and warmth rushed through the still-intact tether.

She wouldn't let go. Her eyes held his. As the knife came down, she prayed silently, yet with more conviction than ever before, that God would answer their prayers and would spare David.

Then Garren was there, catching Amber's arm. Stopping the knife. His words to the demon were clear and firm. "Arioch—demon of vengeance—be done with her."

The knife fell as Cara and David scrambled away. Amber's body convulsed, jolting back and forth spasmodically.

Cara swept up the knife. But Amber's body had fallen in a twisted heap, her legs bent beneath her, her head turned unnaturally to the side. Vaguely, Cara noted that the prayers continued.

David moved to his knees and coughed, lightly at first, then loudly, until his coughing escalated into a hacking. Cara clutched his hand. His face flushed red. Blue veins protruded in his neck.

He coughed so violently, she worried he was choking on something. She was about to try to help him dislodge whatever it was, when he wrapped his free arm around his waist, heaved, and vomited. Small chunks of wood, strands of red string, and black beads trickled out of his mouth in a stream of yellow bile and white, foamy saliva.

Her own stomach clenched and she took a deep breath. A tighter spasm seized her and she pressed her hand to her belly. Something tickled her throat. She gagged and a rush of burning fluid poured from her mouth along with a small mass of black string that unwound and spooled onto the ground.

Disgusted, she stared at the unusual messes beneath her and David. The items that had come from their mouths resembled those

Amber had sewn into their pillows. Cara couldn't imagine how Amber would have fed those things to her and David.

Leaning on one another for support, Cara and David stood up straight. From the relieved look on David's face, he was feeling better, like she was. But the prayers hadn't stopped. This wasn't finished.

# FORTY-THREE

Archbishop Egan knelt at Amber's side. The long Latin chant came to an end as he laid his hand on top of her head. Amber groaned and her eyes opened wide.

Arching into a sitting position, Amber's jaws sprang open, wider than humanly possible. A black, ballooning cloud of what looked like powder spewed from her mouth. The black cloud materialized into a small, misshapen human form with wings like a bat's.

The sulfuric smell in the air intensified until Cara's nose burned. She watched in disbelief as the black cloud flew through the air and over the water, where a transient orca chased two gray whales toward shore. The demonic cloud descended upon the transient, pushing it closer to the grays, who Cara now recognized as Crossback and Bobbi. Crossback's markings showed clearly as her back rose out of the water and her breath spouted high into the air.

Amber moaned loudly, then whimpered, "Stay with me, David," momentarily drawing Cara's attention away from the whales.

David squeezed Cara tighter and she leaned into him as her attention switched back and forth between Amber and the whales. Archbishop Egan sat on the sand and propped Amber's head on his thigh. She lifted her hand to stroke the archbishop's face. For a long moment, Amber gazed at him. Then she snatched her hand away.

Amber searched for people around her until her eyes rested on David. Tears slid down her cheeks. "Please love me, David. Please help me."

The grays were drawing closer to shore. Too close.

Amber kept calling for David, until her words faded into a nonsensical babble. "Da-da, dadada, da . . ."

"The spells this woman cast are recoiling against her," Archbishop Egan said. "Can someone help me get her to a hospital?"

"I'll help you," Ms. Clark said, kneeling next to the archbishop. "Is she falling asleep now, like Rachel did when the demon left?"

"She's suffering the intensified effects of her spells," he said. "I'm afraid she's losing her sanity."

*As if she hasn't already.* Worried more about her whales, Cara jumped to her feet and pulled David with her to run down to the water. Cara's mom, Rachel, and Ethan followed.

The demonically possessed transient had driven Crossback and Bobbi into the shallows. The transient's jaws opened as though it was smiling, then clamped down on Bobbi's snout. Cara screamed at the transient to stop. It dragged the baby underwater.

Seconds later, Bobbi's and Crossback's bodies rolled onto the beach. The water retreated and left them stranded.

Falling to her knees between the grays, Cara put a hand on each whale, in hopes of soothing them. Their giant eyes blinked at her, causing tears to blink out of her own. Streams of blood flowed from Crossback's flippers and Bobbi's snout, creating miniature red rivulets that trickled down to the water.

The sun had escaped the dark clouds and had sunken halfway beneath the horizon. It blazed orange, intensifying Cara's blazing rage toward the killer demon who swam slowly back and forth through the shallow water. Watching.

Cara turned to Ethan. "Call Liberty Charters and have Captain Rick send help. Crossback and Bobbi could only last a few hours on the beach, and that's if they weren't injured. We don't have much time."

"My phone's in the car," Ethan said and ran for the stairs.

Garren, determined to finish the deliverance ritual, dragged the drum to the water and scattered the ashes of Amber's curses in the waves. Then he submerged the can and swirled it around to clean it.

Cara called over to him. "Garren, the whales . . . they need to stay hydrated. Maybe bring some water over in the drum?" She put a hand over David's, which rested on her shoulder. "Will you help him carry it?"

David's mouth opened and his eyes widened. Cara followed his gaze as Garren lifted a full drum of water and carried it across the sand as though it were as light as air.

"It doesn't look like he needs help," David said.

No one spoke as Garren poured the contents of the full drum over Bobbi and Crossback.

"Whoa." Rachel's loud proclamation broke the awestruck silence. "What are you?" she asked Garren as he set the drum down. "Some kind of superhero?"

Garren's face remained neutral as he shook his head. He turned toward the whales, knelt, and ran a hand over Bobbi's snout. Cara watched in amazement as the transient's bite marks instantly pulled together and disappeared. Garren did the same with Crossback, trailing his hands over her pierced flippers. Rumbling sounds poured from the grays' mouths.

Cara clung to David's arm and they slowly stood to watch as Garren faced the water and raised an outstretched hand toward the killer.

"Be gone," Garren commanded.

The transient's snout rose and its mouth fell open. A high-pitched shriek sounded and its body lifted high above the water as it breached. It landed with a loud splash and vanished.

For several moments, Garren stared at the spot where the killer had been, his expression somber. Then he addressed the group behind him. "You'll need to move farther back on the beach."

Everyone scrambled backward, stunned into silence. Garren raised both his hands and drew them backward. A small tidal wave of water rushed forward and cascaded over Crossback and Bobbi. Then Garren pushed his hands forward and the wave pulled the grays back into the water. Seconds later, Crossback spyhopped not far offshore and Bobbi raised his tail flukes to wave good-bye before the grays dove below the water's surface with the sun.

Still holding on to David's arm, Cara stared at Garren in reverent confusion. Light shone on him, though the sun had disappeared with the whales. Cara looked to David, then to Rachel and her mom. Their eyes were all riveted on Garren.

Rachel's voice again broke the silence. "So if you're not a superhero, what are you?"

Garren aimed a soft smile at Cara. "You still haven't figured out who I am."

Cara was surprised to form a coherent statement. "I know you're one of the good guys."

"I thought I gave you too many clues. Maybe you weren't meant to know until now. I'm an angel, Cara. Your angel."

Cara gaped at him. She had wondered if he was attracted to her, or Rachel, or if he was gay and shy, or called to be a priest, or from a family of witches and warlocks. The last thing Cara expected to hear was that he was an *angel*.

"That actually makes sense. Sort of," Rachel said. "But why did you let this go on so long? And why didn't *my* angel show up? I'm the one who was possessed."

"Cara was the one Amber targeted when she summoned a demon to get revenge," Garren said. "And if Cara had joined you for lunch with Ethan that first day of school, she might also have ended up possessed. There might not have been anyone to help save you."

"Why didn't you stop Amber—or the demon—from the beginning, then?" Rachel pressed.

"I can only act as a guide," Garren said. "Unless my help is specifically requested and granted, under extraordinary circumstances."

Rachel planted her hands on her hips and turned to Cara. "You've never been good at asking for help."

Cara grimaced at her.

"So is this over now?" David asked, holding tight to Cara's hand. "Is everyone safe?"

Garren nodded. "Because of the deliverance ritual, all the spells have been permanently broken. The binding spell temporarily broke when Cara touched you, David, because her bond with you is strong enough to break any other bonds. That's why the two of you were brought together earlier than intended, in hopes you would make the choices you did to prevent the full extent of the damage these spells could have caused."

David wrapped both his arms around Cara and she hugged his side, secure in the divine knowledge that they were meant to be together.

"Wait a minute," Cara's mom said, stepping to Cara's side. "I still haven't processed quite what your role is here," she said to Garren.

"But you can't seriously be saying that these two are soul mates. There's still an imbalance of power between them."

David shook his head at Cara's mom. "I would never hurt Cara."

Garren looked between Cara and David before he spoke to Cara's mom. "Happily ever after isn't a guarantee for anyone in this world. But Cara's and David's feelings for each other are genuine. Trust us."

Garren flashed his enchanting smile and Cara's mom rubbed Cara's shoulder and miraculously remained silent.

When Garren took a step toward Cara, she knew his job was finished. At least, his work helping to thwart this particular evil was over. Somehow she believed he'd remain with her, in an unseen state. Now, though, she sensed he was getting ready to say good-bye.

"Will I see you again?" she asked.

"Let's hope not. I only show up when there's serious trouble."

She smiled, but tears filled her eyes. "I'll miss you."

"I've always been with you and I'll always remain with you." He brushed her tears away as they spilled down her cheeks. "I love you, Cara Markwell, more than anyone on Earth."

Taking her hand, Garren pulled her away from David. He touched her finger and the edges of her wound wove together and turned pink. The skin returned to its pre-cut condition within seconds. He kissed the top of her head and her scalp tingled. She touched the spot and felt neither pain, nor any raised area to indicate there had ever been an injury there.

"Take care, Cara," he said, and the light surrounding him became so intensely bright that Cara had to squeeze her eyes shut. When she opened them, Garren was gone.

# Epilogue

Christmas in Liberty was rarely a white one, but this year, as David drove Cara home from church, fluffy snowflakes fell like tiny tufts of cotton. After church service, Cara's mom had invited David over for dinner, as well as Rachel and Ms. Clark, and—much to Rachel's annoyance—Ethan.

David helped Cara down from the cab of his truck just as her mom and Ms. Clark disappeared behind the front door. Rachel waited on the walkway for Cara, although Ethan was waving her over to his Malibu.

Rachel rolled her eyes. "I don't get how he thinks I'm just going to forget what he's done to me." She glanced over at Ethan, whose hair was combed stylishly so that it partially covered the right side of his face. Cara didn't miss the hint of a smile that touched Rachel's lips when she saw the acoustic guitar he held.

"He's been through a lot, too," Cara said.

Rachel sighed. "I know, I know. I guess I should hear him out." She half stalked, half sashayed away.

David grinned. Cara let out a light laugh.

Inside, David took her coat, then shrugged off his own and hung both on the rack in the entryway. Cara reached into her jacket pocket and pulled out the shiny blue package she'd wrapped for him. Knowing no gift could adequately express her feelings for him, she'd struggled with what to get. Finally, she'd settled on a wallet that held her picture and a small duplicate of the photo of the two of them at the Anchor. Maybe he'd show the pictures to his dad. If nothing else, he'd carry a reminder of her with him wherever he went.

They walked to the family room and sat down on the couch. David eyed the package she held out for him and he kissed her on the tip of her nose in thanks before he took it and opened it. Right away, he shifted his things from his current wallet to the new one. Then he slipped the new wallet in his back pocket and reached into his front pocket to retrieve a similar-size box. It was wrapped in green-and-white–striped paper and was tied with a red ribbon.

She accepted the present and tore off the paper. Inside a velvet-lined box, a silver whale tail pendant hung on a thin chain. She held the necklace in her hand and beamed at it.

David took it and motioned for her to turn so he could hook it around her neck. He lifted her hair and draped it over her shoulder before he fastened the clasp.

She faced him and reached out to cup the side of his face in her hand. A smile lit up his eyes as he moved closer. His lips met hers and warmth filled her. The tether drew them closer together as she sank into his soft, sweet kiss. She had faith that she was exactly where she belonged.

He pulled back, kissed her forehead, and picked up their wrappings. "Let me throw these away and see if the other ladies need any help in the kitchen. I'll be right back."

As soon as David left the room, a tiny bell tinkled on the Christmas tree. Cara walked over, knelt down, and picked up a perfect white rose. The flower was free of thorns, fully fragrant, and fresher than they naturally come.

She stood and spoke to the suddenly sweeter-smelling air. "Merry Christmas, Garren."

David walked back into the room, came to her side, and appraised the rose. "What do you have there?"

She held up the flower. He shared his lopsided grin with her and held out his hand. She set the rose in his palm and clasped her hand around his.

"It's a gift," she said. "Just like you."

# Acknowledgments

More people have helped me on my road to publication than I could ever list here. Still, I hope every single person who contributed to my experience with this book, and to my success, will know how much I truly appreciate them.

Specifically, I'd like to thank my family, particularly my husband, Tom, for his continued support, and my kids, Tabitha, Tommy, Nicholas, and Brogan, for their patience while I skimp on certain duties to write and revise.

My heartfelt thanks to my early readers who encouraged me: first and foremost, Christine Renzie, as well as my mom, Carol Wilder, and Raschelle Dickerson-Holland, Siri Herzog, Jessica Mark, Morgan Richter, Amaryllis Scott, and Katy Word.

Huge thanks also to my fantastic critique partners from my mentor Barbara Rogan's writing and revising courses, as well as from CritiqueCircle.com, especially Natalia Jefferson, Susan Bickford, Sue Schaefer, Sybil Ward, Tiffany Allee, Deniz Bevan, Julie Doherty, Sally White, Elaine Dominguez, Emily L'Huillier, Dawn Altieri, Mantissa Creed, Tanvi Berwah, Rebecca Gibson, Jen Hicks, and Jennifer DiGiovanni, as well as Theresa Hernandez. Special thanks also to fellow Swoon Reads authors: Sandy Hall, Katie Van Ark, Temple West, Karole Cozzo, and Kimberly Karalius, for being such a great group of supportive girls with which to share this experience. A shout-out is also in order for Gretchen Stelter of Cogitate Studios, for being the first editor to provide a thorough and helpful edit on an early draft.

I'm ever grateful to Barbara Rogan, who took me on as a student when I most doubted my abilities, and set me on a path toward improving my craft. Other teachers who also deserve thanks are Holly Lisle, Randy Ingermanson, Margie Lawson, and Larry Brooks. Perhaps the most significant of my teachers would be Tony Robbins, whose motivational books and materials moved me to write half of a novel at the age of eighteen. If I'd continued to listen to him and hadn't given up on writing fiction for so many years, I'm certain I would have achieved publication much sooner. Better late than never, anyway.

Finally, thanks to the experts who provided online information and e-mail correspondence with expert advice: Andrea E. Lee, MD, for her expertise regarding medical matters, and Lisa Lamanna-Adams, a police officer employed by the City of San Antonio, for her help with police procedure specifics. Only after I finished this novel did I discover Carrie Newell, a professor of Marine Biology and gray whale researcher based out of Depoe Bay. I based *Save Me*'s fictional town of Liberty in part on Depoe Bay, and not only is the main character's name (Cara) similar to Carrie's, they share similar physical characteristics, as well. This was just another sign to me that this story was meant to be.

Last, but certainly not least, major thanks to my amazing fit of an editor, Holly West, and to the fearless Swoon Reads leader, Jean Feiwel, as well as to the entire Swoon Reads staff for all of their help and support. I look forward to meeting and working more with all of you!

Turn the page for some

Sw❤❤nworthy

Extras . . .

# Recipes from SAVE ME

 **Roasted Elephant Garlic**

*Serves 2 to 4 per head of garlic*

**Ingredients:**
1 or more heads elephant garlic
Olive oil

**Directions:**
Preheat oven to 425 degrees F.
Slice off the top of the garlic head. Place on a piece of aluminum foil and drizzle olive oil inside the head until it's completely filled and just starting to run down its sides.
Wrap tightly in the foil and place on a cookie sheet. Bake until tender and fragrant, roughly 35 minutes. Remove from the oven and let cool.
Peel outside of bulb of garlic, then gently squeeze each clove out.
Use in the recipe of your choice OR spread on bread; tastes great dipped in a mixture of olive oil and balsamic vinegar.

 **Avocado Elegance Salad**

**Ingredients:**
6 medium avocados, chopped
1 head iceberg lettuce, chopped
6 medium on the vine tomatoes, chopped

*Serves 4 to 6*

Lemon pepper, added liberally to taste
1 large sweet onion, chopped
Salad Elegance, added liberally to taste

**Directions:**
Combine all ingredients, toss, and serve.

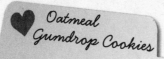

## Oatmeal Gumdrop Cookies

### Ingredients:

*Yields 2 dozen cookies*

¾ cup all-purpose flour
1 large egg
½ teaspoon baking soda
½ teaspoon vanilla extract
¼ teaspoon salt

1 ½ cups rolled oats (not instant)
¾ cup packed light brown sugar
1 cup spice gumdrops, coarsely chopped
8 tablespoons unsalted butter, melted and cooled

### Directions:

Preheat oven to 350 degrees F.
Line two large baking sheets with parchment. Combine flour, baking soda, and salt in a small bowl. In a large bowl, using an electric mixer on medium speed, beat together butter and brown sugar until well combined. Beat in egg and vanilla. Stir in flour mixture until just combined. Fold in oats and gumdrops.
Drop dough by heaping tablespoonfuls onto prepared baking sheets, leaving 2 inches between each cookie. Bake until golden around edges but still soft on top, about 15 minutes. Let stand on baking sheets for about 5 minutes. Transfer to wire rack and cool completely.

## Goulash

*Serves 6 to 8*

### Ingredients:

1 lb. ground beef
1 medium onion, chopped
4 or 5 stalks celery, chopped

2 cans stewed tomatoes
2 cans dark red kidney beans
1 pkg. 16 oz. extra-wide egg noodles

### Directions:

Chop celery and onion.

Brown ground beef with celery and onion, in skillet. Drain fat. Add stewed tomatoes to skillet and simmer 20+ minutes (the longer the better, to enhance flavor). Add kidney beans to skillet and simmer 25 minutes.

Boil large pot of water for pasta and prepare per package directions. Drain pasta and return to large pot. Add contents of skillet to large pot of pasta and mix well. Add salt and pepper to taste, and serve.

# A Coffee Date

with author Jenny Elliott and her editor, Holly West

## *"About the Author"*

**Holly West (HW): What was the first romance novel you ever read?**

Jenny Elliott (JE): You know, I think it was *Jane Eyre*. I read it at a pretty young age. I was like twelve, so it wasn't the easiest reading for me. My mom said that we should watch the movie, then read it again, so I'll understand it. I prefer the version with George C. Scott; I love that one. I've read it many times now and I think I liked the spookiness at least as much as the romance. I started out wanting to write spooky stuff, but then the romance kind of crept up on me. I love *Jane Eyre*. It is probably still one of my favorite romances.

**HW: What's your favorite way to spend a rainy day?**

JE: I lived in Seattle for almost ten years and I LOVE that kind of weather, crazy as I am. When it's overcast, that's my favorite time to go out in nature. Because, especially in a place as crowded as Seattle, if the sun comes out, which it doesn't do often, everyone comes out in droves. And I prefer solitude. So, a lot of times on overcast days, I can find a lot of solitude in nature, and I love that. But sometimes if there's sideways rain, I can't stand that, and that's just the perfect excuse to read and write, watch movies, listen to music, engage in social media, or be lazy. We all need those excuses, so I'll take them whenever I can.

**HW: My mother used to call days like that, when it was nice and overcast but not actively raining, Eeyore days, and they were always my favorites. Do you have any hobbies you are willing to share?**

JE: Well, writing is a profession now—which is nice! Reading is, of course, big. And, like my main character in *Save Me*, I'm a huge Scrabble addict. I don't play against the computer quite as much as I used to, but I'm still pretty good. Sometimes, it's hard for me to play against a person if they don't know the strategy, like the three-letter words and the tricks and all of that, because it can take them a long time to make a play, so I have to have my phone on the side or something. I'm also a huge moviegoer. Not necessarily at home, because my kids will almost always take over and I have to watch *Chitty Chitty Bang Bang* over and over. But I have been known to see a movie in a theater up to five times. For me, there's something about the big screen and the darkness when combined with the action and the music . . . it really inspires me. I kind of treat it as an investment in storytelling training, because it's not the cheapest hobby.

**HW: What kind of movies do you go to?**

JE: They've made so many movies out of books that I've read and it's so interesting to see what they change and to figure out why they changed it, and how the different mediums would appeal and how I can maybe mix the two or switch it up. I'm always looking for a way to change things up a little bit. But I also have kids, so sometimes, I'll go see a movie like the new *Amazing Spider-Man* movie. And I know a lot of people think it's too action-packed, but there's still such a wide appeal, and I think it's important to figure out why people are really enjoying it, and to at least take pieces of that as a writer and as an artist, and try to work it into our own work. So, I kind of try to see a little bit of everything just so I can get proper training, so to say.

## "The Swoon Reads Experience"

**HW: Let's talk a little bit about the Swoon Reads experience. How did you find Swoon Reads? How did you hear about us?**

JE: I am a part of a writers' group, well, several groups, and in one of the groups, a friend had submitted to Swoon Reads, and her novel was being really well-received. She was getting a lot of feedback. I mean, when you're in critique groups, you get a lot of feedback, but nothing like the level of feedback you get if people are reading your book on Swoon Reads. I really liked that idea at first, but an agent was reviewing my full manuscript, and that can take months. She got back to me right before Thanksgiving and I thought, I've been playing this game for a while now with such near misses and it's almost like an agent has to want to marry your book before they take it on. And they're scared. And I don't know how the industry is right now. But it just seemed like they were a little more timid than usual, so I thought, I'm just going to go straight to the publisher and at the very least, I'm going to get this great feedback from readers and writers. Obviously, I'm glad I did that.

**HW: I'm so glad that you did as well. Before you found out you were chosen, what was your experience like on the site?**

JE: It was really good. I reached out and read a bunch of manuscripts because I learn a lot from reading and critiquing other people's work. I tried to help others as much as I could and I really appreciated the reciprocation when they came back and did the same for me. There're some really great writers on the site, so I was really grateful for the feedback and I hope I gave them something useful as well.

HW: Once you were chosen and we contacted you, what was it like getting that e-mail?

JE: Oh, my gosh. I was so in shock about the possibility of it that I thought that maybe I'd won that tote of books, and they are just letting me know that. Honestly, I thought it had to be something else. I kind of was in denial about it until I actually talked to Jean. I think I even said something to her and I heard her kind of trip up for a second. I was like, "Oh, I was hoping that's why you were calling" and she kind of paused, probably thinking, Well, why else would we be calling you? I honestly was in denial until I heard the words come from her mouth.

HW: That's one of the best parts, talking to authors directly and saying, "Yes, we love your book and we totally want to publish it." After we had that conversation and you were able to come out of denial, how did you celebrate?

JE: I did the basic dinner and drinks kind of thing and got congratulations from people. That was nice, but I swear we were all in shock, and we still might be in shock until the book is in hand. I really think the true celebration will happen when the book's finally out, when it's finalized, and when it's done.

SwoonReads

# "About the Book"

**HW: Where did you get the idea for *Save Me*?**

JE: I was working at a book fair at my kids' school and everyone was insane over the Twilight Saga. They started telling me about the books, and it really reminded me of Anne Rice's books when I was a kid. And I thought, I'm going to have to read this because I've never seen teenagers so excited about books. I read it and I loved it, and I loved the simple style. It's easy reading, but very entertaining, and there's so much story there.

But when I read the books, I thought, You know, I really would like to read about a forbidden romance that could happen in real life. It was something about kissing a stone-cold vampire that could kill you at any second. She made it really swoonworthy, but I'd rather have the forbidden romance between people that could really happen with maybe more realistic thrills and a deeper meaning—at least a deeper meaning for me. That's what set the wheels in motion for me, and over time, the romance started taking over.

**HW: This version of *Save Me* is pretty different from the manuscript that was originally posted on the site. What was the biggest change for you and which one was the hardest?**

JE: The biggest change was the mother-daughter relationship and making sure I showed their closeness and conflict at the same time. I found with my early critiquers that a lot of people have very different experiences of what a relationship with a mother is. A lot of times, they're not really willing to believe something outside their own experience could be a possibility, and I wanted it to not be all just how my mom would be, though my mom's pretty open-minded. She probably wasn't as strict as Cara's was. But with your help, I came up with what I hope is a really good balance there.

I think the hardest thing was enhancing the romance while still keeping David's actions above reproach, which is easier said than done when you're working with a nontraditional student-teacher relationship. But I'm happy with what we came up with and I'm excited to see what people think.

**HW: I am proud of the changes you made with both those relationships. What was it like for you getting the edit letter?**
JE: It was daunting, but you were very kind, telling me not to panic and whatnot. And you are a really great fit for me as an editor because you were so specific in what you ask for in the changes you want, so I don't stress and pull my hair out thinking there's five different ways I could try to accomplish what she asked. And what does she want me to do, you know? You spelled it out specifically. We had really constructive talks. Poor thing, I kept you on the phone for I think two hours both times. We got the answers and I think we got everything in the right direction and it really wasn't that bad. It was a good experience.

### "The Writing Life"

**HW: When did you first realize you wanted to be a writer?**
JE: I was just e-mailing and reminiscing with a friend recently, and I remembered that I wrote in journals since kindergarten, and I loved reading, and when I was in fourth grade I decided I wanted to write a book. But I was so intimidated by the scope of the project that I thought I needed to enlist a couple of helpers, and I think

there were two girls that I asked to help me write a book, but I only remember one specifically. They were really excited at first and we came up with this outline and we started writing it, but their enthusiasm waned pretty quickly and mine never did. I kept trying and kept going; it was what I looked forward to the most every day. I think that's when I got the gist that storytelling in some form or another was what I wanted to do.

**HW: What's your process? Do you outline things? Do you just sit down and start writing?**

JE: I'm a huge outliner. I think that's one of the first things that made me feel comfortable when I came back to fiction writing. I took a hiatus for a while before coming back to fiction. I thought, Wow, how am I going to organize this whole book that I'm envisioning? Then I found Randy Ingermanson's snowflake method and that saved the day. It presents just a skeleton, but there are techniques for fleshing it out. And I swear by Larry Brooks' *Story Engineering*, it is like the bible for me in making sure that I have my story laid out the way I want it. Those are basically the things I stick to the most, the blueprints, I guess.

**HW: Do you ever get writer's block?**

JE: Oh, yeah. I get scared often that my well of ideas is going to dry up forever. And I just throw whatever issue I have at my subconscious and ignore it completely and do something else. You know, like go to a movie, or something that will stir creativity or let me totally escape, like reading a book. And invariably in that half-awake, half-asleep state, when it's still dark outside, I'll wake up. Inspiration will strike, though I wish it'd strike at an opportune time in the

afternoon, but nighttime's usually when it does. Then, I'd get out a notepad and a pen that I kept by my bed, though half the time, I couldn't even read what I'd written later on. I can never remember what I was thinking when I'm in that state, anyway. But now, they have phones and I can tap out something that's pretty understandable to me anyway, much to my husband's chagrin. My phone's always the first thing I grab in the morning.

# SAVE ME
## Discussion Questions

1. The title of the book is *Save Me*. Who do you think is being saved? Who is doing the saving?

2. Cara and her mother have always had a close, honest relationship, but then Cara defies her mother to be with David. Do you feel that Cara's mother was right to protest their relationship? Did Cara make the right choice when she decided to be with David anyway?

3. Rachel and Cara are best friends at the beginning of the book, but once Rachel starts dating Ethan, she pulls away and changes dramatically. Is this situation something that you've seen happen in real life?

4. Food is a unifying theme in this book. Cara bonds with her mother over cooking, while Rachel rejects gifts of food while possessed. Can you think of other instances in the book where food is important? Do you use food as a bonding tool in your own life?

5. Garren says that angels can only act as guides unless their help is requested in order to preserve free will. Are there scenes in the book where things turned out better because of Garren's advice? Are there any places where people made the wrong choices?

6. Despite the drastic change in Rachel and the strange occurrences she has noticed, Cara has a difficult time believing in the ideas of magick, witchcraft, and demons. Do you think that this

is a realistic reaction? What would you have done in Cara's place?

7. Cara loves the ocean and whale watching, but after being knocked overboard, she's afraid to go out again. Have you ever had a bad experience ruin something you love?

8. In *Save Me*, you have two hot new guys who come into town and who are in love with the heroine, yet it is not a typical love triangle. Did you enjoy both of these relationships, or were you disappointed that Garren and Cara's love was not romantic?

9. Amber, who is upset about losing her boyfriend, is possessed by the demon of revenge, while Rachel, who is upset that Cara has drawn the attention of both of the new guys, is possessed by the demon of jealousy. What demon do you think possessed Ethan? Could you pinpoint other characters' fatal flaws?

10. Rachel and Ethan quickly return to normal after their exorcisms and Cara easily forgives Rachel for the things she said and did while possessed. But Amber suffers for the things she did, as the consequences of her spells turn against her. Why do you think her situation is different?

Want to host your own
*Swoon Reads Book Club Party?*
Download our *free* event kit at
*www.swoonreads.com/partykit!*

Swoon Reads

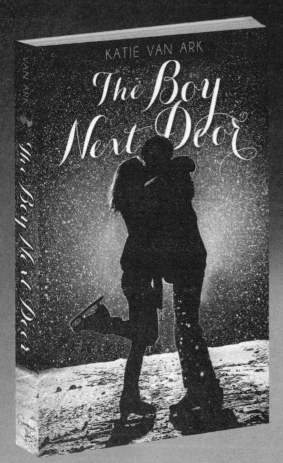

**First rule of dealing with vampire bodyguards?
Don't fall in love.**

Aspiring designer Caitlin Holte's whole world has been turned upside down, and that was *before* she accidentally attracted the attention of a demon. Fortunately, her hot, bad-boy neighbor Adrian—who also happens to be a half-demon vampire—has appointed himself her bodyguard. But, when their pretend relationship starts feeling a little too real, Caitlin starts to wonder if she needs him to protect *her*—or her heart.

I WAS WARM. That was all that mattered. I was warm and perfect and sleepy. So, when the soft *"Caitlin"* floated past my ear again, I wanted to ignore it, to snuggle deeper into the blankets and dream. But someone whispered my name again, and a stubborn part of my brain felt obliged to acknowledge it.

"Hmm?" I mumbled.

"So, you *are* alive," the voice said. It sounded an awful lot like Adrian. Which was silly. Why would Adrian be in my bedroom? Ridiculous.

"What are you smiling for?" he asked as I wriggled my head under his chin.

"You smell good," I mumbled into his collarbone. After all, it didn't matter what you told people in dreams. In dreams, if nowhere else, you should be honest. I pressed my cold nose against his warm neck and wrapped my dream-arm around Dream-Adrian's waist.

He was surprisingly solid.

"Caitlin, you need to wake up now. It's four-thirty."

*"Nurrr."*

"Come on, Caitlin, up," he murmured. His hair tickled my face and I scrunched up my nose. Burrowing closer to the source of heat that was Dream-Adrian, I realized that my shirt was sliding off one shoulder—which was weird, because my pajama shirt wasn't large enough to slide off my shoulder. I reached up and felt the fabric at my neck and realized that it wasn't the heavy cotton

I was used to, it was angora. I sure as hell didn't own any angora. In fact, I only knew one person who *did* own angora.

Slowly, I opened my eyes.

It was dark at first, and I wasn't completely sure I'd actually opened them. Then the hazy form of Adrian's face materialized above me. I was huddled, leech-like, along the right side of his body.

I blinked.

"You all right?" he asked after a moment.

I blinked again. He was still there.

And I still had my arm wrapped around his waist and my leg hooked around his knee.

Oh, dear god.

"How do you feel?" Adrian tried again, starting to look concerned.

*Stupid.*

"Fine," I mumbled, my voice hoarse and froggy as I disentangled my limbs from his until we could both sit up.

"We need to get you back to Trish's," he said, already scooting away, dragging his legs over the edge of the bed and walking to his desk and . . .

. . . taking his clothes off?

I watched, absolutely fascinated, as he tossed a pirate shirt onto the back of his chair and pulled on a black sweater that clung to his body like Saran Wrap. He swiped a hand through his hair and scanned the floor, looking for something.

Maybe I *was* still dreaming.

I wanted to ask what time it was, why I was here, why I needed to go back to Trish's, why, why, why, what, where, when, how? but my tongue was all sloppy and I couldn't form any coherent thoughts.

He looked for something in a drawer, found whatever it was, and took off his pirate pants.

*Oh, my god, he took off his pirate pants.*

He was dressed in nothing but a sweater and tight, black boxer briefs. Even in the dim moonlight, I could see that Adrian wasn't just in shape; he was *built*. Decathlete built. FIFA World Cup soccer champion built. Not bulky, really, but solid. Just muscles for days, lean and beautifully arranged. I was staring, and I didn't care. He didn't seem to notice, however, and slipped on a pair of jeans.

I must be dreaming. Not only had *I* been mostly naked in Adrian de la Mara's room, *Adrian* had been mostly naked in Adrian's room. I mean, that made sense, since it was his room, but I was there, and *what the hell was happening?*

"I don't have any boots your size," he said, turning to face me once more, "but I stole these from my aunt. They're probably a couple sizes too big, but it's all I have."

He held up a pair of sandals, but I wasn't really looking at them, not when the image of his mostly naked body was burned into my retinas like a film negative.

"You're not really awake yet, are you?" he asked.

I blinked at him.

He stared at me and said, "Hmm" in a low, rumbly sort of way.

I blinked again, pinching my eyes shut and then opening them wide. The room came into a bit clearer focus. Slowly, I sat up, the wide neck of his sweater slipping over my shoulder again.

"Adrian," I said, over-pronouncing his name.

"Yes?"

"Your house?"

"Yes."

"Your room?"

"Yes."

I looked down at myself. I was practically swimming in the clothes I wore.

"Your pajamas?"

He smiled. "Yes."

"Time?"

"Four-thirty."

"A.M.?"

"Yes."

I touched a hand to my head. "Jungle Juice?"

Adrian tried to suppress another smile. "Yes."

"Ah," I said, as if that one word summed up everything that had happened over the past five hours. A moment passed as we stared at each other. "I don't really know what to say right now."

"How about I go grab you something to eat while you think about it?"

"Okay," I agreed.

He left and I was grateful I had a moment to pull myself together.

How stupid did I feel? *You got drunk*, I told myself. *You got drunk and Adrian had to drag you all the way to his house so you wouldn't embarrass yourself. And then you* cuddled *with him.*

**Jenny Elliott** is a lifelong resident of Washington State and lives in Spokane with her husband and four kids. Writing fiction is her favorite method for avoiding insanity. Other avoidance techniques include reading, playing Scrabble, and browsing social media sites. *Save Me* is her first novel.